PRAISE FOR THE VE
THE FIRST KATRINA STONE NOVEL

"Gripping. Fascinating. Entrancing. *The Vesuvius Isotope* is 2013's top thriller!"

-Carolyn Hart, author of *Escape from Paris*

"Elise takes us into historic, cultural, medical, and scientific arcana likely to surprise you at every turn... in this brainier-than-Dan-Brown mystery journey."

-Dan Burstein, co-author of *Secrets of the Code*

"I really enjoyed this mystery. There was obviously a lot of research that went into the writing of this story and I feel as if I learned a lot, but it didn't feel as if I were being 'taught.' By the end, I really cared about the characters, and the pages almost couldn't turn fast enough to find out what happened. Very exciting!"

-Catherine M. Walter, author of *The Harmony of Isis*

"A fast-paced mystery based partially on scientific possibility and partially on ancient historical conundrum, this story kept me intrigued... First-person narrative and thrilling escapades make the story an exciting escape while the subject matter makes it interesting."

-Joyce Brown, mystery author

"Katrina Stone is a smarter, sexier version of Robert Langdon. If you like a great murder mystery with a strong female lead, this is for you!"

-KK, Seattle, WA

"This novel is an absolute pleasure to read, its fast pace action combined with history and science liken it to Indiana Jones!"

-Kanaida, Waterlooville, U.K.

"Simply superb. I started reading this one, and abandoned the rest I had been reading along with just to finish this."

-Sakshi, Bangalore, India

"A perfect beach read with a little bit of mystery, adventure and a lot of suspense... If you enjoy stories about travel, history, libraries, archives, and especially ancient Egypt, then you will surely enjoy this."

-Khaola, Constantine, Algeria

"This book captures you from the very beginning. It is filled with murder, mystery, magic, medicine, and history. The author delivers the story in a unique and page turning way. I enjoyed every minute of it."

-Kristine, Ontario, Canada

"This is a gem!… Being an Egyptian… I was a bit apprehensive starting it. Because whenever I read something related to either Ancient Egypt or the modern one, I get this cringe and I'm always disappointed… This book restored my faith—there's someone out there who gets it. Great work, clearly, my new favorite author."

-Kariema, Giza, Egypt

"This was my 69th book of the year and my favorite so far. Set in San Diego (my hometown), Italy and Egypt, the story is rich in history and kept me enthralled throughout the entire book. Kristen Elise has written a smart, intellectually stimulating, medical mystery that kept me on the edge of my seat. This is a book I highly recommend. I am eagerly awaiting her next book."

-Jeanine, San Diego, CA

"*The Vesuvius Isotope* was a gripping adventure through the Mediterranean as well as through time."

-Hari, Raleigh, NC

To Wilma —
Viva Con Science!

Enjoy

THE
DEATH ROW
COMPLEX

Murder Lab Press
San Diego, CA

P.O. Box 178963
San Diego, CA 92177
www.murderlab.com

Library of Congress Control Number: 2015905633

ISBN: 978-0-9893819-2-5 (print book)
ISBN: 978-0-9893819-3-2 (ebook)

Ordering information: Quantity sales. Special discounts are available on quantity purchases by corporations, associations, and others. For details, contact the publisher at the address above.

Manufactured in the United States of America

For my husband

THE
DEATH ROW
CMPLEX

KRISTEN ELISE, PH.D.

Murder Lab Press

San Diego, CA

Author's Note

*B*acillus *anthracis*, the bacterium that causes anthrax, is one of only six microorganisms classified by The Centers for Disease Control and Prevention as Category A: Highest Priority. Defining characteristics shared by these microorganisms include ease of transmission, replication, and dispersal, and high mortality rates. Their potential as biological weapons is apocalyptic.

Vaccines against anthrax have been in use in the United States since the 1950s. Their efficacy in humans is highly controversial, and their use is prophylactic only. Once infection has occurred, anthrax vaccines have no effect.

Confirmed cases are treated rigorously with antibiotics. However, antibiotic treatment is only effective prior to the onset of early symptoms, which resemble the flu. Subsequently, the bacterium releases a toxin, termed lethal factor, which does not respond to antibiotics. This toxin is ultimately responsible for the devastating effects of anthrax.

The following work describes a fictional strain of anthrax that has been genetically engineered to exhibit exceptionally high potency. With the appropriate starting materials, such a bacterial strain could be generated in any molecular biology laboratory. It is for this reason that the Department of Homeland Security strictly controls access to these starting materials in the United States.

This story is fictitious, but the science is accurate and based on legitimate research. In fact, it was my own work with anthrax, and a chilling discovery I made by accident, that inspired the events in this novel.

PROLOGUE

By the time they caught up with him, he had forgotten to keep running. Lawrence Naden was incoherent and scarcely recognizable—the sloughed, discarded skin of a human being.

It had been a rainy week in Tijuana. A small river of brown water carried trash along the gutters of the squalid street. Piles of refuse collected in rough areas, creating dams that would eventually break with the weight of the water and garbage behind them.

A burst of static abbreviated the heavily accented warning from a megaphone. *"You've got nowhere to go, Naden!"* The officer holding the megaphone motioned, and several *federales* carrying M16 rifles moved steadily across a sloping yard.

Except for a handful of onlookers, most of them ragged children, the street was deserted. The majority of adults had characteristically fled at the first rumor of approaching law enforcement.

This time, however, the uniformed team filing through

the *barrio* was not in pursuit of drugs. The *federales* were looking for a single individual.

A few stepped onto the porches of flanking shacks, peering suspiciously through dirty windows or through plastic taped over holes where windows had been. But most congregated at one rickety house. As they surrounded it, they shouldered the rifles and instead began drawing pistols.

Another burst of static. A brief command from the megaphone. And the front and back doors of the house were kicked in.

The men entering the house were greeted by the rank combination of sweet-smelling rotting food, human waste, and burning chemicals. The front room was abandoned but had recently been occupied, as evidenced by a smoldering spoon on a card table against one wall. Needles and syringes, plastic bags, and glass pipes littered makeshift tables, moldy couches, and the concrete floor.

Silently, the *federales* crept through the house with firearms raised. As those behind him assumed formation along the wall of a narrow hallway, the leading officer kicked a bathroom door, and it flung open as he shrank backward against the doorjamb.

The evasive maneuver barely saved the officer from being shot in the face.

As the bullet cut through the thin drywall behind him and embedded into a rotting wall stud, the officer instinctively leaned in and flicked his index finger three times. The brief staccato of semi-automatic fire rang out, and the shooter fell gurgling into the bathtub.

The officer lowered his pistol to look down at the body. Then he turned to his team. "*Esto no es lo,*" he said coldly. *This isn't him.*

Two additional doors were visible along the narrow hallway. One was wide open. The leading officer caught the eye of the man nearest it and cocked his head toward the room. The flanking man stepped in, gun drawn. He strode to the closet and opened it, then stepped back out into the hallway and shook his head.

The attention of the team turned to the other hallway door. It was closed.

After making eye contact with the rest of the team, the leading officer repeated the motions of kicking in the door and then stepping out of the line of anticipated fire. This time, there was none. Cautiously, he followed the barrel of his weapon into the room, noticeably relaxing as he did.

Across the room, a man was sitting cross-legged on the floor with his back against the wall, his gaunt body slumping to one side. A trickle of fresh blood flowed down the inner part of his forearm from a newly opened wound. The entire area of flesh was scarred, scabbed, and bruised. As the officers entered the room, the man's half-opened eyes registered a slight recognition. A needled syringe dropped from his hand and rolled toward the officers in the doorway.

The brief lucidity that had graced Lawrence Naden's eyes faded as the heroin flooded his bloodstream. His pupils fixed into a lifeless gaze onto a spot on the floor, and then the rush overtook him.

PART I: THE MESSAGE

The image was lovely in a somewhat odd, geometric way. A bouquet? Or maybe a tree? The flower heads were a jumbled mess, but the stems were perfectly arrayed—an intertwined cylinder spiraling downward from the wad of flowers on top. The overzealous rainbow coloring of it all was unlike anything existing in nature.

The leaves around Washington, D.C. were turning, and it was already getting cold. Rain was beating against the windows, and White House intern Amanda Dougherty scratched her back with a letter opener while frowning curiously at the bizarre image on the front of the greeting card.

The card had probably been white. It was now a slightly charred sepia from the UV irradiation. Despite its ugly signature on the paper, Amanda had felt much more comfortable about taking this job after Mr. Callahan had explained that decontaminating irradiation was a mandatory process for all incoming White House mail. It was done in a New Jersey facility after processing and sorting at Brentwood, the facility that had made national headlines years earlier when anthrax spores intended for U.S. government officials had infected several people and killed five.

Today, by the time the mail reached Amanda, it was safe.

Amanda flipped open the greeting card. "Oh, my word," she said quietly. The handwritten text was small and neatly aligned, but Amanda most certainly could not read it. She thought the repetitive squiggles before her might be Arabic, or Hebrew, or Farsi—she could not tell those languages apart.

After a moment of thought, Amanda got up and walked to Mr. Callahan's office, where she rapped softly on the door.

He yelled through the door for her to come in.

"I'm sorry to bother you," Amanda said timidly. "We got a greeting card in a foreign language. I don't know what I'm supposed to do with these."

"What language?"

"I don't know. Something Middle Eastern. It has all those funny double-you looking things with dots over them."

Mr. Callahan motioned for her to enter and took the card from her. He glanced briefly at the brightly colored bouquet on the front and then flipped the card open to look at the text inside.

"It's Arabic, but I don't speak it. I'll give it to an interpreter. Thank you, Ms. Dougherty."

On the other side of the country, a prison guard watched from across the visiting room as a man and a woman conversed at a small table.

Both leaning forward, the couple spoke intimately, his dark hands enveloping her black-gloved ones on the table. The standard-issue solid blue jumpsuit of the prisoner was a stark contrast to his visitor's traditional Muslim attire—her formless black robe and the headscarf that shielded her downcast face.

Their conversation seemed hurried, urgent.

The guard nonchalantly crossed the room, slowing ever so slightly as he passed by the couple in a casual effort to overhear them. For a few seconds, he could hear the man impatiently reassuring his mate.

"It's OK, I've taken care of it. You don't have anything to worry about. So shut up already."

The woman said nothing. She glanced up, and her dark face was partially revealed for just a moment from within the folds of the headscarf. She looked afraid. The inmate's expression was one of defiance. To the seasoned guard, it was a familiar combination. He strolled away to watch over another visiting couple.

Overhead, electric eyes were faithfully recording the scene.

𝕏

Ten minutes later in Washington, D.C., Jack Callahan handed the greeting card to an interpreter who had just entered his office.

The interpreter frowned.

"What?" Jack asked.

"This card may have a cute bouquet on the front, but the text... " The interpreter trailed off, skimming silently down the card. Then he began to read aloud, slowly translating from the Arabic:

Dear Mr. President,

Your nation of puppets will soon know at last the price of fighting against our Islamic State. Those of you who survive Allah's justice will reflect upon 11 September of 2001 and consider that date insignificant.

A small taste of the pain we promise has already been put to course. Make no mistake that the blood that will flow is on your hands. Let it paint for you an image of our strength and resolve. Let it serve as a reminder that you cannot defeat Islam.

You will stand powerless and witness this small shedding of blood, and you will then have the privilege of living in fear for two months, as our faithful brothers and sisters have lived in fear of your Christian Crusaders.

And finally, on your Christmas Day of this year, there will begin a cleansing of your country unlike any you can possibly imagine. It will blanket your nation and no man, woman, or child will be safe. Only Allah will decide who may be spared.

Our Muslim brothers and sisters have been imprisoned by the western leaders for too long. The world will now see that you are the prisoners, and Allah will praise the final victory of ISIL.

⋈

The prisoner watched over his shoulder as the guard walked away. Turning back to his visitor, he raised one dark eyebrow and gave a subtle nod.

The visitor disentangled one gloved hand from the prisoner's and lowered it to reach beneath the small table. The hand snaked into a fold of the loose black robe and then re-turned calmly to assume its former position. The guard was now on the other side of the room.

Couples were beginning to kiss goodbye, and the room was clearing out. The visiting hour was almost over.

"Stay in contact," the prisoner whispered. "I will be call-ing on you."

His visitor's eyes flared in shock. This was supposed to have been their final meeting. *"What are you talking about?"*

The prisoner smiled menacingly, revealing a broken fence of rotten teeth. "Oh, did you think it was going to be that easy for you, bitch? That I'd do all the work and you'd get the glory? I know a good negotiation when I see one. Don't fuckin' think I'm kidding."

"Forget it, then! I'll get someone else!"

"Too late, lover," the prisoner said with a grin. "The cat's already out of the bag."

✕

As the prisoner and his visitor were saying their goodbyes, an inmate in a remote wing of the prison was vomiting into his private cell's toilet for the second time that hour. He half-heartedly cursed the prison food, but he did not really think he had food poisoning. He felt like he was coming down with the flu.

✕

The interpreter paused and looked up, his dark eyes a question mark.

Jack Callahan seemed relatively unconcerned. "We get messages like that all the time," he said, shrugging. "They almost always turn out to be a hoax."

"This one might be too," his colleague concurred. "The

11

Arabic is unusual. I was paraphrasing, of course—most of what is here doesn't translate directly, including the abbreviation 'ISIL' itself. But... this reads like it was written by someone who might not be a native speaker. I don't know exactly. Also, the handwriting. It is sort of, ah, overly meticulous. Like someone who doesn't speak or write Arabic is trying to copy something he saw written... it's not like how someone writes in his native language."

Jack made a related point. "It does seem strange to me that the ISIL organization is mentioned but the author gives no other details. Usually, when we get a direct threat from ISIL, or they claim responsibility for an attack, there are very specific references, things that had to have come from them in order to lend credibility. And since when does ISIL send a greeting card to general White House mail, instead of making some kind of grandiose announcement over international airwaves? Those bastards thrive on publicity."

A moment of silence passed as each man considered the card again. Then Jack mused aloud, "So, there's allegedly something about to happen. And then something else on Christmas Day...

"E-mail the translation to me when you've completed it. I still need to log it into the database, and I'll send the card to the Postal Inspection office for analysis. But I assume if no shit hits any proverbial fans in the next couple of weeks, then we're probably fine."

Twenty hours passed, and death row was redefined. Convicted murderer Nathan Horn struggled for air as he lay dying on his bed. Every feeble breath felt like lightning in his chest.

Much of Horn's present state was ironically akin to the once-familiar sickness of heroin withdrawal—a sensation he had not experienced in twenty-two years. His lungs had become increasingly weak over the last hour, and he now continuously felt light-headed and nauseous. There was nothing left to vomit, but he was vaguely aware that he had soiled himself again. Horn had stopped getting up a few hours ago, after he had fainted in the throes of a violent retching spell and hit his head on the concrete floor hard enough for blood to trickle down his agonized face.

Too weak to care that his body was shutting down, he could only be grateful that the violent illness he had been engulfed in throughout most of the morning had finally subsided.

The rotten meat smell of the sores was everywhere. Someone was screaming. Someone else—or maybe it was the same man—was vomiting.

Horn had no choice but to lie in misery and absorb the sounds and smells of the mortally ill. Mercifully, his vision was totally gone. He could not see the disgusting mess that had become of the six-by-eight cell where he had spent the last eighteen years of his sentence. He was also unaware that Buzz, the child molester on the other side of the wall, had been dead for three hours, or that Sam—who two years earlier had raped and murdered his own sister at the age of nineteen—was now on his hands and knees as he sobbed, mumbling an inarticulate prayer to a God that had never existed to him until that morning.

Drifting in and out of consciousness, Horn's ravaged mind was a collage of people and events from his past. His mother. His parole officer. The sixteen-year-old girl he had shot in the chest in her apartment because it turned out that she didn't have any dope after all. A parade of lawyers.

The judge who had asked God for mercy on his soul. Horn had laughed out loud.

The sores were like fire, and their flames were spreading. He could no longer feel the distinct patches of corroded flesh; they were all melting into one surreal torture. Internally, he was being slowly devoured. Externally, he was burning alive. His last semi-lucid thought was a forlorn one.

They had all been right. Nathan Horn finally believed in Hell.

"What in God's holy name happened in here?!"

The faint Southern drawl of Special Agent Sean McMullan echoed as his rich voice boomed through the concrete corridor of San Quentin's North Seg. The corridor had otherwise fallen silent. It was a first for the prison's original death row wing, the wing eternally cacophonous with the rage of dead men walking.

Now? Men, yes. Dead, for sure. None walking. Two tiers of thirty-four cells. Sixty-eight dead men, not walking. Death row indeed.

Treading gingerly down the hallway with an ashen prison director on his left side and the CDC Associate Director of Epidemiology on his right—all three men in full-body, air-supplied, positive-pressure biohazard suits—the veteran agent silently counted to ten to maintain his composure.

Sean McMullan had been a special agent with the FBI Biological Countermeasures Unit—the BCU—for ten years. But he had never seen anything like this.

Each private cell was a new stage set with another scene

of the macabre. A few of the bodies were lying next to steel toilets, but most had died in their beds. IV poles stood at many of the bedsides, and needles, still plunged into stiffening flesh, attached clear tubing to half-empty fluid bags. Some of the bodies were in oddly contorted positions, and most were lying in one form of bodily discharge or another. Some exhibited the sores; others did not. All of them had expressions of terror and agony frozen to their faces.

McMullan turned to the pallid man walking next to him and asked how the deaths of sixty-eight inmates could possibly have gone unattended.

"They did not go unattended," the prison director asserted. "Death row inmates are checked routinely throughout the day and night. These inmates were all fine yesterday morning.

"At one p.m., a guard checked on them and made a note that an inmate had vomited. That inmate indicated he thought it was the food, and he declined to go to the infirmary. By nine p.m., there were two dozen sick men. Vomiting. Diarrhea. Fevers. Chills. Stuff like that. They were unanimously blaming the chicken from lunch.

"When the guards began bringing sick inmates to the infirmary, the doctor on duty assumed he was seeing an outbreak of food poisoning or stomach flu. He sent some swabs to the lab to be tested for *Salmonella* and *E. coli.* He gave the sick inmates fluids, began antibiotic regimens, and prescribed anti-nausea medications. There are no appropriate treatments beyond that, and we had insufficient space in the infirmary. So the doctor began returning them to their cells and prescribing bed rest.

"He also called in our entire medical staff to attend to the sick inmates through the night. Then, at about seven o'clock this morning, some of them began to break out in sores. That's when we called the CDC."

Even before the CDC team arrived, inmates were already dying. It had taken only a cursory evaluation of the situation before the CDC had solicited assistance from the FBI BCU. And by the time Sean McMullan arrived in the evening, San Quentin's North Seg death row wing had been completely depopulated.

It had only been thirty hours since the first inmate became symptomatic.

McMullan stopped in front of a still-locked cell and peered through its bars. The man lying dead inside the cell must have been in his early thirties. His muscular, tattooed arms were clearly the product of extensive weight-lifting. McMullan had every reason to assume that the inmate had been healthy before yesterday.

"OK," he said. "I'm going to need someone to draw a map of this cell block. I want each dead inmate pinpointed on that map, showing where he died and whether or not he had made it to the infirmary for treatment. I want to know who was puking at one p.m., which ones were sick at nine p.m., and the order in which they began getting sick after that. I want to know the order in which they died. I want notation of which ones have the sores. And I want to talk to the infirmary. Is the infirmary doc sick?"

"No, but he's quarantined. And three inmates from other wings of the prison are also dead. Those bodies are still in the infirmary."

McMullan dismissed the prison director, and, when he was gone, turned quietly to the CDC epidemiologist. "Dr. Wong, is there anything else about this that I'm missing?"

Guofu Wong blinked and cleared his throat. "No, sir," he said. "Unless you're missing the fact that this is the most virulent biological weapon the world has ever seen."

Two days later, CDC Associate Director of Epidemiology Guofu Wong stood at the head of a conference table in the J. Edgar Hoover Building in Washington, D.C. Behind him, a large screen projected a slide from his laptop computer. Sean McMullan and several additional FBI agents were among the audience, scrawling into notebooks and punching laptop keys as the doctor spoke.

"The sixty-eight death row inmates at San Quentin State Prison died from anthrax poisoning," Wong said.

Someone gasped. The man sitting nearest to where Wong was standing shifted his chair backward as if to physically distance himself from the epidemiologist who had been at the prison.

"The skin lesions that many of the inmates developed," Wong continued, "were in some ways indicative of textbook cutaneous anthrax. They exhibited the classic black moldy appearance from which the name *anthrax*, which means *coal*, was derived."

Wong projected a slide upon which two photographs were

displayed side by side. Each photograph showed a section of human skin blemished with the black sores of which he spoke. One image was labeled "Normal Anthrax Lesions" and the other "Death Row Anthrax Lesions." The sores on both photographs were similar in appearance.

"But anthrax lesions are usually painless," Wong continued. "The prison staff said that these men were screaming in pain. Furthermore, cutaneous anthrax is rarely fatal, and the lesions are typically small and few. Gastrointestinal anthrax could have caused the nausea and vomiting, and inhalational anthrax would definitely result in the shortness of breath some of the men were experiencing. But it sounds like a number of the inmates had all of these symptoms.

"Moreover, the symptoms of normal anthrax occur slowly, over the course of several days or even weeks. This infection was one hundred percent fatal within little more than a day."

Wong clicked a laptop key and a new slide appeared. On it was a small square, slightly glowing in a light lavender hue. Several haphazard patterns of unevenly spaced fluorescent lines trickled down the square like a collection of old ladders missing multiple rungs.

"So we conducted an analysis, called PCR, of the anthrax from the prison. What we learned is that an additional gene has been incorporated into its DNA. The new gene"—Wong circled one of the fluorescent lines with a laser pointer—"comes from a small, mobile DNA molecule called a plasmid. The plasmid encodes a small protein. Computer-based molecular modeling analyses suggest that this new protein can interact with the dominant toxin produced by the anthrax bacterium, a protein called 'lethal factor.' This interaction results in the formation of a larger complex—meaning, a group of proteins that function together as one molecular machine. The presence of the genetically engineered element in the larger complex potently activates the toxin, leading to dramatically increased virulence... "

A squat, balding man raised his hand.

Wong acknowledged the man. "Yes, Mr... ?"

"Special Agent Roger Gilman. Can you explain that again, please, and leave out the scientific gibberish for those of us that work in law enforcement?"

"Certainly," Wong said. "The anthrax that infected the prisoners is genetically enhanced. Its DNA encodes an additional protein that activates its major toxin. This makes the Death Row strain much more potent and much more rapidly acting than your garden-variety anthrax. The strain would not have been very difficult to engineer in a laboratory."

"If you say so," Gilman said, "but I don't understand why someone would bother genetically engineering a strain of anthrax in the first place. Can't we treat anthrax with antibiotics? Do we not have vaccines against it?"

"Those are good questions," Wong said. "Unfortunately, vaccination against anthrax is strictly prophylactic, and antibiotic treatment is only effective at the very beginning of exposure.

"The issue is that once anthrax has been in your body for a while—a short while—it begins to release the deadly toxin known as lethal factor. Vaccines can potentially block an infection, and antibiotics can kill the bacterium, but neither can neutralize lethal factor. So ultimately, if you're not treated essentially *before* you ever have symptoms, it's already too late."

A wavering voice from the back of the room all but whispered, "Is this new strain contagious from person to person?"

Agent McMullan cleared his throat. "If it was, the entire prison would be dead by now."

✕

Eight miles away, at the Naval Medical Research Center in Silver Spring, Maryland, a distraught research technician was faithfully recording his final analysis of data from the San Quentin outbreak. He could not believe what he was seeing.

Once the corpses had been documented and removed for disposal, a HazMat team had swarmed the facility. An average of fifty locations in every cell of the quarantined wing had been swabbed, as well as all of the facilities that served North Seg inmates. The swabs were used to inoculate Petri dishes for bacterial cultivation.

Normally, anthrax inoculated on a Petri dish is only detectable after overnight incubation. These cultures were flourishing within an hour after the swabs were taken.

That's impossible, the technician thought.

But what disturbed him even more was the source of the contamination. It was the swabs collected near the kitchen that yielded the highest titers of anthrax. The bacteria were most concentrated in the outside dumpster, within the remains of the trays of rice that had been served with the inmates' lunch.

Someone had deliberately poisoned the death row inmates.

✕

As Wong finished speaking, the conference room fell silent for several moments. At last, BCU Director Bob Wachsman spoke. "Next agenda item?"

A man who had not yet spoken stood and cleared his throat. "I'm Jack Callahan from the White House Office of

Correspondence. I was cc'd on this meeting because the prison outbreak cross-referenced with a piece of information I had placed into our database. It was a piece of mail received at the White House with a very vague reference to a prison in the text. It also contained a terror threat of cataclysmic proportions, to be carried out on Christmas Day of this year.

"The original document was written in Arabic. I'm circulating copies of the English translation for each of you. Upon initial examination, certain elements suggested that this document could be a hoax. The Arabic is very, uh, dodgy. And while the author claims to represent ISIL, the text is highly inconsistent with normal ISIL methods of operation. Of course, the reference to imprisonment, and to prisoners, has lent much more credibility to the threat in light of the outbreak at San Quentin. I'm concerned that the prison anthrax outbreak might have been the 'small taste of pain' that they 'promised.'"

"Where is the original document now?" The question was from Guofu Wong.

"I've sent it to the US Postal Inspection Services lab for tracking, forensics, and graphics analysis."

"Graphics analysis?" Wong pressed.

"Yes. The message was handwritten inside a greeting card. There was also a picture on the front of the card."

"Of?"

"Flowers."

"Flowers?"

"Flowers."

"Interesting."

A lengthy pause ensued as the task force members read

their copies of the document translation and considered the incongruous image.

Director Wachsman finally spoke. "It is physically impossible for us to vaccinate the entire country against anthrax before Christmas Day," he said gravely, "or to stockpile a sufficient supply of antibiotics to treat a nationwide outbreak. And even if we could do either of those things, the evidence I have heard here today suggests that antibiotics and vaccines developed to treat normal anthrax might not even work on the genetically engineered strain."

Wachsman looked up at Wong, an unspoken plea for contradiction. To Wachsman's dismay, the epidemiologist nodded solemnly.

"Director Wachsman is right," Wong said. "Against the Death Row strain, our current treatment arsenal is likely to be utterly useless." Wong clicked into his laptop to close the file for the slideshow he had just presented. Then he closed the laptop and dropped it into his briefcase. The rest of the task force sat immobile, most of its members staring vacantly at the conference table. Agent McMullan sighed.

"I may have an alternative solution," Wong offered then, and all eyes looked up to focus upon him. "There is a scientist in San Diego who may be able to kill this bug."

Professor Katrina Stone stormed out of her office at San Diego State University and slammed the door behind her.

From behind a large machine in the main laboratory, the perfectly greased head of Joshua Attle appeared. Thick glasses seated low over his nose, Josh watched over their ponderous frames as his graduate advisor darted through the lab, her volatile blue-gray eyes scanning for something that they did not appear to find.

"Where's Jason?" Katrina demanded when she saw Josh.

"Uh oh," Josh said. "You have that 'I just got another shitty grant review' look on your face."

Katrina sighed. Her face softened as she walked toward Josh and the machine he was operating. "That's because I just got another shitty grant review. I need to talk to Jason about the revisions and they need to happen fast. If I'm going to resubmit, I have to do it by the first of February. Have you seen him today?"

Josh shrugged. "Maybe he had another court appointment?"

Katrina shook her head and sighed again. "I know his divorce is dragging on, and believe me, I can sympathize—but between you and me, I wish he'd get it done. I need data from him. Badly."

For a few moments, she stared absently at the whirring machine, apparently deep in thought. Josh stole cautious glances in an effort to read her.

Only when he was standing right next to Katrina did Josh notice that she had visibly aged in the four years he had been her student. The vertical crease that always appeared between her eyes when she was annoyed or in deep concentration had finally begun to form a permanent wrinkle. He could now see a few sporadic, defiant white hairs in her reddish waves. Moreover, Josh thought she looked really tired.

Katrina Stone was only thirty-four years old.

DNA

Four years earlier, Josh had been pleasantly surprised when Katrina—back then, he still called her Dr. Stone—walked into Molecular Biology 610 and he saw her for the first time. He was not alone. Among the two-dozen first-year graduate students enrolled in the beginner course, several immediately took notice. In a field heavily dominated by middle-aged men, attractive young women were rare. It was only when she approached the podium at the front of the room that Josh realized the woman he had just been thinking of asking out was actually the professor.

"Good morning," she said and flashed a friendly smile to the room. Behind the smile was a sadness that Josh could not place. "Who has worked in a lab before?" Five or six hands went up, and she continued. "For those of you who have some experience, what would you say is the molecular biologist's best friend?"

"Um, a pipette?" one of the students offered.

"Enzymes?" suggested another.

"Well, those things certainly *are* very important in the molecular biology laboratory. But I'd like to suggest that *the* most important things are—bugs. Bacteria. We can't live without them." Two of the students who had raised their hands were now nodding.

"For those of you less familiar with the significance of bugs, don't worry. You'll get to it. But to begin with, let's talk for a moment about what amazing things we can do in a molecular biology lab because of these little guys.

"In short, we can make anything we want. And lots of it. Because bacteria have two qualities that are essential to molecular biology." She picked up a thick marker and wrote on a white board behind her as she spoke. "Number one: we can easily manipulate their DNA. We can drop a small piece of DNA, called a plasmid, into a population of bacteria, zap the bacteria with an electric shock, and they'll open up and take the plasmid inside of themselves.

"Number two: they replicate like crazy. So we pop our DNA plasmid, encoding any molecule we want to generate, into bugs, and as the bugs reproduce, they will make copy after copy of *our* molecule of interest. And we can harvest it and use it however we choose.

"For those of you who pull the short straw and end up in *my* lab," she said, and a few chuckles followed, "you'll be using this technology to bite the hand that feeds you. Because we use molecular biology and these helpful little bugs—to work on killing other bugs.

"The focus of my lab is anthrax research. We are dedicated to identifying molecules that can bind anthrax toxins, forming a larger molecular complex that can inhibit those toxins. Specifically, we want to block a protein toxin called 'lethal factor.' This aptly named molecule is *the* business end of anthrax. If we can inhibit lethal factor, we can reverse the effects of an anthrax infection... "

The memory of his earlier graduate work fell away from Josh when a needle on the computer screen jerked upward and then back down to draw a defined peak.

Katrina, too, visibly snapped back from wherever her mind had wandered to. "Is this a new group of molecules?" she asked.

"Yeah," he said. "I'm just getting started with it though, and our hundred-year-old HPLC"—he patted the side of the machine he was operating—"had a senior moment yesterday which took me all day to correct. Sorry. So I don't know if there are any good molecules in the new group yet."

"Any good news on the previous group? I could use some."

"Actually, there may be. I've done an initial screen and found some pretty strong lethal factor inhibitors. It's a little early to give you numbers, but later in the week I should be able to."

"Awesome. Well, keep me posted. If the data hold up it would be great to include in the grant resubmission." She smiled softly. "Maybe the NIH would take us more seriously if they knew what kind of anthrax inhibition we're getting here in our cheesy little lab."

Guofu Wong sat down at the conference table and lowered his briefcase to the floor. "Very recently," he said, "I was on an NIH grant review committee that received a very elegant proposal from a promising young anthrax researcher. The researcher's name was Katrina Stone.

"Dr. Stone proposed studies designed to continue and expand upon work in her lab aimed at identifying inhibitors of the lethal factor toxin. Her approach employs a robotic technology more sophisticated than any other on the market. This enables her studies to proceed at an exceptionally rapid pace. Unfortunately, it is also very expensive.

"Dr. Stone's preliminary results are stellar. Even in the absence of adequate funding"—he looked directly at an elderly man to his left while making the point—"she has already isolated and characterized *several* potent inhibitors of anthrax lethal factor.

"The application was rejected for a number of reasons, against my recommendation. But in light of the San Quentin outbreak, my team has taken the liberty of using our molecular modeling software to simulate interactions between Stone's inhibitors and the Death Row anthrax proteins. The compounds interact almost perfectly."

Wong turned to face Gilman. "To put all of that in lay terms, Agent Gilman, there is a scientist who may already be very much on the right track to a molecule that can block anthrax. And not just any anthrax, but *this specific*, genetically engineered strain. Therefore, it is my strong opinion that the grant rejection should be reversed at once and that the NIH should immediately fund this grant. I think this woman's preliminary data is *key* to inhibiting the Death Row complex."

✕

The elderly man to the left of Guofu Wong, toward whom Wong had pointedly glanced when mentioning the rejection of Katrina Stone's grant, had been calmly observing throughout the meeting. He had not spoken.

Now, he stood. "I'm Dr. James Johnson," he said. At mention of the name, several people registered recognition and even awe. "I, too, was on the committee that rejected the grant of Katrina Stone"—he rolled his eyes—"*against* the recommendation of my friend and colleague Dr. Wong. And I'll tell you why we rejected it.

"This scientist is only five years out of graduate school. I know that in many professions, five years of experience is a lot. However, scientist years are like reverse dog years. Until you've been in the field at *least* ten years, you're still a pup piddlin' on the carpet. Nobody gets a federal grant of this magnitude five years out of grad school, because they have no track record to prove that they will use the resources wisely. We're not talking small potatoes here, folks. An NIH grant is worth hundreds of thousands of dollars.

"Needless to say, of the *very* few that manage to obtain this kind of funding so early in their careers, most are stars in their field. They are doing research that is beyond anything the world has seen—"

Guofu Wong interrupted. "Jim, at the risk of getting into the same debate again, Stone *is* a star. She *is* doing research beyond anything the world has seen."

"Based on the information I had at the time we reviewed her grant," Johnson said, "I did not consider her a star. Her research was innovative, yes. But she was also competing with large, well-oiled labs that could carry out similar studies in one tenth the time it would have taken her to do it."

"You mean, like yours... "

A collective discomfort began rippling through the room as the task force members shuffled awkwardly in their chairs.

James Johnson glared at Guofu Wong and drew a breath. "OK, look Guofu," he said. "First of all, if I was so greedy as to bulldoze some pissant girl for funding, I'd be running a multi-billion dollar pharmaceutical company right now, not working for the government. I'm not quite that desperate."

He laughed softly, and several others laughed with him. The two women at the table—not laughing—exchanged a glance.

"You and I both know," Johnson continued, "that I'm a pioneer in infectious disease research. I've been doing this since *you* were a child, and I'm most certainly *not* in competition with young Katrina Stone."

He turned to the rest of the task force. "Now, the fact is: the decision not to fund this woman's grant was made before the emergence of the so-called Death Row strain of anthrax. I would like to review the data that Dr. Wong and his team have put together. If I agree with his conclusions, then I will *absolutely* agree with Dr. Wong. If Stone's inhibitors are as potent as he claims they are, then she is definitely the most promising researcher to combat this biological weapon. However, I have a much bigger concern."

He turned to once again address the other scientist exclusively. "How do you know she didn't engineer it?"

Katrina Stone left the grant review on her desk and walked through the lab toward the robot room. As she passed the pH meter setup by the door, she noticed that, as usual, the two most commonly used bottles were uncapped. Even repeated safety violations and tongue-lashings from Katrina had not broken her students of the habit. Sighing, she donned a pair of latex gloves from a box on the table and capped both bottles before throwing the gloves away.

Katrina passed through the open door that led out of the main lab and into the robot room. Nobody was inside. The massive liquid-handling robot, affectionately nicknamed "Octopus," was active as usual.

Katrina walked past Octopus toward the adjacent room just as the machine's Robotic Manipulator Arm—ROMA— was reaching an opening slit in a tall octagonal incubator. The laser at the tip of the ROMA scanned the barcode on a reaction plate. The claw squeezed the sides of the plate and pulled it out of the incubator, placed it precisely over its designated location on the workbench, and then slowly lowered it down into its slot.

As the ROMA retraced its path, a second arm swung into position. The pipetting arm moved over a large, liquid-filled reservoir and aspirated a precise volume into its tips, then carried the liquid to the reaction plate that had just been placed. The pre-programmed procedure scrolled along the computer screen.

Taking care to steer clear of Octopus' moving arms, Katrina passed by the robot through yet another door into the cell culture room. She was greeted by a conspicuous, bright red "BSL-2: Biosafety Level 2" sign, on which were listed the "moderate risk" biological agents permitted inside the room.

Li Fung, Todd Ruddock, and Oxana Kosova looked up, extended distracted hellos to Katrina, and turned back to their work. Todd and Oxana were each sitting in front of a laminar flow hood with their arms inside, using automatic pipettors to dispense pink liquid media into flasks of cells. They each wore blue latex gloves. Neither wore goggles or a lab coat.

Li, dressed in jeans and sneakers with a fully buttoned, calf-length white lab coat, was peering through the microscope at a dish. She pulled a black marker out of the chest pocket of the lab coat and made a notation on the top of the dish.

"Has anyone seen Jason?" Katrina asked.

"He had to go take care of some divorce thing with his lawyer," Oxana replied.

Katrina frowned. "Has he been over to the BSL-3 facility today?"

Oxana shrugged.

"I don't know," offered Li. "Is everything OK?"

"No," Katrina said. "Everything's not OK. If I can't procure some funding soon, our lab is going to be shut down."

At that moment, postdoctoral fellow Jason Fischer had two things on his mind: getting his work done and getting to his band's gig. But right now, he could do neither. Traffic northbound on I-15 was at a bumper-to-bumper standstill.

Jason wriggled to a partial standing position in the driver's seat of his ancient Honda to yank his cell phone from the front pocket of his baggy pants. As he sat back down, a thick lock of his long black hair snagged on the metal hinge to his rearview mirror and was ripped out. *"Mother fucker!"* Jason shouted.

After glancing at the clock on the screen of his phone—the clock on the dashboard had been broken for years—Jason clicked into the touchscreen to make a call.

"What's up, ass lick?" his singer Zack answered.

"Hey, Zacklies, what time do we go on stage tonight?" Jason asked.

"The show starts at eight, but we don't go on till ten."

"That means at least ten thirty."

"Maybe," said Zack. "Why, you're not going to be late, are you?"

"Nah, I think I should be there by about nine thirty. But right now I'm sitting in a parking lot on the 15 aimed the wrong direction. I have to go to Sorrento Valley and whack some infected mice before the show."

In his D.C. hotel room, epidemiologist Guofu Wong was eating dinner when an e-mail popped up on his laptop. The subject was "Operation Death Row." Wong scanned the body of the e-mail and then placed a call to an FBI agent in San Francisco.

"Hello, Dr. Wong," the agent said when he picked up. "I assume that you've gotten my e-mail."

"Yes, I've just finished reading over it," said Wong. "So the source of the anthrax was the rice. I'm not entirely surprised. It seemed that the majority of victims were suffering primarily from gastrointestinal anthrax, and I can see how others could have become inoculated through skin contact with the food or through inhalation while eating and ultimately displayed various symptoms. So what does that mean in terms of suspects? Who else had access to the kitchen?"

"A number of people. The food is cooked and distributed by inmates, under the supervision of a prison employee, of course. The three dead inmates who were not living on death row were all kitchen workers who had been preparing and serving the food for North Seg that afternoon. So the contamination was definitely introduced into the rice specifically fed to that wing of the facility. We have questioned everyone who would have been involved with the process."

"Nobody on the Terrorist Screening Center list, I assume?" Wong asked.

"I'm afraid not," the task force agent responded. "We did get a lead during the questioning, but it's weak. One of the kitchen workers was clearly nervous when we questioned him. After some pushing, he admitted that even though he had duty in the kitchen for that entire week, he had not performed it on one occasion."

"Why is that?" Wong asked.

"Because someone paid him two hundred dollars to not show up. He didn't know the guy. For two hundred bucks plus getting out of work, he wasn't asking questions. So it looks very likely that someone—probably another inmate— gained access to the kitchen and poisoned the rice."

"Did he give a description?"

"Just a racial slur against Hispanics."

"Oh, great," said Wong. "So, basically, our possible suspect list includes anyone at San Quentin of Hispanic or Latino origin. That narrows it down."

"Yes, to about two thousand suspects," said the San Francisco agent. "I'm waiting for the sketch artist, but I'm not putting too much weight on what that might yield. Meanwhile, we *are* cross-referencing prisoners of Latino or Hispanic origin at San Quentin with terrorist factions. We are focusing those efforts on ISIL, based on the information from Jack Callahan about the greeting card. So we are also looking at people of Mediterranean or mixed descent who might look Latino to an inmate not paying attention, and focusing on Arabs since the text was written in Arabic.

"Of course, these are death row inmates we're talking about. They tend to have a lot of people who hate them. I have assigned a team to track down the extracurricular activities of the victims of these particular inmates and *their* families. It's a huge task.

"But we are also considering the possibility that this could have been orchestrated by a disgruntled scientist."

Thirty minutes later, Jason Fischer cleared security at the BSL-3 facility and rushed into the lab to do his work. As it turned out, there was less work to do than he had planned on. He only had to sacrifice half of his mice.

The control group, which had been inoculated with anthrax in the absence of Jason's test inhibitor, was already dead. The experimental mice, those Jason was using to test his most promising inhibitor of lethal factor, were alive and did not appear to have any symptoms. Jason smiled at the efficacy of the compound.

"*Ding, ding, ding*, we have a winner," Jason said under his breath as he euthanized the animals. With the precision and speed of a gourmet chef, he began isolating internal organs for his standard biological work-up, handling each mouse as if it were a vegetable and not a concentrated reservoir of deadly bacteria. After dissecting dozens of mice and properly storing their organs, he hurried through the decontamination procedures, exited the animal facility, and entered the clean room.

Once out of the Biosafety Level Three area, Jason snatched

a paper towel out of the rack by the sink and scribbled down some notes. On the way out of the building, he shoved the paper towel into his pocket.

※

At San Quentin State Prison, an inmate was just returning from the showers. His cellmate's bed was empty. *Good, the dickhead is gone,* he thought. *Too bad I can't have my own room like those pieces of shit on death row.* The thought brought a grin to his face.

The prisoner raised a dark, heavily tattooed arm and grabbed the metal frame of the bunk to swing himself up onto the bed. Looking around to make sure nobody was watching, he reached down and found a familiar slit in the mattress. He shoved his hand inside and withdrew a thick wad of cash. The prisoner counted the money. It was almost enough.

He shoved the money back inside the mattress and covered it with loose cotton.

The prisoner jumped down from the top bunk and peered into the corridor. Satisfied that nobody was coming, he returned to his bunk once again and reached into another hiding place within his mattress. He pulled out a handful of small glass vials. One was empty.

The prisoner still had two vials left, and two would be more than sufficient.

※

"Dude, we didn't think you were gonna make it," Zack said with annoyance as he helped Jason pull his guitars and amp from the car and carry them toward the club's entrance. A large red-on-black poster next to the door read "Lethal Factor! Performing Tonight!" A second sign read "Welcome

42

to The Metal Shop. We are not responsible for the loss of wallets, purses, hearing, or teeth."

The two young men pushed through the line of patrons to bring Jason's equipment inside. It was ten fifteen.

"How much did we make?" Jason asked as they approached the stage.

"Seven fifty including both ticket sales and door draw."

"Thank God. I need my cut for my rent before we leave tonight."

The rest of the band was already on stage and had done their sound check without Jason. Hook, the affectionately nicknamed bass player who was missing a finger, looked emphatically at the clock on the wall and shook his head when Jason mounted the stage. As Jason hurried to set up his equipment, Hook flashed one of his remaining fingers toward Jason behind his back.

Jason worked as quickly and expertly on the stage as he had earlier in the lab, connecting his guitar, amp, and accessories and checking his tuning. As he did, a scantily dressed young woman brought a pitcher of beer and a shot of whiskey to the stage. Jason winked at the stranger and tipped back the shot, then drank deeply and quickly from the side of the pitcher. He offered the girl the pitcher, and she licked the side from which Jason had drunk.

Satisfied that his guitar was tuned, Jason gave Zack a nod. Zack grabbed the microphone off its stand and threw the stand into the crowd, then motioned to the soundman behind the audience. The lights went down and the house music was cut. The violence in the crowd began.

"*How's everyone doing out there?*" Zack screamed into the mic. "*WE ARE LETHAL FACTOR!*"

OCTOBER 16, 2015
4:27 A.M. PDT

The phone rang. Katrina slowly emerged from sleep and then rolled over to look at the clock on the nightstand. The phone rang again, and she picked up. "Hello?"

"Katrina, it's Tom." Her ex-husband sounded distressed.

"What's wrong?"

"Don't panic," Tom preempted. "Lexi is OK. But she has been picked up by the police for DUI. I'm on my way to go get her. She's at the precinct on the corner by my house. Do you know the one?"

"Oh my god, Tom. I'll be right there."

She found him in the hallway of the police station. "What was she doing driving, Tom?" Katrina snapped as she strode toward her ex-husband. *"She doesn't even have a license!"*

"Katrina, I'm just as upset about this as you are," Tom said with exaggerated patience and a roll of the eyes. "Just because this happened on my weekend... it could just as easily have happened when she was at your house and you know it!"

"*No!* This would *never* have happened at my house! It happened at *your* house because you and Kimberly let her get away with murder. Because you're more interested in being cool than you are in raising your daughter. Where was she? Did you let her go to a party where people were drinking?"

"*Hell no!* She snuck out. I didn't even know she was gone until the police called me. I have no idea where she was."

"Oh well *that* doesn't surprise me. Way to be responsible, Tom!"

"Katrina, spare me! Where do you get off? *You* are the goddamn workaholic. *You* are the one so wrapped up in your precious research that you don't give a rat's ass about... " He stopped as a uniformed officer came through a nearby door with their fifteen-year-old daughter.

Alexis was wearing a black miniskirt and a red T-shirt that showed her midriff. There was vomit on the front of the shirt. She was shivering violently; the knee-length black jacket that hung open over her clothing, while fashionable, was thin and offered little protection from the early-morning October chill. Thick black lines of mascara streaked down from both eyes, and a stain of wiped lipstick was smeared across her cheek. Her shoulder-length hair was wildly disheveled.

When she saw her parents, Alexis began to cry. "I'm so sorry, you guys," she said. "I only had one beer, I swear."

"Then what's with the puke on the front of your shirt?" Tom asked.

His daughter's tears stopped as suddenly as they had begun. "Oh, gee *Dad*, I guess you haven't noticed, but I've had stomach problems most of my life. But yeah, I guess any time I puke I *must* be drunk. Whatever!"

"Only when you just got a DUI," Tom countered.

"Honey, what happened?" Katrina asked. "Why were you sneaking out?"

Alexis began to cry again. Thick rivers of mucus streamed from her nostrils, and she wiped them with the back of her hand.

"I knew if I asked Dad he wouldn't let me go," she sobbed. "This guy's parents were out of town and he was having a party. Dylan was going, and this shady ass ratchet bitch Melinda was going, too. She's always, like, totally hitting on Dylan, and she's such a total *slut...* I *had* to go. He's *my* boyfriend, not *hers!* I went with Erin and Jennifer, and Jennifer was supposed to be driving, but she got totally trashed. I just thought I should drive."

"Do you *know* how much trouble you're in?" Tom yelled. "Getting a DUI without a license is some serious shit, young lady!"

"Lexi," Katrina said quietly, "I know you think that your dad and I are too strict. You're right. He would not have let you go to that party, and I wouldn't have either. But, honey, we're strict because we love you. It's for your *own good!* We are just trying to protect you. You have no idea how many psychos are out there."

Alexis rolled her eyes at the comment and then looked away melodramatically. "Yes, I *do* know, Mother! As if you could protect me from any of them."

Jason Fischer woke with a splitting headache and a stranger.

The young groupie from the previous evening was sitting up in the bed beside Jason, her bedcovers draped around her hips, her bare breasts exposed. She was looking through his wallet. As Jason blinked to focus his vision, she withdrew a business card. "You have a Ph.D.?" she asked, reading the card.

"Yeah," he said. Not bothering to veil his annoyance, Jason took his belongings away from her. He stuffed the business card back into the wallet and flipped through the cash. The money from the gig was still there. He sank back onto the pillows of the girl's bed as a wave of nausea hit him.

She tried to nuzzle his bare chest. Jason shrugged her away.

"I saw your car," the girl said. "I thought you were broke."

Jason threw the covers aside and staggered out of bed. "I am," he said and then ran down the hall to her bathroom.

1:12 P.M. PDT

That afternoon, Katrina was in her office obsessing over her latest rejected grant application to the National Institutes of Health. The February 1 deadline for resubmission was already less than four months away.

Katrina was thrilled with the first reviewer's comments. The reviewer had enthusiastically wanted to fund her project. She read over the comments several times to highlight and commit to memory the specific points mentioned as favorable.

But the sentiment conveyed by the second review contrasted starkly. As she examined the reviewer's comments, Katrina wondered, *Did this jackass even look at my data?*

Five years earlier, Katrina's graduate work had been exceptional. Rumor of her being offered a faculty slot at the university—a scarcely heard of event—began to circulate even before she defended her dissertation.

Later, in accepting the new position, Katrina made some

enemies. Some were other junior faculty, but most were fellow graduates in her class.

The unfortunate majority of Ph.D. candidates graduating in her field would have no choice but to endure a postdoctoral stint under a faculty mentor before they were even considered for a faculty post. Postdoc positions paid miserably and subjected researchers to excruciating hours and, often, a total lack of appreciation or respect by their advisors. Tradition dictated that any contributions they made to the field were attributed primarily to their mentors, and so the credit they received for their own work was minimal. To those who had just worked for so many years to acquire a shiny new Ph.D. and the esteem of their colleagues, it was an insult as well as a lesson in mental and physical endurance.

The lucky ones finished their postdocs after only a year or two. The unfortunate were stuck in them for five years or longer. Katrina was among the rare few to bypass the process entirely. The price she would pay later was huge.

Five years after graduation, as Katrina sat fuming over the comments of the second reviewer of her grant, it was clear that her youth and lack of experience had cost her yet another opportunity for funding.

1:21 P.M. PDT

While Katrina was agonizing over the rejection of her latest grant, two federal agents were wandering uninvited through her laboratory. Casually observing and taking mental notes, Agents Sean McMullan and Roger Gilman made a slow, deliberate circle around the central lab space.

Two large, rectangular work islands stood in the center of the room with workspaces for four people per island. Dozens of clear bottles labeled with colored tape cluttered the benches, along with test tube racks of various sizes. Each bench also held several pieces of equipment, most of which were unidentifiable to the FBI agents. Many of the machines were connected to computers.

Around the outside of the room were several large refrigerators and freezers that produced a loud, constant background hum. A shelving area held chemical stocks divided and color-coded with stickers according to their physical properties and the health hazards that they presented to humans. Next to the shelves were a shower and an eyewash station. On a bench leading out of the main lab and into an adjacent room was a small appliance labeled, "pH Meter," with several vials and bottles next to it. Two of them, labeled "Concentrated HCl" and "10M NaOH," were uncapped.

Gilman peered through the window into the adjacent room just as a large mechanical arm stretched suddenly into view. A metal claw opened, grabbed something, and then backed out of view. Gilman took a leaping step backward and exclaimed, *"What the devil is that?"*

From behind him came a response with a slight Russian accent. "Oh, that's Octopus."

McMullan and Gilman turned to look at the girl who had spoken.

She stood in an area overtly labeled "Cytotoxic Compounds." She was wearing latex gloves and a lab coat, and her medium brown hair was tied back into a ponytail. Her arms were extended into a fume hood and she was transferring miniscule quantities of liquid from a vial into a small tube. A lollipop was clamped between her lips.

"What does it do?" Gilman asked.

The girl closed the vial and tube and pulled her hands out of the hood. She peeled off her gloves and tossed them into a waste container before popping the lollipop out of her mouth. "The robot? It runs biological assays for us. Right now, it is looking for inhibitors of an enzyme. It works much more quickly that we can, so it can screen thousands of molecules at a time. It's a very efficient way to do the kind of work we do here."

McMullan chuckled. "Then what do you do?" he asked jokingly.

"Someone has to program Octopus," the girl replied, smiling. "Besides, there are a lot of things that need to be done around here that require a human being to do them.

Robots can work incessantly, but they can't really think. Not quite yet."

"You're not from OSHA, are you?" the girl asked.

"No ma'am," Gilman said, "We are looking for Professor Katrina Stone. Is she here?"

⋈

Katrina's attention was diverted from the grant review when Oxana Kosova poked her head in.

"Some guys are here to see you," Oxana said.

The two men entered the room and Oxana closed the door behind them on her way out. They fanned out and stood in front of Katrina's desk.

She visually dissected them both. Both wore full suits, which none of her colleagues ever did unless they were presenting at a scientific conference. Clearly, these were not scientists.

One of the men was slightly shorter than the other and looked quite young in the face but was balding considerably. Katrina could not decide if he was young and his balding made him look older, or if he was older and his baby-face made him look young. He seemed uncomfortable.

The other man was taller, and muscular, with salt-and-pepper waves and kind green eyes. A vertical scar ran partially down his left cheek, and his face was weathered and tanned. He extended his hand, and the tip of an old tattoo peeked out from beneath his cuff.

"Dr. Katrina Stone?" the taller man asked in a slight Southern drawl. Katrina nodded and smiled. As she reached forward to shake his hand, he said, "I'm Agent Sean McMullan and this is Agent Roger Gilman—"

Katrina's smile disappeared and she pulled her hand away as if a spider had landed on it. "Oh, for Christ's sake!"

she interrupted. "I just talked to Homeland Security two weeks ago, for an hour!"

"What do you expect, lady?" the short one named Gilman blurted out. "You work with anthrax!"

McMullan gave his partner a scowl and lowered his hand to his side following Katrina's rebuff. "I'm sorry, Dr. Stone," he said. "We are with the FBI, not Homeland Security. This is not a routine review of your research."

Katrina flinched. "I'm sorry for my rudeness; please sit down." She gestured toward the two seats facing her desk. "What can I do for you?"

The agents sat down, and he continued. "Dr. Stone, before we proceed, I need for you to *very fully* understand that we will be discussing matters of strictest confidentiality. Please, do not repeat this information to *anyone.*

"We are here to solicit your help. A new strain of anthrax has been discovered, and this strain contains an unusual element. There is a plasmid incorporated into its DNA that encodes a potent activator of anthrax lethal factor. What does that mean to you?"

Katrina was silent for a long moment. She cast her eyes between one agent and the other, sizing each of them up before speaking. "That sounds like a biological weapon. A plasmid is a mobile DNA element that can be inserted into a cell at the will of the researcher. And lethal factor is the toxin that causes the clinical symptoms of anthrax. A strain of the bug carrying a plasmid-encoded activator of lethal factor would presumably be much more virulent than wild-type—I mean, eh, ordinary anthrax."

"It is," McMullan said and shuddered slightly.

Katrina glanced down at the rejected grant application on the desk before her. When she looked back up, she was scowling slightly. "What do you want with *me?* I have recently been reminded once again by the NIH that many other researchers worldwide are working on the anthrax problem, and that most of them are more experienced and better equipped than I am."

McMullan and Gilman exchanged a glance. "One of our scientific consultants was on the review committee for your last grant application to the NIH," McMullan said. "The preliminary data for inhibitor compounds generated in your lab stood out in his mind as exceptionally promising."

"He wasn't impressed enough to fund the project," Katrina said bitterly.

"Actually, he did want very much to fund it. He was overruled by others on the committee."

Katrina thought back to the critiques and realized that McMullan was referring directly to the two reviewers who had provided the comments for her grant application.

McMullan continued, "Anyway, that was before the discovery of this new strain. Your grant application has now been reviewed once again in light of the discovery of the new strain of anthrax. And the NIH committee believes that your compounds have the potential to be developed rapidly into effective therapeutics. So the government has decided to offer you whatever you need in terms of funding, equipment, and staff, to complete the project detailed in your proposal as quickly as possible."

🧬

Twenty minutes later, Gilman and McMullan stood to leave Stone's office, and each of them shook her hand politely.

"It is a lot to consider," said McMullan. "Your lab will be effectively turned upside down. It will be a very large intrusion into your life and the lives of your staff. However, we *will* need your decision as quickly as possible." He reached into his pocket and pulled out a business card. "We'll be in touch." He handed her the card. "And, again, please do not discuss this matter with anyone except Agent Gilman or me. Do not discuss it over the phone or the Internet with *anyone*."

"OK, I understand," Stone said. She took the business card and peered at it quickly before opening her top desk drawer to tuck it inside.

Gilman was glancing absently at the framed degrees on the wall behind her. There were three of them, all from different schools across the nation.

Next to the diplomas was a full-sized poster of what looked like a subway map. The subway stations were nonsense words, such as "mTOR" and "p53." The caption at the top of the map read, "A Subway Map of Cellular Pathways." Another full-sized poster on the wall to the left was a jumbled mess of overlapping, zigzagging, crossing and merging arrows and brightly colored shapes. It was entitled "Apoptosis Signals."

Gilman shook his head and turned to leave, but then he stopped short. For a few moments, he could only gape in disbelief at the large poster on the wall next to the door that had been at his back through their entire conversation. He turned to his partner who was also staring at the artwork.

Wordlessly, Gilman reached into his briefcase and took out a document. It was his copy of the greeting card from the White House. The one with the funny bouquet on the front.

The high-resolution poster on Katrina Stone's wall was in full color. The small picture in Gilman's hand was the smeared black and white of a cheap photocopy. Otherwise, the two images of the bouquet were identical.

The agents whirled back around in unison, guns drawn.

"*Get your hands up, NOW!*" yelled McMullan.

4:56 P.M. EDT

In Washington, D.C., United States Postal Inspector Teresa Wood stepped out of an underground Metro station. A tall black-and-white pillar announced that she was at the Archives/Navy Memorial station.

In Teresa's right hand was her briefcase; with her left she was shoving the entire second half of a hot dog into her mouth. A fierce gust of wind blew past her at exactly the wrong time, sending a shoulder-length tuft of her fine straight black hair directly into her mouth along with the food. Rubbing her face onto her shoulder to detach the hair from her mouth, she crumpled the foil wrapper from the hot dog and tossed it into a trashcan on the sidewalk as she passed. She did not stop walking.

Still chewing the large bite, the USPIS Assistant Director of Forensics progressed briskly up the familiar stretch of Pennsylvania Avenue, her long legs taking half as many strides as those of a man walking nearby to cover the same distance.

The Navy Memorial was spread out on her right beyond the fountains separating it from the sidewalk. A former Navy girl herself, Teresa liked to refer to the memorial as proof that the US is at the center of the globe. The joke was a tongue-in-cheek jab at the large map of the world stretching across the concrete, with North America clearly defined in the center and the other continents fading out around it. And at *The Lone Sailor*—a Navy *man*, of course, standing over it.

West of the memorial, Teresa ignored the signal at Ninth Avenue and dodged traffic as she headed across the street toward the main entrance of J. Edgar Hoover Building. As she did, her cell phone rang.

"Shit," Teresa muttered through the half-masticated food in her mouth. Hurrying to swallow, she absently wiped her face as if her caller could see her. When she could speak somewhat clearly, she answered the phone, "Wood here."

"Teresa!"

Her caller sounded a little distressed. "Ken?" she asked.

"Yeah, it's me," said her colleague from the graphics department. "You're not going to believe this."

"Ken, I'm in D.C. I have a prioritization meeting at FBI headquarters." She dusted the remaining hot dog crumbs off of her suit jacket where they had come to rest upon her sizable breasts.

"Well, they're going to want to see this, too. It's going to change some of your prioritizations. Look at this."

Teresa's cell phone clicked as Ken hung up. Bewildered, Teresa stared at the face of the phone for a moment until it began to vibrate. A bubble on the screen indicated a new text message.

Teresa opened the message. The small embedded graphic was one she had seen the previous day for the first time. The little bouquet. How cute, except that it came with the threat of a nationwide terrorist attack by ISIL.

As Teresa began reading Ken's text message beneath the image, her rapid pace toward FBI headquarters slowed to a standstill. Her heart began to thud in her chest and she sank heavily onto a nearby bench.

"*Holy Christ*," Teresa said aloud, still staring at the screen of her phone.

☒

Katrina's hands flew up as she stood wide-eyed behind her desk, panting. "*What!*" she practically shouted, her eyes moving from one agent to the other.

"*Explain this!*" Gilman spat, throwing a sheet of paper down onto her desk.

Katrina slowly and deliberately reached for the page, watching the agents and the guns pointed toward her. She picked the paper up with hands that were now trembling. On one side of the page was a black-and-white copy of the image on Katrina's wall. On the other was a long message handwritten in Arabic script.

"I can't explain it," Katrina said. "I don't speak the language." Before laying it back down, she flipped it over to glance once again at the picture.

"Where did you get that?" McMullan asked, jabbing a thumb backward to indicate the poster.

"Nature," she replied.

"Very funny," said Gilman. "It's a computer graphic."

Despite her trepidation at the guns still pointed in her direction, Katrina suppressed a smile. "I meant *Nature*"—she bent the first two fingers of both hands in the air to simulate quotation marks—"the scientific journal." She then pointed for emphasis to a printed issue on her desk of the same publication.

McMullan and Gilman lowered their guns. Gilman picked

up the journal and flipped through quickly. Katrina gestured to a section of one of the built in bookshelves on the wall next to the desk, where she had three entire shelves dedicated to the same publication.

"What would this... *artwork*... be doing in a scientific publication?" Gilman demanded.

"It's not artwork," Katrina said.

McMullan stammered. "You mean, *anyone* who has read this particular... journal... entry, or whatever, would have seen this picture?"

"Of course," Katrina said. "Any half-decent anthrax researcher will *absolutely* know this paper. In 2004, it was arguably the biggest accomplishment in the field." Her eyes darted from one FBI agent to the other as they sat down in front of her desk once again.

Gilman reached back into his briefcase and pulled out another sheet of paper. Looking back at McMullan, who nodded his approval, he handed it over to Katrina.

"OK, Dr. Stone," he said, "this is the English translation of the Arabic text you just looked at. The original image and text came from a greeting card received at the White House on the same day that the activated strain of anthrax was discovered. Now, what does the bouquet on your wall have to do with either of those events?"

Katrina skimmed over the English translation of the card. "Gentlemen," she said slowly. "This is not a graphic image of a bouquet. It is a crystal structure detailing a molecular mechanism. What you are looking at is the membrane pore formed by anthrax toxins upon interaction with their host cell receptor. This is the structure that allows infiltration of anthrax into a human cell."

"If you promise not to shoot me, I'll show you," Katrina said with a bit of sarcasm.

The agents finally holstered their weapons.

Katrina sat back down at her desk and clicked into the reference library in her computer, then grabbed a yellow Post-It note and a pen. She quickly wrote "Santelli, E. (2004) *Nature* 430: 905." Then she stood and walked to the bookshelf, from where she selected the appropriate issue of the journal. With both agents looking over her shoulder, she flipped to page 905. Katrina turned two more pages to reveal another full color print of the same image.

"There, you see?" She set the journal on the desk and walked to the wall poster. Pointing at one of the brightly colored clusters, she said, "I know; it does look like flowers. See these seven pieces?"—she encircled each of the differently colored groupings with a forefinger—"the flower heads, if you will? They're all identical to each other. These are called subunits. Each is one copy of an anthrax protein called protective antigen. It interacts with a receptor produced by the host cell, shown here." She traced the neatly arrayed hollow cylinder protruding downward. "The receptor is what looks like the stems of the flowers, but it is actually a pore. When the anthrax proteins interact with the receptor, this pore shuttles the lethal factor toxin into the cell, and that is where the toxin's effects are exerted."

"Why would the cell do that?" Gilman asked, incredulous. "It's as if the cell commits suicide by bringing these toxins inside, right?"

"For lack of a better way to say it," she responded, "the cell doesn't know any better. The receptor is a normal cell surface protein. Its job, so to speak, is to bring beneficial molecules inside. The anthrax proteins infiltrate by hijacking the machinery, so the cell brings the toxin inside instead."

"What do the toxins do to kill the cell?" McMullan asked.

Katrina shook her head and looked down at the floor. "We still don't know," she said. "Despite all the research that has been conducted since 9/11, we still don't know *exactly* how anthrax kills people."

In Washington, D.C., Teresa Wood sat with White House Postal Operator Jack Callahan and FBI Case Director Bob Wachsman. The three of them were reviewing her colleague's brief for a second time.

"It was never flowers at all," Teresa said.

Jack nodded. "And I think we can be assured of three things: that the greeting card was not a hoax, that the activated anthrax strain is the threat referred to in that card, and that what happened at San Quentin four days ago is going to happen to the rest of us on Christmas Day."

2:56 P.M. PDT

After the two FBI agents left her office, Katrina sat at her desk waiting for her heart rate to return to normal. The words of Agent Sean McMullan were echoing through her mind. *A new strain of anthrax has been discovered, and this strain contains an unusual element.*

Katrina took several deep breaths and let them out slowly. She grabbed a Kleenex from the box on her desk and blotted her perspiring face. *There is a plasmid incorporated into its DNA that encodes a potent activator of anthrax lethal factor.* She stood and stepped out of her office. It was Jason she needed to see.

Oxana was still in the main lab. Katrina approached her and spoke with her quietly for a few moments. Then she passed through the main lab and entered the robot room. As if to say hello, Octopus swung an arm toward her. It picked up a reaction plate and filed it away into the incubator as Katrina swerved around it and walked through to the cell culture room.

Jason Fischer and Todd Ruddock were inside. Jason sat

before a laminar flow hood, dousing every square inch of its workspace with ethyl alcohol from a squirt bottle.

Katrina came up behind him. "Fischer! You *are* an alcoholic!"

"Heh heh. Well, if I'm not at the bar, I'm sterilizing something."

"It *is* good for all occasions that way."

"What's up?" he asked without turning around. He wiped up the ethanol with stack of paper towels and then threw the towels into a bright red Biohazard Waste can.

"I was wondering how late you're planning on working tonight and what you have planned when you're done."

"I still have to feed my cells," he said and uncapped a bottle to begin transferring liquid into a small plastic dish. "I'm just getting started and it'll take me, um, probably about an hour."

"And then?"

"Hmm," he stuck his nose in the air and mused in a horrible British accent, "I think maybe I'll take the yacht out for a spell."

Katrina chuckled and poked her finger through a gaping hole in his faded black sweatshirt. "Maybe you oughta sell your yacht and buy some clothes, dude," Katrina said.

"Actually, I'm going home afterward," Jason said, dropping the British accent. "I feel crap-tacular. And I like my clothes just the way they are, thank you! They dispel the grossly unjust myth that everyone with a Ph.D. makes a shitload of money."

"They also dispel the myth that everyone with a Ph.D. is a stuffy geek," Katrina commented.

"As do you," Jason said with a smile.

Katrina thought Jason looked pale, and his face was covered with perspiration despite the cool temperature in the room. "Now that you mention it, you *look* crap-tacular," she said.

Jason looked up at her and raised one eyebrow.

"No offense," she added.

"None taken."

"Rough night last night? You had a show, didn't you?"

"Yeah, but if this is a hangover it's the worst one I've ever had in my life. I think I have the flu. I woke up with it this morning. I'm getting some serious rest this weekend."

Todd Ruddock stood up from where he had been sitting at the adjacent hood and took a tray out of an incubator. He laid the tray on the counter next to the microscope and began picking up culture plates one at a time to inspect them under the scope.

Katrina kept talking to Jason. "Damn. I need to talk to you. I was hoping to take you out for a beer."

"Am I in trouble?"

"Haha, no. Actually, I want to talk to the whole lab. There's been a bit of a development. It's a long story; hence the beer idea."

She posed the same question to Todd. "Hey, Todd, are you free in about an hour for a beer?"

"You buying?"

"Yep."

"Um, let me think. Yes." Evidently satisfied with what he saw under the scope, Todd returned the tray of culture plates to its shelf in the incubator, nodded at Katrina, and breezed out of the room.

Katrina watched Todd walk through the robot room and back into the main lab. Then she closed the door. "Jason, listen," she said.

Jason finally stopped working and turned from the hood to face her, his face questioning. Katrina never closed doors.

She glanced through the window and into the robot room one more time before speaking. "Where is the activator data, and how many people know about it?"

McMullan and Gilman were quiet as they drove away from Katrina Stone's lab. When McMullan finally broke the silence, his words seemed out of place. "She's an anthrax researcher!"

"Yeah, I figured that much out," Gilman responded. "So?"

"So, Homeland Security has her entire life on file."

Gilman smiled for the first time since being assigned to this case.

Jason had never seen Katrina so poorly composed. Her face was flushed, and she looked as if she, too, had been sweating. Jason wondered if she could be coming down with the same bug he had woken up with at the annoying groupie's house. It would be no surprise. Between the close quarters within the lab, the excessive workload, and the lack of rest they were all burdened with, when one person got sick, the whole lab usually caught it.

He did not answer her question right away.

"Well, I *have* talked to people about the data," Jason

finally said, "right after I found the activator. I found it, like, a week before the Keystone conference, remember? So I was sitting with a group of anthrax people at the conference during lunch one day, and something came up that made me think of it." He paused long enough to raise an eyebrow. "I didn't think it was a secret."

Katrina said nothing.

"A bunch of the people at the table were doing inhibitor screens like ours," Jason continued, "looking at all different types of molecules. I mentioned that we had stumbled upon some activators of lethal factor while we were looking for inhibitors. Some of the other people said they had seen them, too. I guess it's pretty normal, every once in a while, to come across something that activates the enzyme. But nobody had seen the three-hundred-fold increase in lethal factor activity we saw with the 37B-17 compound.

"I remember this guy from Stanford said, 'Well, if you ever want to make a biological weapon you're all set.'"

Katrina visibly bristled.

Jason remembered having made a similar remark the day he found the activator. He had gone to her office to discuss his inhibitor data, and in the course of the conversation he had mentioned the activator as an offhand remark. To Jason's surprise, she had asked him to elaborate. He told her that there were several, but that one in particular was extraordinarily potent.

"Keep the data and set the compound aside," she had instructed him. "If we aren't finding any really good inhibitors, we may want to talk to the chemists. A minor structural change can potentially convert an activator into an inhibitor. So we might still be able to use it... "

Now, Jason thought that Katrina looked a bit off kilter as

she turned to look once again through the window into the robot room. "Anyway," he said, "the data is at my desk. You want it?"

Katrina took a breath. "OK here's the deal. I just had a visit—not a phone call, a visit—from two FBI special agents. They described a strain of anthrax carrying an activator. And they showed me a document threatening a bioterror attack.

"They want to fund our research to stop it. But they don't trust me. At all. At one point in our conversation, they literally pulled their guns on my ass. I think there's a strong possibility that in the near future, there will be feds crawling all over our lab. They have some rudimentary information about the activator strain that they found. I don't think we should share anything about *our* activator, because I don't know how close in structure it might be."

In his reflection on the sash of the tissue culture hood, Jason could see that he had turned from gray to white. He slumped in his chair, panting. His flu felt worse every second. "Wow," he said weakly. After a lengthy pause, he swallowed and then sighed. "Yeah, I guess you're right. What would they think if they found the data?"

Katrina continued, "I still want to keep the data for the same reasons I did before. But it has to be somewhere they can't find it—even if they turn our lab and our offices completely upside down, which I think they might. I don't want it at my house, nor do I recommend that you take it home. Who knows if they'll raid our residences. So what can we do with it?"

Jason shook his head. "Hold on a minute." He turned off the tissue culture hood and returned his cells to the incubator.

Together, Katrina and Jason walked out into the robot

room and began looking around, as if regarding the familiar laboratory for the first time. Other than a few cabinets and the large stations supporting the robot and its incubator, there was not much in the room.

They walked back out into the main lab. Oxana was now gone, and the laboratory was vacant. Jason led Katrina to his desk. He pulled down a jumbled notebook crammed with loose pages of data and flipped through it until he found what he was looking for. He removed the pages of interest and set the notebook down on the desk.

"This is all of it," Jason said. "None of it is really written up for anyone to read other than me, since we never followed up with these compounds. And I never bothered entering it into the computer database. I can delete the one raw file from Octopus that identified the compound."

They wandered back out into the lab and continued looking around. Katrina looked up at the ceiling. "You think we could put it in a light fixture?" But then she added, "Oh, duh. It would cut off the light. Nevermind."

Jason began to consider the option of destroying the data entirely. "You sure you want to keep it?"

"Yes," Katrina said emphatically. "We might need it to work on an antidote for the activated strain. We can't destroy it. I'm at a loss."

Jason looked deeply into her face, wanting to know more about the antidote project, wondering what to do with the activator data. And then suddenly, he knew.

He could not contain the grin that now spread over his face. He turned without a word and began walking.

Curious, Katrina followed.

Jason walked briskly back through the robot room into the cell culture room. He turned and grinned at Katrina, dramatically batted his eyelashes, and then cast his gaze across the room.

In the corner opposite the door stood a large, silver tank connected to two steel reservoirs that fed a constant supply of liquid nitrogen. A digital gauge monitored the dangerously cold element, keeping the temperature at negative 196 degrees Celsius. The tank was equipped with a monitored alarm system that would notify university security if the cooling system failed.

Inside the tank were the most precious items in the lab— all of the mammalian cells and viruses that had been generated since the lab had first been initiated. Years of Katrina's research. And Jason's. The tank's contents would be destroyed if thawed. So the tank could never be emptied without relocating everything inside to another cryogenic location, a task that presented a logistical nightmare.

The FBI would never have reason to look inside the liquid nitrogen, and even if they did, the scientists had a strong argument to stall the effort.

A stepstool alongside the cryogenic tank granted access to the heavy hinged lid, that, when open, almost reached the ceiling. A padlock with a four-numbered code secured the lid.

Jason's eyes moved back to Katrina.

Finally understanding, she giggled. Wordlessly, she began opening drawers and cabinets in the storage island by the door of the room, rifling through the contents as she went.

Jason, who knew the whereabouts of materials in the room better than his boss did, crossed directly to the correct drawer and pulled out a medium sized cryogenic bag. He pulled it open and dropped in the several pages of data.

Then he turned and sealed the bag with the heat-sealer that sat next to the microscope.

After mounting the stepstool to reach the padlock, he clamped the heavy plastic bag between his teeth and then rotated the numbers on the lock to the correct sequence. He popped the padlock open.

When Jason swung the heavy door upward, a white cloud of sublimation billowed from the tank. He waved his hand to disperse the upper layers of the thick fog in order to see the towers of cryogenic vials that rested beneath it.

Katrina reached toward a nearby shelf and grabbed a pair of thick, blue, cold-resistant gloves. She handed them up to Jason, and he pulled them on. He then pulled out one of the cryogenic towers, dripping smoking liquid nitrogen onto the cracked linoleum floor.

After pulling out three more towers and setting them beside the first, Jason dropped the bag containing the activator data into the liquid nitrogen tank and watched as it disappeared beneath the murky surface of the vapor.

Jason replaced the metal towers filled with boxes of cryogenic vials, swung the lid back into place, and replaced the padlock. He removed the gloves and turned back to Katrina.

"Well, I guess that about does it," she said.

Jason furrowed his brow. "Now that we've done that, exactly how are we ever going to get the stuff out again?"

Katrina thought for a moment and then smiled. "My daughter volunteers at the humane society," she said. "I have an idea."

4:21 P.M. PDT

Katrina chose a corner table at the bar. She, Oxana, and Todd were quickly joined by Josh Attle, who had shown up at the lab as she was on her way out. The four of them sat sipping frosty pints of beer and sharing a platter of appetizers while Katrina spoke.

Changing the subject abruptly every time a waitress approached, she first told them in broken sections about her encounter with the FBI. She described the activated anthrax strain and said that they had been asked to work on an antidote. She did not mention the activator that Jason had found.

She then began telling the three students about the threatening card that had been sent to the White House.

Josh interrupted her with, "ISIL sent a greeting card? Is their Twitter account suspended?"

The four scientists laughed, a welcome break from the tension, and then spent a few moments reflecting on the particulars of the card. Katrina only had a vague recollection of its text, which she had quickly skimmed while being held at gunpoint by two federal agents. She wondered if she could obtain a copy, but she anticipated that this aspect of the investigation would be deemed 'none of her beeswax' by the feds.

"Listen, you guys," Katrina warned. "If we elect to take on this work, the FBI will become a continuous presence in our lab. I'm sure that probably means media exposure and God knows what else. Will the exposure be good for us as a lab? Hell, yeah! But it will also mean total invasion of our privacy— and no room for error.

"These guys are high-strung about this. One second they were shaking my hand. The next, I was looking into the barrels of both of their guns, and I swear I almost peed myself."

The comment drew another laugh from her students.

"I think the tall cute one likes me a bit," Katrina said with a mischievous smile. "But the short one—I think his name is Gilman—obviously had a beef with me right off the bat. He's going to be a thorn in my side."

She then turned to the reason she had invited them to the bar. "If we are going to do this, we need to go big or go home. I want it to be a unanimous decision. I want all of you working on the project. You know it better than anyone, and I trust you all. Truth be told, Jason and Josh are both so independent at this point that they're much more in tune with their own work than I am."

Josh smiled. "Well, you keep up well enough, but I'm glad you don't try to micromanage me after four years."

Katrina smiled back at him and kept talking. "Todd, Oxana, since you still have at least a couple of years left in grad school, I assume you weren't planning on leaving my lab anytime soon. Same thing goes for Li. However, the dynamics of your projects will change a little bit.

"Todd, we had decided you would take your qualifying exam this spring. That could still be a go, but I would suggest that we change your research proposal to incorporate work on the activated strain in the rest of your doctoral project."

"Do you think I'll still have enough time to prepare for the exam?" Todd asked.

"I think so, but you'll have to go balls-to-the-wall."

"How long did you prepare for yours?" Todd asked his advisor, and it was immediately obvious he had asked the wrong question.

Josh looked wide-eyed toward Katrina and then looked down.

Katrina said nothing at first. She blinked twice and then swallowed before saying, "Well, mine was a little unusual, Todd... "

✖

The qualifying exam represents a commencement in the career of a budding scientist; it is the test that, once passed, authorizes the researcher to embark upon his or her first independent project. For Katrina Stone, the exam marked the absolute decimation of the life she had known.

The week before Katrina's exam was scheduled, she sat at a crowded kitchen table, boring through a mountain of research papers. Beside the papers were an aging laptop computer and a thick molecular biology textbook. Another textbook, entitled *Infectious Diseases*, lay opened to a chapter on anthrax.

In the adjacent kitchen, an empty Hamburger Helper box and a frozen vegetable packet were on the counter, and the sink was piled with dishes from several consecutive days. Tom's share of the Hamburger Helper was congealing in the skillet on the stove.

The phone rang, startling the twenty-six-year-old woman out of her concentration. She dropped the pile of papers onto the table and leapt from her chair. Crossing the living room to retrieve the phone, she danced over a minefield of stuffed animals and the hard plastic toys that Tom angrily referred to as "ankle-breakers." As she passed the coffee table, she grabbed the remote control and switched off the TV, which had been loudly projecting without an audience for the past two hours. She glanced at the clock. It was 9:35 p.m.

"Hello," Katrina said irritably as she picked up the receiver.

"Hey, babe," Tom said casually on the other end.

"Tom, where are you!" It was not a question, but a demand. "You missed dinner again."

"I know—I'm sorry. My car broke down, and my cell phone battery was dead, so I couldn't call until now."

Katrina rolled her eyes and flipped through a stack of bills on the table next to the phone. Several of them were marked in red as overdue. "You sound pretty cheerful for someone stranded at nine thirty on a weeknight."

"I had to get my car to the mechanic, and the tow truck driver took forever. By the time I got here, they were closed, so I had to figure out where I could leave the car overnight.

"It's funny what happened though. I borrowed this jar-head's cell phone. He was just walking by and I could tell he was in the Corps. I showed him my Navy and medical tattoos and asked if I could use his phone. He goes, 'Anytime, Doc.' Anyway, I'm waiting for a taxi now so I'll be home pretty quick."

Katrina glanced away from the stack of unpaid bills and looked at the caller ID. Her stomach knotted. She clicked back to the number from an earlier call, and her knees suddenly felt weak.

Katrina lowered the receiver of the phone to take a deep breath and let it out. Then she returned the receiver to say, "Well, your jarhead friend must have really meant that you could use his phone any time. That same number called our house this morning at ten o'clock."

Silence.

"How do you think that happened, Tom?"

"Look! I don't want to hear your paranoid bullshit right now, Katrina! I'm stuck here with no car—"

"*Save it!* You know, the least you could do is come up with an excuse that makes a little bit of sense when you call me from your girlfriend's fucking phone. I don't have time for this, Tom. I have a qualifying exam to take next week, and I'm a little busy trying to prepare for it while raising two children. Excuse me, three. So... just enjoy your affair, *Doc.*"

Katrina slammed the phone down and stood panting beside it for several moments. Then she blinked back the tears that were threatening and bit her lip to maintain her composure as she walked down the hall to check on the children. She peeked into Alexis' room first.

The seven-year-old was on the floor in her lavender Care Bear nightgown, happily playing with her ponies. She was quietly talking both to them and for them, altering her tiny voice to create different characters. Her waist-length, straight hair was still held back with the pink bow Katrina had tied around it that morning. The ribbon was now disheveled and drooping to one side, and Lexi's hair was tangled from the long day's activities.

Katrina was initially surprised to find her daughter still awake, and then she remembered with a pang of guilt that she had promised to help her into bed at least an hour earlier.

Alexis looked up at her mother in the doorway and smiled sweetly.

Katrina forced herself to smile back. "It's way past your bedtime, honey," she said quietly. "Brush your teeth and get into bed. In a few minutes, I'll come tuck you in."

Katrina crossed the hall to glance into Christopher's room and confirm that her son was asleep. When she opened the door, the five-year-old made a light cooing noise but then settled back down. Katrina watched him for a moment.

Christopher's blonde curls sprang wildly from around his cherubic face, and one chubby fist was resting against a rosy cheek. His blanket had pulled down in his sleep, and his pudgy belly was peeking out from beneath a soft flannel pajama top.

Blinking back tears, Katrina tiptoed toward her only son and pulled the cover over him. Then she crept away and quietly closed the door to his room. She stepped into the hallway bathroom—the only one in their house—and closed the door. She pulled back the auburn hair that fell in thick waves down her back and knotted it quickly into a bun. Then she splashed a few handfuls of cold water on her face and gulped down a few quick breaths of air. The threat of tears gradually subsided. For a long moment, she stared blankly into the mirror, and the blue-gray eyes of the woman staring back reflected sheer exhaustion.

When she felt calm enough to do so, Katrina fulfilled her promise to her daughter. Sitting on the edge of Alexis' bed, she gently pulled the sagging bow from the girl's long hair and brushed it out, beginning at the tips.

"Is Daddy coming home now?" Alexis asked quietly.

"I think so," Katrina said. "He had a problem with his car, but he should be on the way. So go to sleep. I love you."

Alexis lay down obediently and allowed Katrina to pull her covers up over her nightgown to her neck. Katrina kissed her forehead, and Lexi kissed her own tiny fingers and then planted them onto her mother's lips. "I love you more," Alexis said, giggling.

After leaving her daughter's room, Katrina rushed quickly down the hall into the master bedroom, where she locked the door behind her. She finally let herself break down, and she sat down on the bed weeping as quietly as she could.

Then there was a crash and a breaking of glass. She ran into the living room and screamed.

Her work history was as impressive as Guofu Wong had said, and it showed in her Homeland Security file. What surprised Sean McMullan was the financial status of the allegedly brilliant young doctor. Katrina Stone was broke and had been for her entire life.

McMullan had no idea that Ph.D.-level researchers made so little after going to school for so long. Stone had twenty years of education—and education expenses—under her belt. And she made less money than a successful plumber. *God, what a rip-off,* McMullan thought.

As he skimmed through the financial record, he found a myriad of odd jobs that she had worked, from bartending while in graduate school back to topless dancing in college. The latter was only a six-month employment, and he noticed it ended when she got married. The FBI agent tried to envision the classy, professional woman he had met earlier that afternoon shaking it in a tittie bar, but couldn't.

Then he saw the legal section of the file, and a queer idea began to form in his mind.

McMullan began reviewing his notes from the prison.

At present, San Quentin is home to more than four hundred death row inmates. The majority of dead men walking live in East Block—the largest of three death row areas. While some basic freedoms are granted in East Block, a violation of the rules will land the offender in The Adjustment Center, where the inmate's phone calls, visitation, and other luxuries are stripped from him.

The original death row wing of the prison—North Seg—is now the coveted wing among death row inmates. Those who exhibit stellar behavior must actively petition to reside in North Seg, and once there, the slightest infraction will send them back to East Block.

The anthrax outbreak at San Quentin had been confined exclusively to North Seg—the country club among death row inmates and home of the most well-mannered rapists, murderers, and child molesters in California.

No other area of the prison had been touched.

Sean McMullan had been expecting the legal section of Katrina Stone's file to be mostly blank. Instead, he found several hundred pages of documentation detailing several years of legal struggle.

There was a divorce, which revealed nothing unusual. Joint custody was granted; there was no alimony and little child support. The ex-husband, a Navy Corpsman, was not well to do either.

But there was also another thick section of the legal file. There was a lengthy criminal trial involving a man named Lawrence Naden.

In 2007, Lawrence Naden was captured in a Baja California crack house, a rush of heroin flooding his bloodstream as the *federales* closed in. Hours later, Naden was in jail.

That morning, fifteen miles across the border, an answering machine clicked mechanically after the fourth ring of the telephone. "Hello, you've reached the Stone residence," a woman's voice said. "Please leave a message after the beep."

"Hello Mrs. Stone," the caller began. "This is Detective Martinez of the SDPD. I have some good news for you. Lawrence Naden was caught this morning in Ensenada. He is being extradited from Mexico and sent to the San Quentin State Correctional Facility. He will be tried here in the United States."

The caller paused briefly and then continued. "While I'm sure it is little consolation, you can probably be confident that Naden will be convicted and will never be able to terrorize another family again. The case against him is very strong. Please call me if you have any questions. You have my card. I will keep you informed of the details as they develop... "

As the last sentences rang through the empty living room, the front door opened and a woman raced to the phone. A small child followed her into the house. Except for her hair—short and blond, rather than long and auburn—the woman resembled a slightly older version of Katrina Stone almost eerily. She hastily picked up the receiver. "Hello?"

The woman was answered by the dial tone.

"Shit," she said under her breath.

"You're not 'apposed to say that," said the small child at her side.

The woman smiled softly. "I know, sorry kiddo. Listen, Lexi, why don't you go play in your room for a few minutes. I need to talk to your mommy. I'll come in and play with you when we're done though." She leaned over to kiss the girl's forehead.

Alexis trotted off to her room as she was told.

After she heard the bedroom door close, Kathy played back the message on the machine. She began to cry softly while it was playing. When the message was over, she pressed the "erase" button and went into the bathroom to collect herself.

Afterward, she walked to the master bedroom and softly knocked. There was no response. She partially opened the door and poked her head in. Then she opened it all the way and entered the room.

Katrina was lying on the bed, facing the opposite wall. She didn't turn over.

Kathy sat down on the bed and began to gently rub her sister's lower back. "Trina," she said quietly, "the police called. They caught him."

There was no response.

The older woman sat in silence for a few moments, continuing to rub Katrina's back. "Trina," she said again, "I need to talk to you. Please look at me."

Katrina still did not roll over.

"You're my only sister, and you know I love you and I'd do anything I can for you. But I have to go home soon. I'm going to lose my job." She paused for several moments before adding, "And Tom is seeking full custody."

Katrina finally rolled over and looked at her sister. "What?"

She had lost a noticeable amount of weight over the last two months, and her face looked pale and sallow.

"Look, I know he's a bastard and doesn't even deserve the right... " Kathy stopped as her voice began to catch. Then she cleared her throat and continued authoritatively, "You have to go to court. You have to be able to prove you can take care of yourself. He's *marrying* that home-wrecking whore, which—believe it or not—will demonstrate parental stability to the court. I know, it's backward, unfair, and basically ridiculous, but that's how it is."

She was interrupted by the distant ring of the living room phone.

Annoyed, Kathy grabbed the receiver of the phone on the nightstand next to her. Its ringer had been turned off since that night two months ago. "Hello!" she said angrily. "*Tom*? No, Tom doesn't live here anymore. He left his beautiful, intelligent wife to go boink a bottle-blond piece of trailer trash with an *unbelievably fat ass!* So if you're trying to reach him, I'm afraid you're going to have to dial 1-800-HUGE-ASS. Thank you very much and have a nice day!" She slammed the phone down.

Katrina only gaped at her sister.

"Sorry," Kathy said, and shrugged.

Through her tears, Katrina smiled slightly and shook her head. But the smile quickly faded. She closed her eyes and moaned. "God, what am I going to do?"

Kathy cleared her throat. "First, you're going to get custody and child support, because you need both to survive. Then you're going to pick yourself up and move on. Look sweetie, I know it's hard to hear this. But I'm your sister, and I'm telling you that you need to get it together, quick, or you're going to lose everything you have left." Kathy swallowed at the brutality of her own words and rubbed the smeared makeup from her lower eyelid.

Katrina took a deep breath and let it out slowly. She reached down and switched on the ringer of the nightstand phone. She then picked up the receiver and dialed a number.

"Shenanigan's," the voice on the other end said.

"Shawna?"

"Katrina?! Yeah it's me! Oh God, how are you, hun? We've been watching the news… it's just awful… we're all pulling for you down here at the bar… oh, God, I just can't believe it… you know, is there anything I can do? God!"

Katrina sighed. She still wasn't used to these conversations and never knew what to say. "I'm… uh… you know… look, Shawna, do I still have a job? 'Cause I need one, bad."

"Matt's not here right now, but trust me, he'll be happy to have you back. The regulars keep asking where the smart chick is. I'll tell him to give you a call ASAP."

"Thanks, Shawna," Katrina said and hung up the phone. She looked at Kathy and shrugged. "Well, if I can't handle the pressures of fighting infectious diseases, or afford to do it, for that matter, I guess I can always tend bar for a living. How's that for parental stability?"

Sean McMullan jumped when the door connecting his hotel room to his partner's was flung open.

Gilman barged in and threw his copy of the file onto McMullan's bed. "*I knew it!*" Gilman spat.

"Shhh, I'm reading," McMullan said, panting from the start he had just been given.

"Well let me save you the trouble, McMullan! Stone got a faculty appointment as soon as she graduated, which James Johnson said is practically impossible nowadays, remember? So she's unusually smart, but young and inexperienced. I gather that there are a lot of people who are jealous of her success. I'm sure she has a lot of enemies. Sure."

He paused for a breath and then puffed it out harshly. "Nonetheless, there's one enemy that stands out in my mind as being maybe the one she might possibly have the biggest problem with. Lawrence Naden. Picked up in '07 in Ensenada. *And sent to San Quentin.*"

Katrina polished off the last three swallows of her second

pint of beer and turned the conversation back to her meeting with the FBI. "If any of you are uncomfortable with this work, I want you to speak up," she said.

Todd and Josh exchanged a look that said they were both overwhelmed.

"I'm serious," she continued. "I don't want to go forward with this without your *full* support, nor do I want to force you into something you aren't comfortable with just because I'm your boss." She paused while the waitress collected their empty glasses. "That being said," she said then, "I have to add... I think that if you choose not to participate in this, you will be blowing the chance of a lifetime. Very few people make a contribution of this magnitude in graduate school. So please consider that in making your decisions.

"As your advisor and friend, I highly recommend proceeding with this in the best interest of your careers. We can really make a major impact with this work, and your careers would be set for the rest of your lives."

She paused and looked at each of them. "If you think you're tired of working like donkeys and barely scraping by, you'd better believe that I'm even more so. And this could be our break."

5:39 P.M. PDT

Jason Fischer shifted his position on the hard plastic emergency room chair, trying to find a position comfortable enough for sleep. His efforts were useless. His head was throbbing, and the thin flannel shirt he had on over his T-shirt was not offering any protection from the violent chill currently seizing him. Jason pulled the shirt more tightly around his torso.

A few minutes later, wracked with fever, he removed the flannel shirt altogether and used it to wipe a fresh outpouring of perspiration from his face. Not really caring if anyone was looking, he reached down and readjusted his boxers through his blue jeans to allow his throbbing genitalia a bit more space. *Someone needs to teach that chick the "no teeth" rule*, he thought.

Paranoia was slowly forcing its way in, and Jason struggled to mentally relive every step of the safety procedures. He had done the decontamination thoroughly. He always did. The ethanol. The gloves. The booties. The biohazardous waste. He had touched nothing on the way out of BSL-3. He was clean when he entered the clean room.

But the fever was clouding his thoughts.

It only took one spore. And he had been in a terrible rush.

The news had been excellent—the inhibitor worked wonders. But for use against anthrax infection in humans, it was not even close.

After what seemed like hours longer, his name was finally called.

Jason stood, painfully and slowly, and shuffled through the doors behind the nurse.

❉

"I see you've been here twice in the last year," the emergency room doctor commented with a slight slur as he examined Jason's chart.

Jason, in turn, examined the doctor, who looked about his own age. "Yeah, that was different," he said. "Those other times were for broken bones and cuts and stuff that I got during gigs with my band. I'd be rich if I could get paid for time spent in your waiting room. This place is a colossal pain in the ass. I've been here for an hour and a half this time. "

"Only an hour and a half?" the doctor remarked. "We must be having a slow night. Now, what are your symptoms?"

Jason finally placed the reason for the slur in the doctor's speech. The young man's tongue had recently been pierced.

"Fever, chills, muscle aches, and the worst fucking headache I've ever had. I'm exhausted, run-down, and my lymph nodes are swollen. And so is my dick, by the way, but I think that's someone else's fault."

The doctor raised an eyebrow without looking up from his clipboard. He finished his notes and then placed the clipboard onto a tray next to the gurney Jason was sitting on. He reached forward with both hands and felt the glands beneath his patient's jaw. "You're right, they're swollen pretty badly. Let's see the other." He motioned for Jason to drop his pants.

Jason stood up to oblige, gritting his teeth while the doctor performed the examination.

"Well," the doctor said, "other than a few teeth marks that are probably causing the pain you've got there, everything looks pretty normal. I'd venture to suggest you probably have the flu. There is a nasty one going around this fall."

"I'd have said so, too," Jason said, "except that I work with live anthrax."

The doctor took a step backward. "I see." He flipped through Jason's medical record. "I assume you've been vaccinated... oh, yes, there it is. When was the last time you were working with the live bug?"

"Last night, about nine forty-five."

"And before that?"

"Before that it had been a few weeks."

To Jason's surprise, the doctor now laughed heartily. "Well then, of course you have the flu! As an anthrax researcher, you should know there is no way you'd be this symptomatic in twenty-four hours, and if you were exposed weeks ago you would certainly have already known it before now! You can't have anthrax. The incubation period doesn't match."

Roger Gilman looked as if he had been slapped. He sank miserably into one of the chairs of Sean McMullan's hotel room. "Life?" he groaned. "Naden got life? Not death? How can that be?"

An annoyed McMullan pointed to a page of the Homeland Security file in his hand. "It's right here, dumb shit. You were so excited about bustin' Katrina Stone that you didn't read far enough.

"Lawrence Naden had to be extradited from Mexico, and the Mexican government wouldn't release him if the death penalty was on the table. He's serving life without the possibility of parole. He never would have been in any of the death row wings at San Quentin. On top of that, he was transferred to a prison in Texas in 2010.

"So instead of going off half-cocked again, maybe you oughta double check that he's still there. You can also make yourself happy by confirming that he's *not* on the list of dead inmates at San Quentin. My guess is he's alive and well and singing *Deep in the Heart of Texas.*"

"I saw the sparks between you and her."

McMullan looked up from his paperwork. "What are you talking about? There's nothing between me and her."

His partner wordlessly pursed his lips. He paused for a second, but then prodded, "You sure?"

"Of course I'm sure!" McMullan laughed. "You think I wouldn't know? Come on, you must not know me very well. I wouldn't jeopardize an assignment like that. Period. I've met the woman once, and you were there."

"That doesn't change the fact that there's something there, whether *you* realize it yet or not. I hope it doesn't interfere with your ability to do a thorough investigation."

McMullan changed the subject. "What exactly is *your* problem with her? I mean, you're obviously a bit old school when it comes to science, but you also seem like a reasonable guy for the most part. So I don't get it... It's like you're hoping she's the bad guy."

After a long pause, Gilman said, "Frankly? I think for an attractive, allegedly brilliant, thirty-four-year-old doctor, she seemed a little bit interested in my scabby old battle-scarred partner—no offense. And I wonder if there's a motive behind it.

"And I trust James Johnson for the same reason that I trust God and tradition, because both are tried and true. And I think Guofu Wong is way too eager about the technology and way too trusting of his fellow researchers to be objective.

"And, most of all, I can't get past the coincidence of Stone's preliminary data being so closely aligned with the Death Row strain of anthrax. I can't believe it *is* really a coincidence."

USPIS Assistant Forensic Director Teresa Wood sat in front of an ultraviolet light box in the physical sciences unit of the National Forensic Laboratory in Dulles, Virginia. In gloved hands, she tenderly cradled a one-inch-thick gelatinous square. Sliding one hand out from under the gel, she allowed the corner, and then the side, to contact the light box. Gently holding it in place, she removed her other hand, and the gel sat freely upon the glass.

Teresa closed the door to the small room and then switched off the overhead light. In the near-complete darkness, she found a face shield and pulled it over her face. Then she switched on the light box before her.

Bright purple ultraviolet light flooded the room from the small box. Where nothing had been visible in the overhead light, she could now clearly make out patterns of solid pink lines in the gel. Each represented a unique piece of DNA from her PCR analysis.

Teresa only had to glance at the patterns to see that the DNA fragments retrieved from the White House greeting card and its envelope were different from any of the biological toxins she had incorporated into her assay.

Along with other toxins, DNA samples from both normal anthrax and the Death Row strain had been included in her experiment. Neither strain was present on the greeting card. Nor were any of the other toxin controls. There was absolutely no infectious material on the card.

Goose egg, Teresa thought.

Katrina felt ill prepared for the scheduled meeting with the FBI agents. Jason had helped her hide the activator data in the liquid nitrogen tank, but he had never exactly consented to the project. And today, he was not in the lab.

Reflecting on how sick he had looked, Katrina was not surprised by his absence. Jason rarely got sick, but when he did, he was a baby about it, and it seemed to last forever. She blamed the fact that he didn't ever seem to lay off the partying long enough to get well.

Katrina had been hoping it would be the tall agent, McMullan, who would be meeting with her. When the other agent arrived at her office, her spirits sank.

Roger Gilman entered Katrina's office with the flustered appearance of someone who had already had a long day. His morning comb-over's attempt at hiding male pattern baldness had now been surrendered, and the shiny dome of his skull reflected the fluorescent light in Katrina's office. Gilman's eyes were red, and his suit looked as if he had been sleeping in it for days.

Katrina put forth her best effort at a sincere, pleasant smile. "Good afternoon, Agent Gilman. How are you today?"

"I'm fine, thank you. How are you?" Gilman answered with equal cordiality.

The two sat across from each other over Katrina's desk.

"Have you considered our offer, Dr. Stone?"

"Yes, sir, I have considered it in depth, and this is my position. Obviously, I am more than happy to take the government's money to finally be able to do my work the way it should be done. I mean, what scientist would not wish for that? However, I have one very important condition—"

"You want total scientific freedom," Gilman interrupted. "We understand."

Katrina chuckled. "*That* goes without saying. But, no. The condition is this: if I am to work on the Death Row project, I must insist that I keep *all* of my own people. The government may provide additional staff—in fact, I will require them—but my original lab members have seniority and will answer directly to me. Additional staff will answer to them, with no questions asked."

"They're students!" Gilman protested.

"They are graduate students and one postdoc. They're very good. I have handpicked each and every one of them, and they know the work better than anyone. I need them.

"If I were forced to let them go, not only would it be detrimental to *their* careers, it would also be fundamentally damaging to the project. I would be forced to train new people by myself from scratch. It would take months—years, in fact—for me to bring a whole new staff up to speed. This condition is simply not negotiable."

Gilman sighed. "OK. I will include your condition to the contract we will be drawing up. However, your staff will be subject to the same scrutiny as you. I need a list of your people. We will be performing very thorough background checks on every single one of them before we involve them in this. You have *not* discussed the situation with anyone, correct?"

"Of course I haven't," Katrina lied.

"Good. Are all of your people American citizens?"

Katrina laughed out loud.

"What's so funny?"

"I'm sorry," Katrina said. "It's just that American citizens are actually pretty rare in this line of work. In most labs, foreign students and postdocs outnumber Americans about ten to one."

She pulled a small notepad out of her desk and began writing down information as she spoke. "My staff is as follows. My postdoc's name is Jason Fischer, and he *is* an American citizen. My students are Joshua Attle, also an American citizen, Oxana Kosova, who is Russian, Li Fung, who is Chinese, and Todd Ruddock, who is English. You may get any other information you need from our human resources department."

She stopped writing and looked Gilman in the eye. "While we are on the subject of invasion into my staff's privacy, I would like to discuss compensation. You have already assured me that the lab will be well funded for the project. That is wonderful. However, I expect that there will also be reasonable salary adjustments for all of us in consideration of the disruption to our careers and lives, and because of the potential risks we are facing."

"There will be no risks to you," Gilman countered. "As you have noted repeatedly, you will be under FBI surveillance. That also means FBI protection."

"Of course, this is true of the lab," Katrina countered. "But will my staff have twenty-four-hour personal protection? If so, their privacy is invaded even more greatly than I thought. If not, then of course they *are* in some degree of danger. This project is about national security. I am not naïve enough to think that it is perfectly safe."

"There will not be twenty-four-hour surveillance of anyone," Gilman conceded, his face reddening. "We do not feel it is a necessary use of our resources unless you are actually threatened in some way. OK, Dr. Stone. What do you think is fair compensation, then?"

Katrina began scrawling on her notebook again. "My postdoc currently has a job offer in biotech on the table for eight-five thousand a year. This is almost double what he currently makes as a postdoc, which is normal for the transition between postdoctoral work and the biotech industry. But the job he is being offered is a nine-to-five position with no risk to Jason's health and safety. I assume that, considering the factors we've just discussed, he will be compensated for staying on *this* project by at least thirty percent more than that.

"My senior graduate student will be turning down a postdoctoral fellowship offering him forty-five thousand a year. I would like to offer him double that, since he will be pigeonholing his career by failing to carry out a postdoc after graduate school if he takes on this project. Trust me—I know very well how difficult it is to succeed after making such a decision. So, in essence, this assignment will *become* his first professional position.

"As for the remaining students, I believe they are entitled to a twenty percent increase over their current student stipends, which are not even generous enough to pay the rent in this city. And as for myself, I am taking on the heaviest risks and the most responsibility. I expect a forty percent pay raise."

Gilman abruptly stood and pushed back his chair. "Dr.

Stone, this is extortion. My personal opinion, frankly, is that you *and* your staff should be ashamed of yourselves. I will be relaying your demands—or 'conditions,' as you call them—to my superiors in the brief I will write regarding this meeting. But unless you hear from me again, you can assume that our proposal has been withdrawn.

"Forget everything you have heard about the Death Row strain of anthrax on penalty of reprimand by the federal government. We are finished here. Good day."

As he voiced the final words, Gilman strode briskly out of the office without shaking Katrina's hand.

She calmly watched him go. She was smiling.

The FBI had already taken a lot of risks in bringing this situation to her. Someone in the highest sphere of influence was strongly pushing to include her. She assumed it was the scientist who had fought to approve her grant application with the NIH.

Roger Gilman was just a field agent.

It wasn't over.

Gilman stormed away from Katrina Stone's office and jabbed the button for the elevator. Once outside, he gulped deep breaths of air to calm his rage. *How dare she?*

As he walked briskly toward his car, his cell phone began to ring. "Hello, this is Roger Gilman," he said angrily.

"Hello, Agent Gilman. Guofu Wong here."

"What can I do for you?" Gilman asked the CDC epidemiologist.

"I assume you've received the latest update from San Quentin?"

"The last report I read stated that they had narrowed down the search to any Latino or other dark-skinned inmate at the prison, and that the food supply had been the source of the contamination," Gilman said sourly. "And there was a whole bunch of scientific jargon about culturing bacteria, which I assume you will interpret for all of us according to your own agenda."

Wong ignored the insult. "The science is certainly sound," he said calmly. "What of Katrina Stone?"

"I hope she chokes on her own anthrax."

On the other end of the line, Wong was silent.

"The woman is demanding an exorbitant sum of money," Gilman continued, "not just for her research, but also as pay for herself and her staff. And even if she wasn't, I still wouldn't trust her a bit. I'm still not convinced she didn't design the Death Row strain."

Wong paused for a moment before answering. "Agent Gilman, let me assure you of one thing. Stone has done extraordinary work with very limited resources. She has put *everything* into finding her inhibitors. She couldn't possibly have had the *time* after those efforts to create a biological weapon. And furthermore, I cannot stress enough the importance of bringing her technology into the mainstream—"

"You know what, Wong?" Gilman blurted out. "I think you maybe ought to take a step back and look at what this *technology* has created. I mean, even if Stone is not the person directly responsible for the Death Row strain, it had to be someone *like* her, right? It had to be an anthrax researcher that developed this biological weapon.

"The trouble with your *technology* is that it has no higher power, no God, no ethical authority beyond the ego of the inventor. It has no sense of conscience."

To Gilman's surprise, Wong chuckled. "It's funny that you would use that word," he said. "Conscience. Con science. Literally, 'with science.' Agent Gilman, you and I are not that different. Scientists are investigators, just like you are. We both seek the truth based on the evidence before us. And the only way to really get at the truth is to be honest in one's interpretation of the evidence. Scientific reason and ethics are necessarily married."

Gilman scoffed. "James Johnson is a scientist, and he doesn't trust her either."

A long silence passed over the line.

"Agent Gilman," Wong said finally, "there's something I haven't told you and Agent McMullan about the relationship between Katrina Stone and James Johnson... "

Ten minutes later, Gilman was driving between Katrina Stone's lab and his hotel. Ignoring California cell phone law, he clicked off the call from Guofu Wong and speed-dialed Sean McMullan, not bothering to engage the Bluetooth of his government-issued car.

When McMullan answered, Gilman repeated what Wong had said.

"I'm confused," McMullan said. "How does Stone have a relationship with Johnson? I didn't think they had ever even met."

"They haven't met. But they do have a relationship—sort of. Wong says that when researchers are seeking funding, they apply for grants to the NIH. Most of the grant reviewers are researchers just like Dr. Stone. Experts in their fields. Reviewers for any given grant are typically selected based on the fact that they specialize in similar research to that described in the application."

"OK, so what's your point?"

"James Johnson thinks that Katrina Stone plagiarized his data."

McMullan paused. "How could she have done that?"

"Johnson has to write grant applications just like everyone else. When a grant is reviewed, the researcher who wrote it never knows by whom. But they are usually quick to guess, and the longer a researcher has been integrated into the scientific community, the more guesses they have. James Johnson has been in science for a long time. He knows a lot of people."

"Yeah," said McMullan. "From what I gathered in that meeting, it sounds like he is some kind of legend. But why would he have to worry about funding in the first place? I thought he'd be set."

"That's what I asked Wong," said Gilman. "But it turns out that's not really the case. Johnson *is* a legend—for ground-breaking discoveries he made back in the '80s. And he *was* set, for a while, based on those discoveries.

"Then he became comfortable and a little arrogant. He trusted that those discoveries would keep him going, and he became very lazy about keeping up on the latest and the greatest.

"Wong says that science is a fast-moving field and young researchers pass older ones who aren't keeping current. Johnson did his training long before the arrival of many modern advances that are now commonplace. Like many of his generation, Johnson relies on tried and true methods. But many younger scientists believe him to be somewhat out of touch and even a bit fearful of technology. Evidently, he has made relatively few major contributions in the past ten years or so.

"Of course, this is all from the mouth of Wong, who smug-ly educated me that 'conscience' means 'con science,' which means 'with science.' Wong doesn't seem to think scientists can do any wrong, so I don't trust his opinion any more than I trust Stone. But there's even more.

"Johnson is seventy-five years old. Wong says that when a committee is reviewing a grant application in which the researcher asks for several years of funding to the tune of hundreds of thousands of dollars, the committee has to consider the possibility that the researcher might retire before the work is done. Or worse. So in a nutshell, Johnson's funding has been progressively drying up for a while."

"What does all of this have to do with Katrina Stone?" McMullan asked.

"Her grant application. After the NIH committee reviewed the application, Johnson told Wong point blank that it was originally *his* idea to use the types of molecules she was proposing. He suspected that Stone had previously reviewed one of his earlier applications and taken the idea for her own."

12:03 P.M. PDT

Jason Fischer faced a hospital room wall, mindlessly re-reading a wall poster he had already memorized. Over the last nineteen hours, his diagnosis had become all too obvious.

Visions of playing guitar, liters of booze, and late nights spent with one morally devoid groupie after another flooded his thoughts, and he realized he had been lucky to dodge this particular bullet for as long as he had. *What was I thinking?*

The door opened and Jason turned to see the young doctor with the tongue ring.

"OK, Jason, let's see the boys," the doctor instructed.

Jason lifted his hospital gown and revealed a grotesque mess of red sores. They were just beginning to crust over, and the pain was giving way to an intolerable itch. For the first time in distant memory, Jason was horribly embarrassed. He looked away from the doctor as he replaced the gown.

"I assume you have already figured this out," the doctor said, "but you definitely don't have anthrax. Those tests came back negative. Your sterile technique—in the *lab*, anyway—is fine." As he spoke the last sentence, the doctor peered knowingly over the tops of his glasses. Then he continued. "All you've got here is a hangover on top of a vicious case of genital herpes."

Jason tried to push aside the notion that he might have preferred death by anthrax.

November 1, 2015
7:30 A.M. PST

A San Quentin guard watched as visitors to the minimum-security wing filed through the metal detector. His eyes fell upon one woman, and he frowned.

Her long black headscarf flowed over a black robe so seamlessly that the guard could not tell where one ended and the other began. She stepped through the metal detector and then began following the others down the corridor toward the visitation room. Her dark face was downcast, shielded by the headscarf.

"Excuse me, ma'am," the guard said. "I'd like you to come with me."

"Is there problem?"

"No, ma'am, I am sure there is not. But we will need you to remove your headscarf for a moment. It's only a routine check."

The visitor's heavily accented voice remained calm and low, almost submissive. She did not look up. "It is my right to wear hijab in the prison. I read the rules the first time I come here."

"And it is our right to ask you to remove it, in private, for security reasons, at our discretion. Step into the room over here, please. A female guard will join you shortly." He motioned toward a small room to his left. The visitor shook her head and stepped toward it.

In Dulles, Virginia, a phone was ringing. USPIS Assistant Director of Forensics Teresa Wood engaged her speakerphone without looking up from her paperwork. "Wood here."

"Teresa, hi, it's Mason," said her colleague.

"Hi, Mason. Have you got something for me?" Mason had been tasked with tracing the IBI—a barcode applied to mail entering the system—on the greeting card from the White House. It is the IBI that permits the USPIS to determine where a document was mailed.

"Very little," Mason said. "I traced your greeting card, the one with the Arabic writing on it."

"Yeah, I know the one," Teresa said. A photocopy of the Arabic text was sitting on the desk in front of her. She had just been examining it.

"Well, whoever mailed the card was smart enough not to go to a post office or mail it from any other business. All we know is that the card entered the system somewhere in Phoenix, Arizona. The stamp came from a public stamp kiosk with no camera—also in Phoenix."

"Hm."

"What about the handwriting?" Mason asked. "Any luck?"

"We haven't found a match with any known members of ISIL or with anyone else from whom we have an Arabic handwriting sample. The White House interpreter who first read this document made the observation that the handwriting is, in fact, very odd. It looks like it was written by someone who does not speak Arabic."

"Could someone have put the sentences together from a dictionary or an online translator?"

"Not if their reference language was English. The sentence structure is just too different, and no online translator on the market can reproduce it. Whether you entered the English text word for word or as a whole sentence, the Arabic translation would still come out as gibberish. Especially given the content. This text is strange, but it *is* real Arabic. It didn't come from online translation.

"So the FBI linguistics department is working on it as well. They are trying to pinpoint a dialect. Even that task has proven elusive."

A few moments later, the prison guard's female colleague approached. "What now, Fred?"

"Just a routine check. Muslim woman. Bulky headscarf. I want her to remove it. And I want her frisked."

His colleague rolled her eyes. "I'm sure she's a terrorist, just like the seventy-five-year-old grandmother you had me frisk earlier this morning. Do the words 'racial profiling' mean anything to you?" She walked away without waiting for his answer.

Once inside the room, the annoyed female guard closed the door behind her. "Please remove your headscarf," she said to the woman while examining her own manicure. "You may use the mirror." She motioned toward a small mirror mounted on the wall.

The visitor consulted the mirror to reach up with black-gloved hands and remove the hijab. Long thick ropes of equally black hair cascaded over the loose robe. "You touch my body now to check for bomb? Why? Because I am Muslim?"

The guard sighed without looking up from her fingernails. "No, ma'am. Thank you for your cooperation. You may go."

Linguistics analyses were fruitless. Five days after learning that the greeting card was mailed in Phoenix, Teresa spoke to the linguistics specialist from the FBI.

"The card was written in a mixture of Egyptian, Levantine, and Iraqi Arabic," the specialist said, "with a smattering of language from Modern Standard—a dialect that nobody in the Arabic-speaking world actually uses in day-to-day speech."

"What do you mean, a dialect that nobody uses? Is it an old dialect, like Shakespearean English? Then why call it modern?"

"It's modern, but it is only used in official or professional documents, newscasts, and the like."

"Great. So our terrorist is a newscaster from anywhere in the Arab world. How close are the different dialects to each other?"

"Distinct enough that Arabs don't always understand other Arabs."

Three days later, Teresa withdrew the card itself from a sealed envelope with gloved hands. She spread it out on the sterilized metal table before her and drew the head of a CrimeScope toward it. She flicked the scope's power switch and began directing intense light of various wavelengths at the card in hopes of picking up objects or substances that would otherwise be invisible.

Teresa inched the light source across and down the card in a grid pattern. Seeing nothing, she adjusted the filters to change the wavelength of light produced and then retraced the same motion again.

No semen present. No blood. No surprise. It was a piece of mail. There also did not seem to be any ink-to-ink variations that would indicate that the card had been doctored. *Think, Teresa. What would be on this?*

She changed wavelengths again. With painstaking diligence, she ran the beam of light over every square centimeter of the front of the card. A gloved hand tenderly opened it, and she ran the light over the inner leaflets. Nothing.

Teresa ran the CrimeScope's beam over the outside of the envelope. Nothing. She held the envelope open with one hand to direct the light inside. And two new lines became visible.

The first was long and narrow. *Microscopic hair fragment?* The second was fuzzier. Probably a fiber of some kind.

Without deflecting the beam, Teresa reached into the top drawer of the lab bench upon which the scope was sitting. She retrieved a long glass cylinder from the drawer and un-capped it one-handed. Then she withdrew the sterile micro-forceps inside. Without allowing *anything* to touch the sterile tip, Teresa smiled as she reached in with a steady hand to collect the evidence.

Sean McMullan parked his government-issued unmarked car in the dirt lot at the Torrey Pines Gliderport in La Jolla, California. It was 5:35 a.m., Thanksgiving Day, and the lot was mostly empty. McMullan's immaculate black sedan contrasted starkly with the two dusty SUVs parked nearby.

As McMullan stepped out into the early morning mist, a pair of surfers came into view over the crest from the beach below. Both wore full wetsuits, currently stripped to the waist, and carried short boards. Neither wore shoes. They approached the SUVs in the parking lot and waved at McMullan, and he nodded politely.

McMullan briefly wondered if the surfers would go to work that day, or if they even had jobs. He had no idea that one of them was Jeffrey Wilson, a world-renowned chemist from the nearby Scripps Research Institute, or that Wilson had just been awarded the Nobel Prize.

A posted sign warned "Unstable cliffs. Stay off the staircase." In fact, the "staircase" was no more than a treacherous path of embedded rocks, large logs, two-by-six boards, and sandbags that led down to the beach below. Locals called the path Ho Chi Minh Trail. McMullan ignored the warning sign and approached it.

On a dry morning, he could jog down some parts of the trail. On a misty morning like this one, he was forced to move slowly or risk a slip on the slick rocks that could send him tumbling. He trod carefully down the irregular path, taking care to favor the tender right knee that had earned him a Purple Heart in the first Gulf War.

When he reached the beach at the bottom, he turned to begin running along the thick sand above the high tide line. The cliffs loomed above to his left, and the Pacific Ocean spread out to the right under the morning mist.

Jogging toward McMullan was a stark-naked man. As he approached, the two men began dancing awkwardly from side to side in an effort to pass each other, the stranger's limp penis swaying to and fro from the motion. Finally, the man ducked past him and McMullan continued on.

It was Katrina Stone that had recommended this route, but she had failed to mention that the beach at the bottom of Ho Chi Minh Trail was clothing optional. McMullan had been caught completely off guard on his first visit. But after the initial surprise, he came to like Black's Beach for the same reason Katrina liked to run here—it was almost totally secluded. Vehicular traffic to the beach was prohibited; the access road that rose up from the sand was chained off to all traffic except for police vehicles. And with the exception of the trail from the gliderport, additional points of entry were miles away.

McMullan also liked the fact that the run back up the mountain on the access road was a bitch of a workout with no motor vehicles to contend with. Now, as he reached the road, the morning mist was burning off, and the southern California sun was warming the air. He took a few deep breaths and started up the steep switchbacks.

Jogging ahead of him was a large group of men, all sporting the same close-cropped haircut that McMullan himself had worn in the Marine Corps. He found himself marveling, not for the first time, at the density of military personnel in San Diego.

To the south, near downtown and the airport, was the Naval Base San Diego—the largest Naval port on the West Coast. Its neighbor on Coronado Island contained the North Island Air Station and Naval Amphibious Base. In addition, San Diego housed the Outlying Field in Imperial Beach near the US-Mexico border, the Naval Auxiliary Airfield on San Clemente Island, and the Miramar Marine Corps Air Station. Thirty miles north was the one hundred twenty-five thousand acre Camp Pendleton United States Marine Corps Base.

The heavy military presence around McMullan would normally have offered a sense of security. Now, it seemed ominous. As he jogged up the mountain behind the Marines, he was acutely aware that if someone wanted to both punish and cripple the United States, there was perhaps no better target than "America's Finest City." The military would make San Diego difficult to hit with traditional forces. But it was the perfect location for a biological terror attack.

10:54 A.M. PST

Josh Attle halted in the doorway as his eyes fell on the mostly vacant space in front of him. Katrina and a large sweaty man were leaning over a folding card table in the center of the room. Both were wearing hard hats. A blueprint was spread over the table.

"Damn it," Josh exclaimed, and pivoted on his heels to exit.

Katrina and the contractor looked up in unison and Katrina giggled.

Josh turned back around to look at her. "Um, have you seen our molecular biology lab? I thought I left it here."

Katrina laughed louder. "I keep doing that, too. I think our molecular lab is currently in boxes, but if you find a way to do your experiment anyway, I'll give you a Scooby Snack." Katrina smiled sweetly at Josh and then returned to the blueprint.

The lab was now a construction zone, in the process of being expanded to almost twice its original size. Douglas Tsoukas, the immunologist next door, had initially been furious upon learning that he was being evicted from his lab space, effective immediately, with very little explanation. The financial compensation he was offered, and the gorgeous new lab that miraculously began appearing in a new high-tech complex across the street, had quickly smoothed over his anger.

Katrina had wasted no time moving into the former Tsoukas space. In addition to the multiple Ph.D. staff scientists she was provided with, a dozen temporary employees had been assigned to the move and to the development of the lab space itself.

Octopus the Robot was relocated into what had been Tsoukas' main lab space. Within days, Octopus was joined by seven additional robots and their supporting equipment. Two robotics experts were brought on board to man the machines full time under the scientific direction of Jason, Josh, and Oxana.

The three biologists also began a relentless collaboration with a new team of organic chemists that was designing the chemical compound libraries. It was those compounds that would be screened to identify new inhibitors of the Death Row Complex. Li and Todd would follow up with the inhibitors, evaluating lead molecules for toxicity, efficacy, and stability in cells.

When molecules showed potential in test tubes, the next step was to move them into animal testing—first mice and rats, and eventually, primates. Before now, the animal work in Katrina Stone's lab had been severely stunted by a lack of funding. She had established a pulmonary anthrax model in mice—the functional equivalent of inhalational anthrax in humans—at the Sorrento Valley BSL-3 facility. But primate testing had been far too expensive.

Now, lack of funds was no longer a problem. The issue was lack of time.

The San Diego State University vivarium and the Sorrento Valley BSL-3 facility were effectively taken over. Streamlined teams of pharmacokineticists, drug metabolism experts, bacteriologists, and veterinarians assembled to move compounds out of mice and rats and into a new test group of monkeys. The tension in the animal facilities was palpable as researchers struggled to select the most promising compounds prematurely, based on data that was still grossly incomplete.

The greeting card that had been mailed to the White House in October had specified that a terror attack would take place on Christmas Day. It was now Thanksgiving, and the work had just begun.

✕

Josh Attle was halfway out the door of the lab when a young woman in skintight jeans and a babydoll T-shirt shoved him back inside.

Katrina glanced up from the blueprint just as the woman stepped into the lab. The neck was cut out of the tight T-shirt, and Katrina saw Josh cast a quick glance at her prominent cleavage. Aside from her breasts, which were obviously medically enhanced, the woman was very thin.

"*Where the fuck is Jason Fischer?*" she demanded.

"Um, I, uh, I don't know... " Josh stuttered, staggering backward, his eyes darting back and forth as if looking to Katrina for guidance.

Katrina watched the exchange with the composition of a person experienced with outbursts of this nature. She tipped the hard hat off her head and set it casually on top of the blueprint. "Who wants to know?" she asked.

"I'm the chick who's about to kick the living shit out of Jason Fischer. Where is he?" As she snarled the words, the woman brushed past Josh and began to approach Katrina.

Katrina did not back down, but rather, strode toward her confronter. "I'm sorry," she said, "but I'm not going to just offer up my postdoc to someone who wants to 'kick the living shit' out of him. You'll have to provide a little more explanation or you'll have to leave."

"Well, that son of a bitch gave me herpes! How's that!"

Katrina's eyes flashed, but she continued to step forward to meet the girl. The two women stood toe to toe, almost matched in height. Their faces were inches from one another. The younger woman was slightly taller than Katrina, and Katrina's eyes were tilted upward to meet her gaze.

Katrina rose slightly onto her toes to look downward into the woman's eyes. "Look, lady," she said through her teeth, "Jason's personal life is not a drama that needs to unfold in my lab. Now, if you don't get out of here and talk to him on his own time and in his own space, I'm either calling security or kicking your ass myself."

After she spoke the last sentence, Katrina heard a man deliberately clearing his throat. She looked past the woman toward the sound.

Roger Gilman was standing in the doorway, leaning against the jamb. He was chuckling and shaking his head. "Oh that's lovely, Dr. Stone. Are you in the habit of threatening teenagers with violence in front of your students?"

"I'm not a fucking teenager," the woman spat. "I'm twenty-two. And who the fuck are *you*?"

"Special Agent Roger Gilman," Gilman answered cheerfully. He glided toward the two women and offered his hand to the stranger.

She did not take it. Instead, with a last spiteful glance in Katrina's direction, she whirled to pass Gilman and exit the room.

"Ah, Dr. Stone," Gilman said after the woman was gone, "the professionalism with which you conduct your affairs never ceases to impress me."

Gilman had to trot to catch up with the young woman in the parking lot. By the time he reached her, he was panting heavily, and he moved directly into her path as if to block her from moving forward. "Ma'am... " he said between desperate breaths, "I need to... ask you a few questions."

"*What?!*" The woman stepped around him.

Gilman jogged alongside her brisk walk. "We're investigating... a series of murders."

"Good for you. If I get my hands on that motherfucker, you'll be investigating one more."

Gilman fumbled through his pockets for his notepad and pen as he ran. After locating the items, he took a deep breath and let it out quickly, then continued. "What is... your name?"

"I don't have to answer your questions." Her breathing was normal as she maintained the rapid pace through the parking lot.

"Well yes... actually... you do. As I mentioned... I'm... a federal agent investigating... a series of murders... for the government. If you don't... answer my questions... you are obstructing justice... and committing... a federal offense. So lose... the attitude... answer my questions... and slow down!" Gilman stopped jogging, leaned over, and cupped his hands over his knees.

The woman reluctantly stopped walking and turned back toward him. "My name is Lisa Goldstein. What else?"

Gilman wrote the name on his notepad and continued. "What is... the nature of your... relationship with Jason Fischer?"

"There is no relationship. We had a one-night stand. I haven't seen him since. He's probably off giving herpes to some other chick dumb enough not to make him wear a rubber."

"And do you... work at this university? Are you a scientist?"

The woman ejected a sarcastic laugh. "Do I look like a fucking scientist?"

"I don't know." Gilman's breathing was returning to normal, but he was sweating profusely. He reached into his pocket for a handkerchief, which he used to mop his brow. He caught a few more breaths. "I don't really know what a scientist looks like anymore."

"Well, I'm a stripper," the woman said. "And spare me the moral judgment on that, because frankly, I'm not up for it right this minute."

Gilman was uninterested in Lisa Goldstein's choice of career. He was contemplating the notion of a Ph.D. biologist in a band who worked on anthrax and picked up strippers in his free time.

Roger Gilman could not stop smiling as he and Dawn strolled slowly through Lafayette Square. Directly in front of them stood a large statue of Andrew Jackson waving his hat atop a rearing horse. Centered behind the statue was the White House; behind it, the Washington monument stretched toward the heavens.

It was an unusually cold fall in D.C. A light dusting of snow already covered the square, and both Gilman and his wife wore long coats, scarves, and hats. Each of them had removed one glove, and his large hand enveloped her small one. It was just perfect.

"Mary is doing so well," Dawn was saying. "She's reading almost all by herself. When you first left town, she was crying a lot. But then she got this new determination all of a sudden." Dawn laughed at the memory. "She just comes to me and says, 'Mommy, I'm not going to cry for Daddy anymore. I'm going to learn how to read really good and then when he gets home I'll surprise him!'

"So James has been working on it with her. Every day, he

comes home from kindergarten and she's waiting for him to teach her what he learned that day. It's so cute to see them camped out in their PJs, with her sounding out the words while he corrects her by sounding out the same words."

Gilman's eyes welled up. He was not ashamed. He wiped the tears softly with the gloved hand not holding Dawn's, and then stopped walking and pulled his wife into his arms. For a moment he just stood with her, not wanting to miss a moment of this time. "What about the rest of them?" His voice was on the verge of breaking.

"Oh, they're fine," Dawn said. "The older kids are a lot more used to having you gone for a while. They know you'll always be back. They're just going to school, going to church, doing their homework... sports... business as usual... you know."

Dawn fell silent as they began walking again. Wordlessly, they changed direction and began heading east, and then south along 15th street. It was as if Gilman was responding to an inexorable pull, a magnet drawing him toward FBI headquarters.

"What time is your flight in the morning?" Dawn asked.

"My driver is coming to get me at 4:50."

"Ouch!" she laughed.

"I know, but I practically had to beg just to get an overnight stay at all. This meeting is only supposed to last about an hour. Bob was going to put me back on a plane to San Diego this afternoon."

"Well I'm glad the begging worked. The kids are thrilled you'll be there when they get home from school. Speaking of which, I do have to go. Mary and James will be out soon."

For a moment, they stood at the northwest corner of Freedom Plaza, Dawn's kind eyes shining up into his. He sighed. "I need to get to work. But I'll be home as soon as I can."

"Good," she said with a hint of mischief in her voice. "I'm making pot roast." Pot roast was Gilman's favorite dinner in the winter. He smiled gratefully and hugged his wife for a long moment, his round belly pressing into her flat one.

Minutes later, Gilman was across a conference table from Teresa Wood and Director Bob Wachsman. Beside him was Sean McMullan. In front of each of them was a copy of the same status report. Bob appeared to be reading it when Gilman approached. Gilman had familiarized himself with the information on the airplane.

Teresa had written the report. "There are two primary pieces of evidence that have come to light on my end," she said after Gilman sat down. "The first is a fiber from a piece of clothing. I've had this material analyzed and tracked, and it helps us—well, maybe a little. It is most likely a fiber from a white lab coat. There are many other standard-issue white uniforms, all of which are generated by the same clothing manufacturer. But given all of the other evidence in this case, Ockham's razor tells me it's probably a lab coat, probably from a researcher or a doctor.

"Second piece of evidence: there was also a microscopic hair in the envelope with the card. Medium brown and fine, although the fineness of this one tiny sample doesn't necessarily mean your perp has fine hair overall. We've done a DNA analysis. It's from a Caucasian female."

Gilman and McMullan looked at each other. Neither spoke.

"Now, I understand we have some suspects that fit the description?" Teresa continued.

Gilman nodded grimly. "That and every other description

on the planet. McMullan and I have been combing through the backgrounds of all of our San Diego-based suspects since October. Our counterparts in San Francisco are doing the same work at San Quentin. It's taking a long time. The heavy metal guitarist alone has hundreds of friends and even more enemies."

"Well," Teresa said, "get me a DNA sample from your top ten Caucasian suspects—even if they are male, because that could potentially bring a familial connection to light. Obviously, we can't rule anyone out based on the fact that their DNA is *not* on the card, but if we find a match then we have a pretty clear winner."

"We'll get the DNA," McMullan said. "What's your next move?"

"Well guys, I'm at a fork in the road. I have exhausted all of the assays that can be done to the card using non-destructive methods. I have not found any prints, which doesn't surprise me. I'm sure your perp probably had the brain to wear gloves when handling the document.

"I *could* dust the card for prints with fluorescent powder and look using the gooseneck—that would be the most sensitive way to examine it for fingerprints. But that would contaminate the card, and if we *did* pick up a print, I bet it would match the hair sample so it would not give us any new information.

"So I have decided go a different route instead. I'm going to proceed with the ESDA. This will also damage the document, but it might pick up a trace of another writing or other indentation. So it could give us a *unique* piece of information. If your perp is a scientist or a doctor, as the lab coat fiber suggests, then he or she probably writes on a million things a day. We might get something from this."

"Sounds good," Bob Wachsman said. "Make it happen. What about the tracing of the postage? Linguistics? Handwriting?"

"Useless. The language is a mixture, the handwriting is a mystery, and Mason tracked the IBI of the postage stamp as far as he could, which wasn't very far. It was mailed in Phoenix. That's all we know."

"Great," said Wachsman. "So basically, our perp is anyone in Arizona."

"Or anyone in San Diego with a car," Gilman added.

"Or anyone in the world who's not afraid to fly," Teresa corrected.

In the main forensics laboratory at the USPIS, Teresa reached into a plastic bag with a gloved hand. She gently pulled out the White House greeting card and then took a deep breath. After a moment to ensure the entire experiment was ready to go, she laid the card, opened, onto a flat surface in front of her. Instantly, the force of a vacuum sucked the card to the surface where it formed a seal.

Teresa worked expertly and quickly. The ESDA—electrostatic detection apparatus—would pick up invisible impressions in the paper. But the longer the card sat over the vacuum, the less sensitive the assay would become as the force of the vacuum increasingly flattened the impressions in the document. Teresa laid a thin layer of plastic film over the card and the vacuum immediately pulled the film taught. With a hand-held corona wire, she began to deposit a negative electrical charge to the entire surface of the plastic.

Then she waited. The time frame for the experiment was absolutely critical to maximize the negative charge while minimizing the damage done to the document by the force of the vacuum.

Teresa took pride in her skill with the ESDA. When intuition told her she was at the critical moment, she retrieved a vial of what appeared to be colored powder. In fact, the vial was filled with tiny, positively charged glass beads, coated with liquid toner. Quickly, she poured the beads over the plastic, where they automatically distributed to neutralize the charge applied to the document.

Gradually, a series of impressions developed as the beads were sucked into the lowest points on the document. The first indentations shown were those produced by the Arabic text, which became crisper before Teresa's eyes as if an invisible hand had come in with a second pen and precisely traced the writing.

A moment later, a second set of impressions began to emerge.

Teresa began to grin, and then chuckle. "Damn, I'm *good*," she said aloud. She reached into a drawer and grabbed a sheet of sticky, transparent film, from which she then removed the plastic backing to expose the tacky surface. Carefully, to avoid introducing air bubbles between layers, she laid the film over the newly created trace to preserve it.

In a San Diego hotel room, Roger Gilman sat on the bed cross-legged, surrounded by pages and pages of documentation. On the notepad in his lap was a sketched Venn diagram. In one circle, the agent had written the names of suspects who were female and Caucasian—women whose DNA could match the hair sample Teresa had found in the greeting card. At the top of the list was Katrina Stone. Several other names were scrawled beneath that of Stone in the circle: Stone's Russian graduate student, Oxana Kosova, the heavy metal postdoc's soon-to-be ex-wife, Angela Fischer, and his crazy stripper groupie, Lisa Goldstein.

Family. Stone had both a daughter and a sister. Her mother was in the beginning of stages of Alzheimer's disease—not a likely suspect, but still ambulatory. Stone's ex-husband had remarried. Kimberly Stone. Another Caucasian female.

In a second circle of the Venn diagram, Gilman had written the names of suspects who would wear a lab coat or other white standard-issue uniform. Katrina's ex-husband, Tom Stone, had been included. He was a medic. Stone's other female student, Li Fung, was not Caucasian but she did fit into the second circle. So did the rest of Stone's staff.

Asked to provide DNA, Li had willingly submitted as had Joshua Attle. Jason Fischer had said, "Fuck you—come back with a court order," without looking up from his experiment. Todd Ruddock had provided the sample along with a middle finger, and then cheerfully requested with his charming British accent, "Now bugger off, will ya?" Angela Fischer had agreed to provide a sample and then slapped Gilman across the face when he plucked the hair from her head.

Gilman had not managed to locate Lisa Goldstein. According to another stripper at the club where she worked, Lisa had a tendency to go on "vacation" with some of her "clients" and would probably be back at some point.

The area of overlap between the two circles contained only two names—only two Caucasian females who would wear lab coats. Oxana Kosova and Katrina Stone.

A third, non-overlapping circle was reserved for suspects who had no obvious ties to either the hair sample or the fiber. The ISIL network, which had been silent on the matter since day one of the investigation. Other international terrorist organizations. Domestic terrorists. Also in the third circle was the phrase "2000 Hispanic Prisoners," and beneath that, "Prisoners' Victims."

Lawrence Naden was, indeed, sitting in a prison cell in Texas. Not a suspect. Gilman had written his name outside of all circles and then drawn a direct line to the name of Katrina Stone. One woman in the center of the diagram. One woman at the center of it all.

Gilman reflected back on his short, wonderful visit to Washington, D.C. and sighed.

His cell phone began to ring. Gilman crawled over the paperwork on his hotel room bed and began rifling through clothing on the floor. Finally finding his phone in the pocket of a pair of slacks, he clicked into the call. "Hello, this is Roger Gilman."

"Hi Roger, Teresa Wood calling from Dulles. I've got good news and bad news. Do you have a few minutes?"

Gilman scrambled to find a notepad and pen. "Uh, sure. Hang on a minute."

The hotel staff had been given strict instructions to leave the room alone and had evidently been complying. Gilman found what he was looking for and shoved a few papers on the bed aside before sitting down. He uncapped his pen. "What did you find with the DNA?"

"In short, nothing," Teresa said. "I ran the sample against all of the suspects you gave me. There was no familial similarity with any of them, let alone exact matches. You mentioned that two of your potential suspects had not given up their DNA at the time you sent the samples, correct?"

"Correct."

"And have they now?"

"The court order came through and we've gotten DNA from one of them—Jason Fischer. But he's a man, obviously, and he has no family near San Diego. He doesn't seem too close to any of his family at all, so I doubt we'll get anything from his DNA. Even though he's a *punk*."

"Send me the sample anyway," Teresa said.

"Of course."

"What about the other suspect?"

"We still haven't located her. But I doubt she's our perp anyway."

"She? What color is her hair?"

"Brownish. And point taken. I'll find her." Gilman paused and then added, "I was really hoping for a hit on the lead suspects so I could wrap this up and go home."

"Sorry," Teresa said. "I guess it's not that easy this time." A moment later, she cleared her throat. "Uh, Roger, I have another question for you."

"What's that?"

"I hate to insult your intelligence here, but did you include a DNA sample from the intern that opened the card at the White House?"

Gilman paused. "You're kidding, right?"

Another pause. "Um, no. Are you?"

"You mean *you* haven't collected that sample?"

Teresa groaned. "Oh, *God* Roger! Why would *I* have collected that sample! *You* were supposed to be providing me with DNA. I was never under the impression that I was to collect any of it myself. Nor do I have time to!"

"Teresa, do you realize I'm in San Diego? Because I *do* realize that *you* are in D.C. I have collected the evidence here, you collect it in D.C. Make time!"

"No, I'm *not* in D.C. I'm outside of D.C. I don't just pop into the city on a daily basis. And I do *not* have time to be collecting evidence! Gilman, let me tell you something you don't seem to know. The U.S. Postal Inspection Service has had more than twenty thousand incidents to respond to since the anthrax mailings of 2001. FBI and CIA applicants have increased more than tenfold since then. But applicants to be federal postal inspectors—not so much. They don't call us the 'silent service' for no reason. So to put it mildly, we're grossly understaffed.

"I'll get the intern's hair. But you could have let me know! *Shit!*"

"You can say that again!" Gilman said.

"All right," Teresa said, a bit more calmly. "I'll take care of this. I'll let you know when or if it tells me anything."

Gilman heard the click of Teresa hanging up, and then a dial tone. He sat on the bed a moment longer. The mistake had been both of theirs. Gilman desperately hoped that the intern's DNA would *not* match the strand of hair on the card. If it did, his efforts to collect samples from every suspect had been nothing but wasted time.

A moment later, Gilman realized that Teresa had never given him the *good* news.

It took Teresa less than forty minutes to obtain a hair sample from intern Amanda Dougherty. When she called Jack Callahan at the White House, Dougherty was working in the next room.

Amanda was both stunned and thrilled that her own genetic material was actually being examined in a real FBI case. She could not wait.

Jack advised Teresa that because she did not usually conduct business within the White House, it would be easier to bring Amanda to Teresa than to bring Teresa through White House security. Teresa informed Jack that there was no way he was bringing a complete stranger into the National Forensics Laboratory, not even a kid. They decided to meet halfway.

In the time it took Jack and Amanda to get out of the White House, through central Washington, D.C., and across the Theodore Roosevelt Memorial Bridge, Teresa was already waiting at the Iwo Jima monument when they arrived. When she saw Jack, she waved him over. "Thanks for meeting me," she said and turned to the girl. "I assume you are Amanda?"

"Yes, I'm Amanda," the girl said. She was grinning. "So what do you do, just pluck out one of my hairs?"

"Yep, that's it," Teresa said. "Easy, huh? But I need to pull it, not cut it. I need the root."

"I thought so," Amanda said, looking proud.

Teresa pulled a plastic bag out of her pocket and then reached toward Amanda to extract the hair sample.

"Ouch," Amanda said quietly when the hair was yanked out. "So, are you an FBI agent?"

Teresa smiled. "No, I'm a postal inspector."

"Oh," Amanda said with obvious disappointment.

"But I work with the FBI," Teresa said. Amanda looked unimpressed.

Teresa tried again. "We were the first federal law enforcement to use the Tommy Gun, ya know."

Blank stare.

Teresa turned instead to Jack. "This is why I'm understaffed."

The next day, Teresa Wood held a phone to her ear while typing furiously. When the call she had placed was answered, she ceased her data entry and gripped the phone with one hand while leaning backward in her chair.

"Hello, this is Roger Gilman." As Gilman spoke the words in San Diego, Teresa simultaneously mouthed them in Dulles. His greeting never varied.

"Roger, Teresa Wood here," she said. "I have good news and bad news."

Gilman groaned. "Oh no, not again."

"Yeah, no kidding. The bad news is that it was the intern's hair on the greeting card. So we've wasted time that we could not afford to waste. There is no other possibility for DNA. We've come to a dead end on that front."

"That was our best chance at finding the perp!"

"Don't you think I know that?"

"What else?" Gilman demanded.

"Well, I forgot to mention this in the confusion over the intern's hair—but the ESDA picked up a trace of another writing. It's a good trace. But... I don't know what it means. I don't know if it will tell us anything."

Gilman sighed. "It better tell us something. Christmas is in seventeen days."

The ESDA trace told nothing. Eleven days before Christmas, Roger Gilman sat staring at the text in the office he now occupied adjacent to Katrina Stone's new laboratory. Three lines. That was all. And it was gibberish.

WHO1315

DR1630

AL1800

Who? Dr? Dr. Who? What? And who is Al?

Gilman had been staring at the text for the better part of five days. He had read up on *Dr. Who* and decided that if the popular time-travel science fiction series had any connection at all to Operation Death Row, the nation was sunk. He had given the three numbers from the ESDA trace to top FBI code-breakers who had come back with nothing.

It was over.

Reluctantly, Gilman picked up the receiver of his office phone to call Bob Wachsman and recommend that the government prepare for the worst.

⚭

The prisoner was already waiting at the small table when his visitor sat down across from him. Her black headscarf and Muslim robe had been gone for more than a month, along with the Arab alias and bogus accent. Instead, the visitor's dark face was now obscured by long thick waves of black hair. A chunky sweater draped over a skirt that flowed almost to the floor. *She's still ugly as fuck,* the prisoner thought offhand.

The visitor scanned the room for watching guards and then reached into a fold of the skirt. "I can't keep this up," she whispered as she leaned in to hand the money to the prisoner. "I'm going broke."

"I don't really give a shit," the prisoner said. "You'll keep paying for as long as I say. But just to make you feel a little better"—he cocked his head and a grin spread across his face—"I'm almost done with you."

December 19, 2015
9:00 a.m. PST

Following a phone call from Roger Gilman to Bob Wachsman, the terror threat level was increased to red—the highest of the Homeland Security Advisory System. Official government briefings warned the public to remain hyper vigilant and to report any suspicious activity immediately. No specifics were provided.

But then, the classified report detailing the anthrax outbreak at the prison was leaked to the press. Word of the genetically activated strain spread through the nation like wildfire, and the media developed a feverish interest in the sudden massive expansion of an unknown anthrax research laboratory in San Diego.

Katrina Stone and her staff had been amply forewarned that there would be a federal presence in their laboratories for the duration of the project. What they were not prepared for was a full military invasion. Every entrance to the original building and the new facility across the street was now guarded by at least two armed soldiers. Only essential personnel were permitted access to the buildings. Construction workers, scientists, and professors were issued ID access badges and required to wear them visibly at all times. Random searches became the norm.

The building housing Katrina's lab at San Diego State University was still a construction site. Now, it was also a police state.

⋈

It was six days before Christmas when Katrina and Jason Fischer stood over the bodies of three dead monkeys. *"Why, Jason?!"* Katrina was practically crying. "Your compound was completely effective in mice! Why isn't it working in monkeys? What's the difference in the primates?"

Jason shook his head. "I'm not sure," he said. "It could be one of any number of things. Primates aren't mice—we've rediscovered this inconvenient fact a million times. But if the drug doesn't work in monkeys, I bet my life it's not going to work in humans."

"I know that, Jason!"

Jason raised a palm toward Katrina in a gesture for her to calm down. "I have an idea about what might be causing the discrepancy," he said. "But I need another few days to confirm or disprove it."

"Another few days is literally *all* you have," Katrina said.

Four days later, Jason had the answer.

It was the day before Christmas Eve, and Katrina was standing with Gilman and McMullan in the break room outside of her laboratory. Although they stood close together, nobody spoke. All three were gulping large cups of coffee and staring absently at the floor, all three absorbed in their own concerns, all three ultimately consumed with the same thought. *The day after tomorrow.*

Jason burst into the room. "There you are!" he said as he rushed toward Katrina. "I've got it."

Katrina sank into a chair at the break room table. Her hand was shaking as she set the coffee cup loudly onto the table. "What is it then?"

"The inhibitor only blocks TEM8 on primates."

Katrina looked up at him. "Are you sure?"

"Positive. I've used three different assays."

Gilman and McMullan exchanged a glance. "What does that mean?" McMullan asked.

Jason turned to face McMullan. "There are two receptors

that anthrax proteins interact with—they are called CMG2 and TEM8. The toxin can get into the cell through either one of these receptors, and it has to get into the cell to kill the cell.

"My lead compound works beautifully in mice. But it failed in monkeys. I've been racking my brain trying to figure out why. Now, I have done some cell-based testing and confirmed that it only blocks one of the receptors in the monkey cells, but it blocks both in mouse cells. From those pieces of data, I can easily conclude that the reason the monkeys died was that they were still vulnerable to an infection. We need to block both receptors to block the complex."

"What about humans?" Gilman asked.

"It was probably a safe assumption that if it didn't work in primates, it wouldn't work in humans either." He turned to Katrina before adding, "but we don't have to make that assumption. I have confirmed it. I tested the compound in human cells to see if it would block both receptors. It doesn't." Jason turned from Katrina to McMullan, and then to Gilman. "The monkeys have taught us definitively that there's no way our lead compound will be effective in humans."

Gilman went pale. For a moment, he stood breathing quick, shallow breaths, until McMullan stepped forward to guide him to a chair next to Katrina's. Then McMullan sat down as well. "What can you do now?" McMullan's voice was soft as he asked the question to which he already knew the answer.

"We can redesign the compound," Jason said. "But not in two days."

PART II: REDESIGNED

December 25, 2015
12:00 a.m. EST

It was midnight in Washington, D.C. when Gilman placed the video call to his wife. Between midnight and 5:00 a.m. East Coast time, he and his wife shared the intimacies of life-long sweethearts facing the last day of a terminal illness. Every second was more painful than the last, every instant another sliver of borrowed time. Nobody knew when the attack would happen. Or how. Or where.

No longer concerned with the national security he had failed to provide, Gilman's only thought now was that he should have gone home—and, so be it, to hell with his job—when he still had the chance. But now, all U.S. flights were grounded. So it was Skype that would allow him to talk to his wife, Skype that would allow him to be with his family even if the apocalypse crashed down upon them as they spoke.

At 6:15 a.m., the children began to wake up. It was still the middle of the night in San Diego, and Gilman glanced between the black sky through his hotel room window and the oasis of life projecting from his cell phone. Dawn's phone jiggled as she trotted to the living room to watch their children dive into the mountain of gifts that was over-the-top lavish this year.

About 8:00 a.m., the children began to ask about breakfast and church. It was Gilman, and not his wife, who explained that this year—this year only—the family would stay home and pray privately rather than attending Christmas mass. He asked his children to pray hard.

After breakfast, Dawn left her phone charging on the kitchen table, propped up against a book so the video could continue to run. Gilman watched his family career through their daily affairs until he fell back asleep.

✖

It was 2:35 p.m. in San Diego when Gilman woke up. His phone had died. Consumed with an instant feeling of panic, he dug through the clutter in his hotel room until he found his charger, and then stood impatiently by until the phone picked up enough of a charge to be used again. Immediately, he resumed the video call.

His children were in the midst of a lazy Christmas afternoon, seemingly normal except for the fact that Daddy was away. Dawn was preparing dinner for the eight of them, and Gilman once again found himself sad beyond measure that he had not abandoned his duty to the FBI to be home for this day.

As the evening wore on, and the children began winding down, a surreal sense of calm began to creep in, and the nightmare in which he had been living began to feel as if maybe—just maybe—it had been exactly that. A bad dream.

Still, he stayed on the call with his wife after the children were sleeping. When midnight approached once again, and Dawn was dozing off in their bed, Gilman found himself also beginning to relax, as it began to seem more and more likely that the day he had been dreading for months would conclude without incident.

Christmas Day came and went without incident. The nation breathed a collective sigh of relief, and the frenzied bicoastal investigation began slowing from its breakneck pace to a manageable one. But Operation Death Row was far from over.

Katrina Stone and her staff were still committed to redesigning the inhibitor of the Death Row Complex, and the turmoil surrounding her laboratory had not waned. On January 8, she was sitting once again at the break room table with McMullan and Gilman, talking them through the latest data updates from her staff, when a voice echoed through the laboratory toward them. "Get your hands off my willie! I have an ID badge!"

The door to the break room burst open and a pudgy man who appeared to be in his late sixties shuffled into the room. The man wore wrinkled slacks and a button down shirt; the buttons did not align correctly with the buttonholes, and one un-tucked shirttail was longer than the other.

Behind him was one of the armed guards on duty.

"He's clean," the guard said to McMullan and Gilman. "I frisked him."

"Thanks," McMullan said, looking amused.

Katrina looked up apologetically but did not speak.

"Oh, Jesus, Katrina," the elderly man began and then stopped when his eyes fell upon the cookie jar next to the coffee pot. He reached in and pulled out a large handful of broken cookies, which he shoved absently into his mouth before continuing to speak. "This is ridiculous! I can't even do my work anymore!" The pronunciation of the word "can't" was forceful enough to send a fragment of cookie flying out of his mouth and onto the floor in front of him. Noticing the fallen morsel, the man paused to reach down and pick it up. He shoved it back into his mouth and continued. "Please tell me this is almost over!" Another chunk of cookie escaped on the word "please," but this one stayed on the ground. McMullan and Gilman pulled their eyes away from it to ex- change an amused glance.

"Richard, I'm doing everything I can to make this all go away," Katrina said. "We have figured out what was wrong with the compound, and we think we know how to correct it."

"Do it, then," he responded. "I'm not running a circus here, and I'm not the least bit amused by all of this. I'm fend- ing off negative press every day. So when this is all over, there had better be some payoff in the way of good publication to compensate for the damage you've done to our department's reputation. *Science* or *Nature*. I'll accept nothing less."

He reached and grabbed another handful of cookies, then shoved them in to join the partially chewed previous batch. He then turned and left the room, shoving his hand down the back of his pants to scratch an unmentionable itch as he went. The two agents looked at one another again and then both burst out laughing.

"Who was *that* clown?" McMullan finally asked when he was able to speak.

"That's the chair of the biology department," Katrina answered.

"What a wing nut!"

Katrina's frustration dissipated slightly and she allowed herself a giggle. "The truth is, he's a genius," she said. "Molecular cardiology is his specialty, and he has made some of the largest advances in the field. But yeah, in the tradition of many true geniuses, he's a bit socially inept."

"I don't get it," McMullan said. "*You're* not that clueless!"

"Oh, *thanks*, Sean!" Katrina laughed. "Well, the truth is, I work very hard, but I certainly don't have his level of scientific brilliance either. Richard is on the same plane as Einstein. A man who, by the way, was a kleptomaniac, was known for forgetting to wear socks, and often forgot where he was entirely."

As the second full week of January was wrapping up, Roger Gilman sat in his office adjacent to Stone's laboratory. It was Friday evening. Gilman glanced up from his paperwork to polish off a long-forgotten doughnut with the last cold bit of his coffee from the morning. He grimaced. Then he dropped the document he had been reading into the wastebasket by his desk before grabbing his coat to leave.

Gilman glanced out the window and then tossed the coat back onto his chair in disgust. Even in January, San Diego was too warm for a jacket. The fact that he was trapped in one eternal season seemed fitting for this endless assignment. He stepped out of the office to pass through the lab on his way out.

Katrina Stone was alone at a computer, using a mouse to scroll through something. The connected printer was spitting out page after page.

Gilman approached her. "You know what I still can't figure out?"

"What?"

"I still can't figure out how your unpublished data could be so closely linked to the activated anthrax strain with no prior knowledge of it."

Katrina stopped working and glared at him. "Agent Gilman, what exactly are you implying?"

"Nothing, nothing. It's just that there are scientists out there who wonder if you engineered the Death Row strain. Maybe even sent it off to San Quentin to make sure it would work. Of course, *I* would never believe that of you. But, wow"—he sucked air between his teeth dramatically and gestured sweepingly in all directions—"you sure do seem to have made out like a bandit with all this. Shiny new lab, plenty of money to do your work. Not to mention you seem to be some kind of a hero for all this. I hear you've even been invited to speak at the upcoming biotechnology convention? Must be nice.

"I might not mind any of that so much, given that there conveniently doesn't seem to be any real threat after all, except for the fact that *I'm* still stuck here on an assignment I never wanted while you wrap up whatever you're doing for apparently no reason. So do me a favor, will you? Hurry the hell up."

Katrina had not responded but her breathing was quickening. She now turned from her work and strode quickly toward him. Inches from his face, she looked defiantly into his eyes. "Use your brain for just a minute here, genius. If I wanted to kill a prisoner it would be Lawrence Naden. You know who he is, right? I certainly hope so, or else the FBI has been crawling up my ass for the last three months for no reason.

"And *if* I wanted to kill Lawrence Naden, I wouldn't do it with something that is uniquely traceable to myself. I'd just send Naden some cyanide in a Ziplock bag labeled 'Free Cocaine.' Now, if you don't have any other ground breaking hypotheses for me, I'm excusing myself from this conversation."

Katrina turned to leave, and then turned back around. "And by the way, I don't know who *you've* been talking to, but I have hardly made friends around here and I'm certainly no hero. You recently heard a conversation I had with the chair of my department. Yeah, that guy yelling at me with the cookies flying out of his mouth? He's my boss. And he's mad as hell.

"Richard and the rest of the faculty are holding me personally responsible for obstructing their work—as if I have any control over the military presence and press, which nobody at the FBI seems able to do anything about either. You guys can make someone disappear, but you can't make a news van use a different street—which means you have less power to facilitate this work than Cal Trans. So what are you even doing here? You don't seem to be helping things much.

"And you know what else? You're not the only one stuck here, asshole. I'm working myself into the ground over what should have been my holiday season. My entire staff, in fact, has given selflessly to make this project work because you guys seemed to think the country was depending on us. *You* came to *me* about this, remember? I'm doing this because you have asked me for help to do work that the government *will never let me publish.*

"In academic science—which is what I *normally* do here— the rule is 'publish or perish.' If we don't publish work, it's as if we never did it. You heard Richard. *Science* or *Nature*— the two top journals. But I *can't* publish my work on the Death Row inhibitors.

"So everything I'm doing right now is for absolutely nothing as far as my career is concerned. All of my current government funding is only temporary, and the plug can be pulled at any time. And since I've pissed off the entire biology department, they'll never float me. So great, I have a nice new shiny lab, but if I can't get a grant after all this is over, it's going to go to someone else while I end up unemployed.

"The sad thing is, I almost *needed* for there to be another terror attack to justify how I've spent the last three months. How sick is that?

"Taking this project has all but ruined me. I'm thirty-four years old. I still have a very long way to go. So you know what I'm going to do now? I'm going to drink. And you're not invited, fucko."

Katrina turned to grab her purse and keys from her office before storming out of the lab and slamming the door behind her. The printer was still whirring next to Gilman.

Katrina was muttering under her breath as she walked briskly toward the parking lot. After a few moments to think, she pulled her cell phone from her purse to call Sean McMullan.

McMullan sounded out of breath when he answered the phone. "Sean, it's Katrina."

"Hey! What's up?"

"I need to talk to you and I don't want Roger Gilman to be there. Where are you?"

"I'm at the gym."

"Which one?"

"Uh, it's the Fitness Land on the corner of Eighth and E, downtown."

"I'll be there in twenty," she said and hung up.

She found him at the free weights, bench-pressing what looked to be an enormous load. It was the first time Katrina had seen Sean McMullan outside of a work environment.

McMullan's long athletic shorts revealed calves that

were toned and tan. He was wearing a gray T-shirt that read "USMC" across the chest in large navy blue lettering. McMullan's muscular left forearm was covered with a faded tattoo that read "Semper Fi." Katrina briefly remembered the first time she had met McMullan in her office, when she had noticed a tiny fraction of the tattoo below his shirt cuff.

"Want to take a walk?" she asked.

Resigned to the fact that his workout was cut short, McMullan reached into his gym bag and pulled on a sweatshirt. Then he and Katrina headed west into the Gaslamp Quarter.

"So, what's on your mind?" McMullan asked casually.

"Gilman," Katrina answered.

McMullan chuckled. "Heh, you sure I should hear this?"

"What is his problem? I see how he acts toward you, and everyone else for that matter. He's not an asshole to anyone but me. Obviously, I've done something to offend him.

"Truth be told, I don't really care if the dude likes me or not. But he's interfering with my ability to do my job when he comes into my lab and my office flinging accusations at me. I thought talking to you about it might help me to figure out how to deal with the jerk before I accidentally kill him."

Between Eighth and Fifth Streets, the downtown area became noticeably brighter and livelier as McMullan and Katrina approached the buzz of Friday night activity. Well-dressed couples zigzagged along Fifth Avenue between the more scantily clad groups of twenty-somethings. Bars and restaurants overflowed; at the entrances to some, the lines stretched through the doors and down the sidewalk. Pedestrians swerved around each other on both sides of the street, stepping out into the street to bypass the crowds outside of the busier establishments.

The scientist and the FBI agent crossed Fifth Avenue and waited for the signal to cross E street. "Well, Roger is very conservative," McMullan offered.

"And what am I, some kind of hippie? I own a gun, I know how to use it, and my ex was a jarhead and an active member of the NRA!" She laughed.

"Well, fair enough," McMullan said. "But still, your work... you represent... change. Something Roger doesn't do well with. I think if it was up to him, we'd still be in one-room schoolhouses... What in the world is that?" McMullan pointing one block westward to where E street abruptly came to an end.

Katrina smiled. "That's Horton Plaza. I know... it looks like something out of an Escher print. But it's actually just a mall. You ought to check it out sometime—there are all these whacky levels that don't really match up with each other, and escalators only going one direction without a corresponding escalator going the other direction. So you can see the store you want to go to, but you have to travel around a little bit in order to figure out how to get there. Unless you want to run up the down escalator or down the up escalator, which my daughter likes to do." She giggled. "Lexi calls Horton Plaza the Yuppie Ant Farm."

⋈

At that moment, a security guard was making his rounds inside Horton Plaza. As he rounded a corner, a young woman came into his view and his pace quickened. "Excuse me, miss! You're going to have to get down from there!"

The teenager was standing on a bench along the mall's uppermost walkway and leaning precariously over the balcony, the protective stucco wall only reaching to her knees. Below her was a several-story drop to ground level, where shoppers milled about the numerous kiosks in the center of the mall. She was taking a photograph with her cell phone.

The girl glanced in the guard's direction but then turned back to snap three more photographs, the flash of her phone's camera ricocheting from the window of a pet store across the open space before her. Satisfied, she jumped down and smiled at the guard. "Sorry," she said politely.

A young man appeared at her side and put his arm around her.

"Also," the guard said. "No photographs are allowed at Horton Plaza without permission. You'll have to go to our security office."

"Aren't you the security office?" the young woman asked.

"It's not my decision," the guard said. "Just don't take any more pictures until you've gotten permission. The office is closed now, so you'll have to come back tomorrow during the day."

The young couple thanked the guard politely and walked away. A few moments later, he saw the flash once again, this time angled upward from the floor below. The guard lunged down an escalator and approached the teenagers from behind. Without warning, he snatched the girl's cell phone away. "I told you no photographs!"

"Give me back my phone!"

Before the guard could react, the girl's companion lurched forward and grabbed him by the shirt, shoving him backward into a wall. "Who the *fuck* do you think you are!" the boy yelled. Several mall patrons turned to look as he grabbed the phone away from the startled security guard and then pushed him away. He then roughly took the young woman's hand and led her toward the large escalator that would exit the mall onto Fourth Avenue.

Kids, the somewhat shaken guard thought, but he held the butt of his nightstick as he followed behind to confirm that they were really leaving.

The girl abruptly stopped walking at the top of the escalator.

"What?" her companion asked.

"My mom!" she said and turned on her heels.

"Wow, it's crazy down here," McMullan said. "I've been in San Diego for a little while, but I've never been downtown on a Friday night except to go to the gym." The light was still red, and they were still standing on the corner of Fifth and E. "I like the cool old buildings," McMullan said, motioning down Fifth Avenue.

"Yeah. In the 1800s, this area was notorious for gambling, prostitution, drinking... "—she pointed across the street—"That building over there was owned by Wyatt Earp. I think it used to be a brothel."

McMullan looked again at the traffic light holding them immobile. "I guess it's still the red light district," he said.

The girl was trapped.

The Horton Plaza security guard watched, smiling, as she stepped behind her companion to hide from the woman down the street who was evidently her mother.

The girl turned back around to face the guard, who now stood behind her, less than ten feet away. Then the traffic

lights changed, and the woman and her companion began crossing the street. Still hiding behind the boy, the girl
smiled sweetly at the guard and mounted the escalator.

"Who is that with your mom?" the guard heard the young
man ask.

"I don't know. I didn't think my mom had a boyfriend."

"Then find out," the boy instructed as they stepped off
the escalator toward the street.

𝇇

The January air was chilly, and now a breeze had come up.
Katrina shivered and pulled her thin sweater more tightly
around her body. McMullan, still wearing a sweatshirt over
his gray T-shirt, took notice. "You're cold. I can offer you my
sweatshirt, but it's pretty grungy from the gym. Your call."
He smiled sheepishly.

Katrina laughed. "Thanks, but I don't know what my
daughter would think if I came home smelling like a sweaty
guy. I'm having a hard enough time trying to stop her from
acting like a fifteen-year-old as it is." After a pause, she said,
"But I will let you block the wind a little." She stepped closer
to him and McMullan placed a hand on the small of her
back.

As they headed south along Fifth Avenue, a raucous Irish
folk tune began drifting toward them. As they drew closer to
the music, it was accompanied by a mouthwatering scent.
McMullan's stomach growled. "Hungry?" he started to ask,
but Katrina was already winking at him as she stepped toward the door of the pub.

7:14 P.M. PST

J ason Fischer slid out of the seat of his Honda Civic, locked the door from the inside, and then slammed it shut. Habitually, he took a cautionary glance around to ascertain his surroundings as he hopped up onto the curb.

Twenty-five minutes inland from downtown San Diego and ten minutes from the lab at SDSU, Jason's one-bedroom apartment was in the mind-bogglingly cheaper community of Santee. Flipping through his keychain for the correct key, Jason trotted nimbly up the stairs before coming to an abrupt halt at the top.

The door to his apartment was already wide open.

A surge of adrenaline rushed through Jason as he walked into the apartment and flipped on the living room light. The room was illuminated, and Jason dropped the keychain along with the worn-out backpack he was holding. "You've *got* to be *kidding* me!" he yelled.

Jason's garage-sale entertainment center had been flipped forward, and the TV and stereo were smashed beneath it. Compact discs and orphaned cases were strewn about the living room in a random array of squares and circles. Some

of the items were crushed. His Salvation Army couch and loveseat had both been sliced open and large wads of stuffing
were now strewn about the room, enveloping the inverted
coffee table with billowing white clouds of furniture innards.

"Son of a *bitch!*" Jason ranted as he pushed his way
through the debris and into the kitchen. The kitchen cabinets had been emptied and the mismatched dishes—inher-
ited from an aunt who was planning to throw them away—
were now lying in broken piles on the floor. The refrigerator
was open, but most of what little food Jason had was still
inside. An eighteen-pack of Coors Light had been shoved out
and lay on its side in front of the fridge; some of the cans had
exploded and now the kitchen reeked from the small foamy
rivers running across the linoleum.

Jason gave only a passing glance to the destruction in
the kitchen. His kitchenware was shit. His furniture was
shit. Everything Jason owned of value, every cent he could
spare was concentrated in one area of the apartment. His
bedroom.

Guitars. Amps. Cables. Cabinets. Cases of strings. His microphone. His floorboard. His stands. His tuners. Thousands
of dollars that Jason could not afford, invested in his second
true passion. The first was science.

With his heart in his throat, Jason opened the bedroom
door. The guitars had been pulled out of their cases and
roughly thrown to the floor. One had a cracked headstock
that would require expensive repair. Both guitars had at
least one broken string dangling from them.

The amps, normally lining the wall opposite the bed, had
been shoved face-forward. Designed for rough transport between the stage and the home, they were none the worse

for wear. Other items were scattered about, but remarkably undamaged.

It did not appear that anything had been stolen. In wonder, Jason now realized that the TV and stereo, while now useless, were also still lying in the living room. Whoever had broken in was not a thief.

Jason sat down on his bed and cast his eyes around the room for a few moments. Then he reached into his pocket for his cell phone and his wallet. He rifled through an assortment of business cards until he found the two he was looking for. He dialed the number on the first card. There was no answer. He hung up and dialed the number on the other card.

$$\bowtie$$

"Hello, this is Roger Gilman."

"This is Jason Fischer. My apartment has been broken into," Jason picked up a guitar and lovingly placed it back onto its stand.

"What was stolen?" Gilman asked.

"That's what's weird. I don't see anything missing, not even stuff like my guitars that would have been easy to take and that are worth a lot of money. It's like the asshole just wanted to fuck my place up for no reason."

"Or they were looking for something in particular," Gilman conjectured. "I'll be right there."

The comment echoed in Jason's mind as he continued to examine his musical equipment. *They were looking for something in particular.* Like Jason's inhibitor data, rapidly produced since the beginning of the Death Row project. And supposedly under lock and key by the federal government.

Or his activator data, which very few people should have

known about in the first place. Was he just being paranoid? Someone would have had to track down his address, and—

Jason's thoughts were interrupted by a loud knock at the door. It had been less than two minutes since he had called Gilman on his cellular phone. *No way he could have gotten here already,* Jason thought. *And no way he was already in Santee.* As he hurried from the bedroom into the living room, he realized that the knock was a formality only; the door was still wide open and furthermore, Jason's keys were on the floor next to it.

Jason was incredulous to see that Gilman had, in fact, already arrived. But even more shocking was the person accompanying Gilman, standing slightly behind him in the doorway. Her eyes darted to the floor when Jason saw her. Angela Fischer. Jason's estranged wife.

"What the fuck is she doing here?" Jason demanded, looking questioningly at Gilman.

"You're going to be mad," Angela began, but Gilman intervened.

"Your wife called us," he said. "She saw who broke in to your apartment."

"I don't understand," Jason said. "How... " As soon as the words were out, he realized the answer. "Have you been following me, you psycho stalking wench?"

"Look, I just wanted to keep track of what you were doing with your money. I don't have anything to live on, and I don't want my ass handed to me in the divorce because you've spent it all before I can win any alimony in court... and it's not my fault that you're lagging on the proceedings. Now don't give me shit, Jason. I didn't have to come forward with this, but I did. Face it—you're lucky I'm here. Anyway, I was parked across the street and I saw the person who broke in. It was a woman."

Gilman and Jason both looked shocked. Gilman pulled his notepad out of his pocket and began flipping through to find a blank page.

Jason flipped his mutilated loveseat back into position. "Care to sit down?" he asked sarcastically. "Sorry I can't offer you a cup of tea, but I'm remodeling the kitchen at the moment."

Angela sat down on the loveseat and a puff of stuffing drifted to the floor. Jason and Gilman both grabbed an end of the larger sofa and tilted it upright, then sat down.

"So what did this woman look like?" Gilman asked Angela.

"She had long hair and was wearing a long skirt."

"What color hair?"

"I couldn't tell exactly. This area is not well lit enough to make out shit in the dark... which is one of the reasons I'd been nagging Jason for the last two years to move out of Santee"—she threw a haughty glance at her husband—"but I digress. Anyway, the woman's hair was long, thick and some dark color... that's about all I can tell you."

"What about build?" Gilman asked. "Thin? Overweight? Tall? Short?"

"Hard to say with the distance I was at and no reference. She wasn't fat."

Gilman turned to Jason and let out an exasperated sigh. "Well, there are two people who immediately come to mind, my friend. The first is your research advisor."

"No way," Jason objected immediately. "Why do you think Katrina would break in here? Why now? She's known me for years. And anyway, Katrina doesn't have a dishonest bone in her body. I know you have a number of suspicions about her—I'm not blind—but you're totally wrong."

Jason could not say what he needed to. Katrina had absolutely no motive for breaking into his apartment. He had kept nothing from her, ever. She knew exactly where the activator data was. Jason and Katrina had dropped it into the liquid nitrogen tank together. And with federal agents in the lab at all times, there was no way he could have moved it even if he had wanted to.

And maybe he and Katrina should have thought of that when they hid it there in the first place.

"Well, thanks for your input, *Doctor* Fischer," Gilman was saying. "And no offense, but your opinion doesn't weigh any more heavily with me than your mentor's. From what I've seen, you're both about the antithesis to trustworthy, as a matter of fact. And that brings me to the other suspect that comes to mind. Or perhaps several of them."

Jason looked over at Angela. "Can we talk about this in private?"

"No need," Gilman retorted. "I have every intention of finding out what all of your lady friends were doing tonight."

He turned to Angela. "What time was the break-in?"

"Around six thirty, I think," Angela said. "And Jason, I already know about all of your little bimbos. I really couldn't give a flying fuck at this point."

Gilman stood and brushed a stray ball of couch stuffing from his slacks, then stepped past the coffee table and toward the door. Nonchalantly, he turned back before exiting and addressed Angela. "And by the way, thank you for the tip—but you're also far from above suspicion, so don't even think about leaving town."

As Sean McMullan and Katrina Stone stepped out of the Irish pub, the noise level dropped dramatically. Only then did McMullan hear the chime on his cell phone. He pulled it out of his pocket and looked. He had missed a call. There was no message, and he did not recognize the number.

McMullan shrugged. "I guess if it's important they'll call back."

With full bellies and relaxed minds, Katrina and McMullan continued down Fifth Avenue. At first, neither spoke. It was McMullan who broke the silence. "Strip Club?" he asked, tipping his head to indicate an establishment.

Katrina laughed as she looked toward the restaurant. "That's not really a strip club; it's a cook-your-own-steak house." A moment later, she added, "but I bet a strip club would do pretty well down here."

"They could call it the Ass-Lamp," McMullan said.

Chuckling, they reached the arch over the street that marked their exit from the Gaslamp Quarter. Directly in front of them, the jutting peaks and glass curves of the San Diego Convention Center punctured the sky.

"So, *this* is where the convention center is..." McMullan mused.

"Yep, this is where the biotechnology convention will be. I bet all the hotels in this area are already booked solid for that entire week. My personal favorite is the Hyatt, down the street." She pointed along the coast to the pair of skyscrapers that distinguished the skyline of downtown San Diego. "There's a gorgeous view from the bar at the top, and I hear they make one hell of a martini. I've never tried one though..."

They began walking up the several flights of stairs that led to the balconies of the convention center. "It looks so futuristic," McMullan noted, his eyes wandering over the layers of curving glass.

"You should see the UCSD library," Katrina said.

"I have seen it. I jog by there almost every day. Thanks for the tip on that route, by the way. It's awesome, as long as you aren't intimidated by naked strangers." He glanced over at her. Was that a blush?

They reached a semi-circular balcony and for a moment, neither of them spoke as they took in the view of the bay. To their left, the Coronado Bridge formed a gentle arch, its lights speckling the sky over the horizon like an unusually ordered arrangement of stars.

Katrina shivered and wrapped her thin sweater around herself once again. McMullan stepped toward her to block the breeze as he had on the crowded street. She leaned in toward him, her eyes tipping upward to meet his, but when he bent down to kiss her, she stepped away.

Katrina cleared her throat and spoke curtly. "So, you think I should just be a bit more prudish?"

McMullan stepped back. "Huh?"

"With Gilman. If I let him know I actually have pretty old-school values, despite being a scientist, do you think Gilman will lighten up on me a bit?"

McMullan pulled in a breath and let it out slowly. "Ahem... ah, yes, that will probably help. Good idea." He ran a hand through his salt-and-pepper hair.

"Shall we keep walking?" Katrina asked.

"Sure. Where are you parked? I'll walk you to your car."

"I'm all the way up by your gym."

"Oh, yeah. Me too."

They walked in silence back down the flights of stairs leading back down to the street, a full three feet of space between them. Once back on the street, they stopped at the traffic light intersecting West Harbor Drive and Fifth Avenue.

"I'm a little lost," McMullan said. "So we cross here, and then walk back up Fifth Avenue and that will take us back to E street, right?"

"Yep," she said.

A gust of cold wind blew across West Harbor Drive, and Katrina shivered so hard her teeth chattered. She clamped them together. When the light changed, she stepped into the crosswalk. McMullan remained motionless behind her. Katrina turned and gave him a questioning look.

He gestured toward the Hyatt Hotel. "You know what, I think I wouldn't mind trying one of those martinis."

For a moment, Katrina stood immobile in the crosswalk. The crosswalk signal changed from flashing green man to flashing red hand, and then to solid red hand. The traffic light turned yellow. As it turned to red, she stepped back out of the crosswalk and took McMullan's arm, and the two slowly turned to walk up West Harbor Drive toward the Hyatt.

Except for candles on the tables and a few, dim sconces on the walls, the bar at the top of the Hyatt Hotel was dark. An invisible sound system played a soft selection of romantic music.

The bar was attended by two handsome gentlemen in tuxedos. A smattering of patrons, some in jeans, others in slacks or dresses, populated the tables and the bar in the center of the space. McMullan looked down at his gym shorts and T-shirt. "Ya think I'm a little under-dressed?" he laughed.

"Um, yeah. But don't worry about it. You don't stink *too* badly."

He opened his mouth in an exaggerated gesture of shock, and then gave her a soft shove. Katrina chuckled and ducked away.

A few moments later with cocktails in hand, they wandered around the room, peering out the windows at the panoramic view. McMullan sipped lightly at his martini. "Well?" Katrina asked. "How is it?"

"I think I'd rather have gone for a beer." He laughed. "Oh, wow, there's the balcony we were just on." He motioned through a window to direct Katrina's gaze downward. Beyond the balcony, the Coronado Bridge sprawled behind the convention center.

Katrina walked over to an open table with two plush chairs beside it. She set her drink onto the table and sat down, and a waiter approached to ask if they needed anything else. Katrina leaned forward and whispered in the waiter's ear as McMullan sat down at the table next to her.

A few moments later, the waiter returned with a pint of beer for McMullan. He laughed when he saw it, but then drank deeply and smiled. "Much better," he said, "and you nailed my favorite variety. You must have been a good bartender." He offered a wry smile.

Katrina looked up at him, at first surprised. Slowly, she realized that the man in front of her knew almost everything about her. The thought was both unnerving and oddly comforting. "And you must be a good FBI agent," she said.

"How's yours?" McMullan asked, motioning to her drink.

"Actually, I kind of wanted to taste yours," she said and leaned in to steal a passionate kiss before he could remind her that it was probably a bad idea.

The plastic chair of the visiting area creaked as the muscular prisoner sat down. Today, he was expecting a different guest.

The visitor arrived and sat down across from him, and the mirror image from the neck up was striking. Except for a small scar above the right eye of the prisoner, the dark faces of the two men were indistinguishable.

The prisoner wore the standard-issue pale blue of the San Quentin minimum-security wing. His visitor wore a black muscle shirt. Underneath, both men bore the same signature, etched in bold arcs across their powerful chests:

MORALES

"Thanks for coming, *hermanito*," the prisoner said.

His visitor chuckled. "Four fuckin' minutes apart and I'll always be *hermanito*. What do you need?"

The prisoner brought a hand up and across the visiting table. "First, give me some skin," he said, raising an eyebrow.

The visitor's hand rose to meet his, and when he lowered it once again, it was closed. "What was that for?" He pocketed the money his brother had just handed him.

"I need you to take care of something for me. Or maybe I should say, 'someone.'"

A guard approached and casually stood nearby. After a moment of silence, both brothers looking defiantly at the guard, they began to speak again. But this time, it was in a language that only existed between the two of them. A language they had invented as children. A language of twins.

"Who?"

"She'll be here in a minute."

"She?"

"Yeah, is that a problem?"

The guard walked away, and the visitor switched back to English. "Course not, bro. As long as you tell me why."

The prisoner smiled. "Because she's the only link between me and the unfortunate incident that happened in the death row wing a while ago. If this bitch is gone, I'm in the clear."

The visitor thought for a moment. "So what's the plan?"

"Follow her. Find out where she hangs. Then when you can do it, do it. And be careful. Remember that she knows my face—your face. I don't want my baby brother in the other wing of this fuckin' hell hole."

❂

Carlos "Chuck" Morales had been instructed by his four-minute-older brother Oscar to follow the ugly bitch with the thick black hair. He had no idea he would be following her for more than eight hours and five hundred miles.

Fortunately, the Bitch's beat up piece-of-shit car had

been bright red in its earlier days. It was easy to keep an eye on. The red Honda left San Quentin and crossed over the Richmond-San Rafael Bridge, then crawled its way through the Interstate 580 cluster-fuck of San Francisco. Once the 580 turned eastward and headed inland, the traffic lightened up considerably, and by the time they were merging onto Interstate 5 south, Chuck was on autopilot.

For more than two hundred torturously boring miles between Tracy and Bakersfield, Chuck kept his eyes glued to the rear bumper of the red Honda. When the Bitch finally stopped for gas just north of Grapevine, Chuck pulled into the gas station across the street to fill up as well. He was sure she would notice him. She didn't appear to.

The free-for-all traffic of Los Angeles woke him up temporarily. But as he followed the Bitch through Orange County and into San Diego, Chuck was ready to kill his brother. He was more than five hundred miles from home, he was hungry, he had no place to sleep, and he desperately had to take a piss.

The red Honda headed eastbound on Interstate 8 for ten miles and exited at College Avenue, where it turned right onto the San Diego State University campus.

And then he ran into the roadblock.

Chuck was three cars behind the red Honda when he realized that a guard was monitoring the passage of cars up the hill to the buildings overlooking the freeway. The Honda was waved through.

Before he had time to come up with a reasonable purpose for being there, Chuck was stopped by the guard. After five hundred miles of driving, he had no choice but to watch while the Bitch slipped up the hill, around a bend, and out of his sight.

The Doctor was waiting in an underground parking lot when the old, red Honda arrived.

The driver stepped out of the battered car and the long, black skirt draped almost to the concrete floor.

"Have you kept up the payments to the prisoner?" the Doctor asked.

"Of course."

"And?"

"Morales doesn't suspect a thing. He still thinks he has me over a rail."

After the red Honda drove away from the parking structure, the Doctor stood reflecting for a moment. Oscar Morales would not be killed just yet. Morales was still needed. He still had something important. Morales had several vials of anthrax left, and more importantly, he had the skill to keep them contained until the time of release.

Aside from that, Oscar Morales did not even know the Doctor existed.

The next morning, Chuck was staring at the monitor of a rented computer in the pay-per-use business center of a postal annex. All he knew from Oscar was that the Bitch worked with anthrax. What he had learned for himself was that she was affiliated with San Diego State University. From there, it was easy to find her.

Every faculty member at San Diego State University had his or her own laboratory website, linked to a professional bio and photograph. Chuck scrolled through the various pages until one caught his eye, and he smiled.

> Katrina Stone, Ph.D. Professor of biology. Research focuses on anthrax biology and pathogenesis of bacterial/host interactions, including high throughput screening for anthrax lethal factor inhibitors.

Chuck scrolled through the remainder of the faculty listings for the same department. There were no other researchers at SDSU involved in anthrax work. He clicked on the link to Katrina Stone's web page.

The page contained detailed contact information, including a building and room number for her lab. Chuck looked around and found the employee who had seated him at the computer. In his most polite voice, he said, "Excuse me, sir?"

The employee turned around. "How can I help you?"

"I was wondering if I can print something."

"Of course," the employee said, his eyes falling onto the web page. "Well, you'll want to use that printer over there." He motioned across the room. "May I use your mouse for a moment?" The employee reached over and used the mouse to locate the correct printer. "That is our photo printer. It will make this page come out the clearest." The employee printed the page, and then walked over and picked it up off the printer. After a final glance at the page to ensure the quality of the print job, he handed it over to Chuck.

The employee had been right. The color photo of the woman named Katrina Stone, Ph.D. was faithfully reproduced in the printout. Chuck thanked the employee and paid, then exited the building and began walking out to his car. As he walked, he studied the photo intensely.

The woman in the picture had long, reddish hair. The hair of the woman he had followed from San Quentin had been raven black. *Dye job? Wig?* Chuck racked his brain to accurately remember the face of the woman he had followed. As he stared at the photo, he could not. But he did remember one detail: *The bitch from the prison was uglier than a bucket of armpits. This chick, Katrina Stone, is hot.* He briefly wondered how well the average woman could disguise her face with makeup and realized that he had absolutely no idea. Female habits were a total mystery to Chuck, whose transient interest in any woman tended to eject from his body along with his semen.

No matter. It was the best lead he had. And San Diego State University was only a couple of freeway exits away.

🧬

This time, Chuck left his car behind the checkpoint. He skirted his way up through the landscaping to approach the building from behind. Then he slipped past a pair of guards when they were looking the other direction.

Chuck took the elevator to the indicated floor of the North Life Sciences building. When he stepped out, he scanned the various hallway doors for the lab with the correct number. It was then that he realized that the lab he needed was the only one being guarded.

Bitch must be pretty important, he thought. He briefly remembered what Oscar had told him about live anthrax. Not very many people—even scientists—have access to it. Chuck was certain that he had found the right woman.

He approached the guard at the door.

"Do you have an ID?" the guard asked. "Nobody is allowed in this lab without an ID."

"Oh, I didn't know that. I'm looking for Katrina Stone. I'm an old friend of hers."

"Well," the guard said, "unless you have an appointment, which you don't or she would have told me, I'm afraid you're S-O-L. Next time, try the phone."

Chuck considered his options for a moment and decided not to slit the guard's throat in the hallway. Instead, he fixated a long glare upon him and then turned to re-mount the elevator.

He took the elevator back down and stepped out of the building. As soon as he was outside, he reached into his breast pocket for a cigarette, and then remembered for the thousandth time that he had smoked his last one the day before, halfway between San Quentin and San Diego. The mild nausea, severe headache, and nervousness that had been following him all morning as a consequence were not helping his mood. Not one bit.

Chuck shook his head and looked around. He remembered the piece-of-shit red Honda that he had tailed from San Francisco. There was no parking lot near the building that he could see. A few utility vehicles occupied a designated area, and even fewer miscellaneous cars sat in spaces marked for temporary parking. No faded red Honda.

Along the west side of the building was a small food stand. The sign along its top read "The Hotdogger." Outside of "The Hotdogger" was a small collection of cheap tables with two people sitting at one of them. There was nobody else in sight with the exception of a solitary employee attending the stand. Chuck approached the stand and asked the attendant if they sold cigarettes.

The employee laughed out loud. "Are you serious?"

"Yeah, why." Chuck did not see the humor.

"You can't buy cigarettes anywhere on campus, Dude. That's about like asking for meth."

Chuck refrained from informing his new friend that a little meth was also sounding like a good idea, but he'd settle for a smoke. Out of ideas, he turned and sat down at one of the tables.

And then the woman from the photograph in Chuck's hand stepped out of the North Life Sciences building.

※

Katrina Stone, Ph.D., did not seem to notice Chuck as she

walked briskly away from him. Chuck waited for a moment to allow her a lead and then followed.

She passed through another building and crossed a street before approaching a cliff. Then she disappeared, having seemingly walked right over its edge.

Chuck rushed forward. Descending from the top of the cliff was a steep staircase leading to a parking lot below. Stone was already halfway down. Chuck remained standing at the top of the stairs from which he had a bird's eye view of the parking lot. The woman approached a silver sedan, clicked her keychain to unlock the doors, and slipped inside.

Not the piece-of-shit red Honda after all.

5:24 P.M. PST

The sun was gone, the evening breeze cool, when Alexis Stone stepped out of the market. A tuft of her shoulder-length hair—exactly the same auburn color as her mother's—billowed across her young face. Alexis shifted the grocery bag on her hip to free one hand and brush the hair aside. Then she buttoned her jacket while she walked.

A man followed her out of the store. "Excuse me," he said politely.

Alexis turned and looked at the man. He was cute, and probably in his twenties.

"I don't mean to be forward," he said, "but I make great veal parmesan and I was wondering if you'd be interested sometime."

"Thanks," Alexis said, "but I have a boyfriend, and we don't eat meat. Besides, I just can't see myself having dinner with someone who has dead rotting animals inside of him." She smiled sweetly.

The man gave her a strange look and shuffled quickly away, muttering something under his breath. Alexis continued walking and grinned, already envisioning Kevin's reaction to the story. He'd fall over laughing. She couldn't wait to tell him.

Lexi's pace was leisurely as she followed the familiar route home in the dark. Mom wouldn't be there. Not for quite a while. As she approached a corner a few blocks from her house, the evening silence was broken by a single, friendly bark.

Lexi looked up with interest. As she rounded the corner, a middle-aged woman was approaching with an Alaskan malamute on a leash. He looked almost exactly like Eskimo, Lexi's childhood pet.

"Hello," the woman said, smiling.

"He's gorgeous," Alexis said breathlessly. "Is he friendly?"

"Oh yes, go ahead and pet him if you'd like."

Alexis again shuffled the grocery bag and reached down to bury a hand in the thick fur behind the dog's head. For a moment, she closed her eyes, and then she was seven years old again.

🧬

She never really believed what they told her. Not Christopher. Not her little brother. Her "Bubba." He was too little. She told Mommy in private that maybe it was a joke someone was playing, and that soon Bubba would come back and it would be funny how he had fooled everyone.

Mommy and Daddy were always fighting. And then Daddy was living somewhere else, and Mommy was sleeping all the time.

And then Mommy was just too busy. And Daddy had to go away for a long time for his work, all the way to a different country. It was called Eye-Rack. People were afraid that her Daddy might die.

Then Lexi was nine. Her stomach started hurting all the time, mostly at night when she was trying to sleep. None of the doctors could help. And her parents always seemed sad, or mad, or disappointed, and Lexi couldn't understand why they didn't seem to love her anymore.

But someone loved her. Eskimo. Eskimo knew that things were not good. Mommy and Daddy didn't pay any attention to him either. He started sleeping next to Lexi's bed, then at the foot of the bed, and eventually, beside Lexi—her thin arm around his body, her tiny hand buried deep in his thick, comforting fur.

Alexis taught Eskimo to sit, stay, and lay down, to fetch, to open the door for her, to kiss her cheek, to stand on his hind legs and hug her, and to speak. Eskimo was her best friend. One who never cried, never took her toys, never asked for anything, never needed attention from grown-ups, never got mad at her, and was always happy to see her. A best friend who loved her no matter what.

Eskimo died when Lexi was ten. She was not allowed another pet by either of her parents. Dad was on deployment too often, and Kimberly was allergic to dander. And Mom just didn't have time to take care of a pet. Of course she didn't.

Alexis found other ways to keep animals in her life. Now, at fifteen, she took the bus every Saturday afternoon to volunteer at the local humane society. She was active in PETA. It was at a PETA meeting that she met Kevin. And it was Kevin that brought her into the Animal Liberation Front.

"We'd better get moving along then," the Alaskan malamute's owner said softly, breaking Lexi out of her reflection. The woman turned the dog, who looked so much like Eskimo, and rounded the corner. When they were out of sight Alexis wiped a tear from one eye and sighed. The scent of the dog was still on her hand.

10:08 P.M. PST

More than eight years had passed since Katrina Stone—not yet a doctor—was working furiously at a crowded kitchen table in a disheveled house, studying for her qualifying exam and unaware that her life was about to be destroyed. Tonight, the scene at *Doctor* Katrina Stone's kitchen table appeared uncannily similar to that night eight years distant. With one exception. Tonight, the woman at the table was Katrina's daughter, who resembled her mother strongly in appearance but not at all in ideology.

It was late. Her mom had not come home, and Alexis had lost track of time while she worked. She was currently addressing envelopes and stuffing them with flyers she had generated and duplicated. She still had hundreds of envelopes to go and hundreds of emails to send. It was a school night, and she had a test the next day.

Lexi was startled by a noise. She looked up from the flyers and sat motionless for a moment, listening to determine if the noise would repeat. For a moment, she heard nothing. Then it happened again.

The doorknob was being tested.

Lexi looked at the clock and suddenly became aware of the hour. Mom should have been home hours ago; even with her 14-hour a day schedule, she usually stopped by the house around 7:00 or 7:30 to change before dashing off for a run on the beach. In any case, she always entered through the garage and not the front door.

Slowly and silently, Alexis slipped out of her chair and tiptoed across the living room. As she neared the front door, she reached into a pocket in her jacket, which was hanging nearby on a coat rack. Her hand encased a small tube, and she withdrew from the door.

The doorknob made no more noise, but Alexis could see a shadow across the front window. Someone was still standing there.

Lexi poised the tube in her right hand and reached for the door handle with the left. Then, taking a deep breath, she flung the door open. A small, quick burst of pepper spray billowed directly into the face of her mother.

Katrina leaped violently backward, choking and sputtering.

Alexis dropped the vial. "Oh, my god, Mom, I'm so sorry! I thought you were someone trying to break in! Why didn't you come in through the garage?" As she spoke, she raced forward and grabbed Katrina's elbow just in time to stop her mother from flipping headfirst into a planter alongside the walkway.

"*Jesus Christ Lexi!*" Katrina's voice was ragged. "My garage door opener battery died! I didn't... "

Her sentence was cut off by another coughing fit, and in the midst of it, she jerked her arm away from Lexi to turn and vomit into the planter.

✖

An hour later, Katrina's red eyes were the only visible

indication of her recent encounter with her daughter's pepper spray. But for the next two days, her throat would continue to feel scratchy and people would be asking if she was stoned.

Katrina still felt that she could smell the noxious gas even after a long shower. She donned her favorite sweats and slippers and then walked out into the kitchen to confront Alexis, who had now resumed her work at the kitchen table. "OK, Lexi," Katrina said, her voice raspy. "We need to talk."

Alexis looked up with clear annoyance.

Katrina took a deep breath and continued. "You know I'm supportive of your work with PETA and your interest in animal rights, even though I still don't think you fully understand the necessity of animal research."

Alexis rolled her eyes and sighed dramatically.

Katrina ignored her. "I think your actions tonight have made it obvious that you're a bit paranoid these days. I personally think it's your involvement with the Animal Liberation Front and all its whackos in ski masks that are doing this to you. And where the hell did you get a vial of pepper spray in the first place?"

"The source of the pepper spray is confidential, Mother," Alexis spat. "And besides, you can buy it at any army surplus store."

"What are you doing wandering around an army surplus store? Are you running off and joining the armed forces? I thought you hate the military!"

"That's irrelevant. It isn't paranoia—it's preparation. I need to be able to protect myself because I am here alone all the time. If someone really had tried to break in here tonight, my pepper spray would have been my only defense. I certainly would not have had any parents around to help me, and you and I both know how much can happen in the time it takes San Diego police to respond to anything.

"Regarding my activities with the ALF, I think you should consider yourself lucky that I won't let them target *your* research. The San Diego chapter of the ALF has wanted to go after you for quite some time. The only reason they don't is that I'm an active member and we have a deal. They need people like me, so they let your work slide in order to keep me on the team. You should thank me for that. But you're still on their list of Exploiters, so don't blame me if something happens one day. It would be out of my hands."

Katrina raised her eyebrows at the threat.

Alexis continued. "I know damn well what goes on at your BSL-3 facility with all those poor mice and rats. You *deliberately infect them with anthrax* just to watch them die. Do you realize how sick that is?

"And now, you've got monkeys. *Monkeys.* You're a scientist, Mom. Surely you must know that the genetic identities of primates are up to ninety-eight percent identical to humans. Yet, you seem to think it's OK to kill them for research purposes.

"Why don't you kill humans that way? Oh, wait—I know why. Because it's illegal. Because for some reason, that two percent of DNA makes the difference between scientific research and criminal behavior. It's just not right, Mom. Why can't you see that? The ALF is just trying to make right what should have been right all along.

"Two thousand years ago, humans were thrown into the Coliseum with wild animals, to be torn limb from limb for sport. Society finally realized one day that the activities were barbaric, and Roman games were banned. Just like that.

"Yet, eighteen hundred years later, the notion of 'owning'

another human being and forcing him or her to work to make someone else richer was still just fine. But then, again, the voice of reason spoke—and today, we as a collective society consider slavery outrageous.

"The ALF is the voice of reason fighting to liberate the slaves of today. Two hundred years from now, the notion of owning, enslaving, and conducting research on an ape—or a mouse, for that matter—will be considered barbaric as well."

"Alexis, you don't understand," she said. "Without animal research, there is no medical progress. I love animals—you know I do! And it makes me sad to do the things we have to do to them. But we're looking for cures for horrible diseases. Thousands and even hundreds of years ago, people died routinely from things we consider absolutely trivial today.

"You take aspirin, don't you? Of course you do. I've seen you. How do you think that aspirin was developed? And I know for a fact that you're on the pill—you have left the packages out on the dresser in your room. Remember that urinary tract infection you got last year? You thought you were going to *die* from the pain—until we took you to the doctor, and you were given antibiotics and painkillers that were developed through animal research. You didn't think twice about taking them.

"Lexi, I understand your motivations. I really do. And for the record, I myself am opposed to unnecessary animal cruelty. But don't you think it's a bit hypocritical that you condemn the work I—we, as scientists—are doing, while you also sit back and reap the benefits?

"And by the way, monkeys are not apes—so at least get your facts straight if you're going to continue on this crusade."

Alexis reddened. "Whatever. You know what I mean.

Monkeys may not be officially classified as apes, but they are still evolutionarily right next to humans, and you know it. And to demonstrate this point, I will be protesting—along with ten thousand of my closest friends from PETA and the ALF, at the biotechnology convention.

"Yes, I know, you're going to be a big speaker there. You're getting a great, big, fat 'congratulations' for killing the most animals. Well, guess what. I'll be outside. My boyfriend will be dressed as a monkey. I will be holding him on a chain with a knife to his throat. And I will be dressed as you."

Two nights later, the sun had long since set when Katrina pulled into the dirt parking lot at the Torrey Pines Gliderport. It was something to which she was well accustomed. During the winter months and into March, it was dark every moment that Katrina was not in her labs. This evening, with just a sliver of moon peeking out from a foggy coastal sky, the blackness was almost total.

Katrina was happy to see that the rocks on Ho Chi Minh Trail were dry, and she began trotting down the staircase with abandon. The exercise felt freeing until reached the sand and her heart rate and breathing began to increase. It was then that the pain returned to her lungs.

Normally a religious nightly runner, Katrina had just taken an unprecedented two nights off, the residual effects of the pepper spray still too strong for cardiovascular exercise. Tonight, as she tested her ability to return to her routine, she grimaced against the stabbing in her lungs. But she ran even harder.

Tonight, she ran to calm down.

Alexis had all but physically threatened her. And aside from the brief moment of rushed apology, which had seemed more like shock than true regret, her daughter had not *really* seemed disturbed by the fact that she had attacked her mother with pepper spray.

The paranoia. The drastic changes in friends. The attitude. Above all, the fanatical animal rights activities that Katrina could not help but take personally.

Katrina reflected back over the last few years, wondering when Alexis had begun to spiral out of control. In retrospect, it had been happening gradually for quite a while.

At first, it was the occasional snotty remark or lack of respect toward Katrina and Tom. Now, she treated both of her parents with utter contempt. She drank to get drunk. And rather than serve as a wake up call, a DUI had only led Alexis to stop concealing her behavior. Apparently, she no longer felt the need to bother.

The pepper spray incident revealed a horrifying truth to Katrina. She was beginning to fear her own child.

Katrina was literally sprinting as she turned to ascend the steep hill toward North Torrey Pines Road. On the first switchback, she sharply cut the corner, running within inches of the trees flanking the paved street. And as she did, a thick, muscular body emerged instantly from the shadows and crashed into her from the side.

✕

The momentum of Katrina's uphill charge carried the stranger for a step or two, but he was easily twice her bodyweight. The pair crashed sideways to the pavement, Katrina's petite body crushed to the hard surface by the weight of her attacker. A rough, massive hand over her mouth muffled an instinctive scream.

Katrina had been breathing rapidly from her run and the effects of the pepper spray, and now, with her face covered and the weight on top of her, she could not catch her breath at all. As she was violently flipped onto her back, a second hand encircled her throat. Katrina felt the reflexive, choking cough that accompanies compression of the trachea, but there was no air. There was no air.

She couldn't breathe at all. She couldn't move at all. A rush of panic overtook her as her head began to swim. Above her, a pair of dead, black eyes pierced into her from the small holes of a ski mask.

You can't pass out, she barely had time to think before she did.

Chuck Morales straddled the woman lying on her back. Her hair—reddish-brown, not black—fanned out around her on the pavement. A sudden strong stirring arose within his groin. Chuck continued to watch for a moment after the woman's eyes rolled into the back of her head, and then he cautiously loosened his grip on her small throat.

The body was lifeless.

He glanced down at her T-shirt, damp with perspiration, and thin running shorts. In this horizontal position, the T-shirt clung lightly to her breasts and stomach, revealing the outline of her torso. The waistband of the shorts was elastic, but an additional drawstring poked out below her navel in a bow. Chuck pulled the drawstring open and then reached for his own fly. As he pulled down his zipper, a now full erection poked through a thin pair of cotton boxers, and he drew a breath.

Don't lose your head because of your dick, he reminded himself. While his left hand reestablished its grip on her throat, his right reached into a cargo pocket halfway down the right thigh of his loose pants. It emerged rapidly, and in three precise motions, the six-inch blade of a silver butterfly knife caught the thin light of the slivered moon.

But suddenly there was too much light.

The ski mask blocking his peripheral vision, Chuck's eyes jerked upward, and he turned his head toward the source of illumination. Headlights. From above.

"*Fuck,*" Chuck muttered. He quickly reversed his former hand movements to re-sheath the knife, dropped it back into the pocket, and stood up. Tucking his softening penis back into his pants, he jerked the woman upright by her arms and threw her over one shoulder. Then he ducked quickly into the trees.

Chuck had barely gotten off the road, his victim still over his shoulder, when a patrol car rounded the switchback just above him on the road. He waited, motionless, while the car slowly passed.

That's a sign, bro, he heard in Oscar's voice. *Stop fucking around.*

Slowly, almost gently, he lowered the body to the ground before him. He retrieved the knife from his pocket and reopened it, and then straddled the woman once again. Her eyes were closed. His left hand gripped her lower jaw to hold steady her head.

As Chuck's right hand raised the knife to her throat, one of the woman's knees thrashed upward, squarely crushing his scrotum into his pelvic bone. Chuck's groin exploded in sudden, immense, eye-popping, excruciating pain. "*Ooooh,*" he moaned weakly as the pain flooded from his loins through the rest of his body and then turned to nausea.

Chuck fell sideways off the woman and retched. His body convulsed violently several times, each time drawing him into a tighter fetal position. For the next fifteen minutes, he was paralyzed, lying with the side of his face emerged in a small trickle of vomit, hands drawn protectively—too late—to his squashed, deflated testicles.

By the time Roger Gilman arrived, there were four police cruisers lined up alongside an ambulance, and a fire truck stretched down the other side of the street. The lights of the police cars were still flashing, and a section of street had been sequestered from passing traffic, but the sirens had been silenced. Gilman could hear the frantic barking of the four K-9 unit German Shepherd dogs racing through the foliage below.

Had Gilman not been notified in advance, he might not have recognized the woman before him.

Katrina Stone was sitting in the back of the ambulance, her legs dangling out of the opened door. One of them was skinned all the way from the hip to the knee, and a medic dabbed at the still-bleeding road rash. Stone held an ice pack to the back of her head with one hand. The other held a blanket around her torso. She was shivering violently. As Gilman neared her, she looked up and her red, puffy eyes briefly met his before she broke her gaze and looked at the ground beneath her.

Gilman felt a pang of guilt. From the moment of his own

involvement in Operation Death Row, he had considered her the prime suspect in the investigation of an unspeakable crime. Looking at her now, he thought, *there's no way.*

Stone was in the middle of giving her statement. "No, I didn't say that," she said when Gilman arrived, "I didn't know it was a cop coming by at all. I passed out."

"I'm sorry," the police officer said sympathetically. "I must have misunderstood you. Can you please start over from when you were attacked?"

Stone sighed and began again. "I was running, and all of a sudden out of nowhere, this huge guy just slammed into me. I couldn't breathe. He pinned me down. I was out of breath from running, and I couldn't breathe because he"— she let go of the blanket and tried to demonstrate with her free arm—"he pinned me down. He sat on top of my stomach. He was wearing a ski mask. His eyes were like coal."

Her eyes began to well up again, and Gilman reached wordlessly into his pocket for a handkerchief. Stone took it and surprised him with a brief smile of gratitude before she looked down at her feet and broke into sobs.

The officers huddled around her waited. Out of the corner of his eye, Gilman saw a flash of movement and then turned to see Sean McMullan charging toward them.

When he reached the circle of men surrounding Stone, McMullan gripped the shoulders of two of the policemen and pulled them roughly aside to step in toward her. He reached one hand forward to lay on her shoulder; with the other, he tilted her face upward to look into her eyes.

Stone's sobbing was cut short with a slight gasp.

McMullan looked critically into one eye and then the other. He then looked away from her face to the bump on the top of her head, and scanned her body thoroughly. "You hit your head," he said, "can you follow my finger?" He held up an index finger vertically in front of her nose, and then began slowly moving it from one side to the other.

"The EMT already did that," an officer began with a bit of annoyance. McMullan's eyes blazed as he stood upright and glared at the officer, who took a step backward, closing his mouth as he did. As McMullan's attention returned to Stone, Gilman and the officer exchanged a glance.

Stone wiped her face with Gilman's handkerchief and closed her eyes for a moment. As she did, she took three deep breaths and held each, letting the air out slowly each time. Then she looked back up, and for the first time, into the eyes of each man in turn.

Gilman was shocked at the transformation. It was if she had closed a valve that released her emotions. She handed back the handkerchief and gathered the blanket around herself once again.

This time, when she spoke, her voice was strong. Angry. Determined. And logical. "I passed out, and when I came to he had me over his shoulders and was carrying me. There was a car passing. I didn't look up to see it. I kept still. I was hoping he wouldn't know I was awake, which evidently, he didn't.

"He put me down. After the car passed he straddled the top of me again and I could hear him doing something. I couldn't tell what he was doing... my eyes were closed... "

Stone closed her eyes again and paused for a moment, but this time it was not to gather her emotions. Gilman could sense her reliving the moment. She wanted to be sure to remember the details accurately. The data needed to be precise. Otherwise, the conclusions would be wrong. It was almost fascinating.

Gilman glanced at each of the officers briefly, and then settled his eyes upon McMullan. McMullan did not seem to notice. His gaze was focused on Stone, his jaw working, his face flushed, his breathing rapid.

As his eyes darted from one player to another, the sympathy Gilman had been feeling for Stone gradually began to wane. This was an intelligent woman. Out running, alone, on an abandoned beach, at night, in the middle of this investigation. She should have known better. And McMullan was in the palm of her hand. It was possible that she was playing with all of them.

"I felt one hand on my face and something up against my throat," Stone said. "Something cold. I assumed it was a knife. I decided it was now or never, so I kneed him in the nuts as hard as I could. He fell off me, and I got up and ran the rest of the way up the hill. I didn't have my cell phone, so I started heading back toward my car to get it, but then you showed up." The last line was directed at the officer who had been questioning her.

Gilman interjected, "If she didn't call you, then who did?"

"Nobody," the officer replied. "This is my normal route. I had just driven down the hill to the beach and was on my way back up. She must have just beat me to the top."

Sean McMullan interjected. "You mean she *ran* up this hill, after having just been knocked unconscious, faster than you could drive up it? Didn't you hear anything?"

Stone interrupted. "There was nothing to hear, Sean. My mouth was covered the whole time I was awake. I couldn't scream. Then once I got away, I was just running. I wasn't making any noise. I guess I was just trying to get as far away from him as possible. I was lucky this officer showed up. Otherwise, I probably would have just run all the way to my car."

McMullan redirected his interrogation. "What about the dogs? Haven't they found anything down there?"

An officer who had previously been silent answered. "They've definitely gotten a scent but it's led them to the beach. After that, they're lost. I guess the guy went into the water."

"Well if he doesn't drown or die of hypothermia, he has to come back out," Gilman said optimistically.

"He better hope he drowns or dies of hypothermia," McMullan answered, and turned to run down the hill to the beach.

🧬

Five hundred yards up the coastline, Chuck swam parallel to the beach. The late-winter Pacific Ocean was below fifty degrees. As his body turned from cold, to pain, to numb, Chuck remained as submerged as possible – only allowing his nose and mouth to peek out of the water with each subsiding wave, in order to catch a breath. *I'll probably catch fucking pneumonia,* he thought. *The Bitch is going to pay for this.*

An hour later, serenity had been restored to the suburban road atop the police beach access street. Katrina, Roger Gilman, and one police officer were the only three people remaining. On one side of the police cruiser was Gilman's car. Sean McMullan's black sedan remained jutting into the street, its awkward angle evidence of a hurried parking job. But McMullan had still not returned from the beach.

He's probably chasing the guy down the coastline, Katrina was thinking.

"Katrina, seriously," Gilman said quietly. "I realize we can't force you to go to the hospital, but I really don't think you should be driving home. I know it's tough to insist anything with you, but please, let me drive you. I'm begging you— don't drive right now. You're too upset, and you've also hit your head."

Katrina looked into his eyes and was surprised to find that she believed in his sincerity. Even with the veiled allusion to her stubbornness, about which Katrina knew he was right, his intentions seemed to be truly in her best interest. She was both skeptical and relieved.

"Who's going to drive me?" she said. "All three of you have your own cars, and if one of you takes me, then my car will be stuck here. Otherwise it's a bunch of driving around for more than one person. Just take me to my car and let me go home."

Gilman paused for a moment. "Where is your daughter tonight?"

Katrina grimaced and threw a hand over her eyes. "Oh *shit!* What time is it?"

"Almost nine fifteen."

"I'm late to pick up Lexi from her dad's house."

Gilman reached into his pocket and pulled out his cell phone. "Well, he's probably worried something happened to you. And by the way, something did. So tell him to come pick you up and drop you and your daughter off at your house."

Katrina shook her head at him, but for the first time that evening, she smiled.

Ten minutes later, Gilman had dismissed the uniformed officer. He and Katrina were alone, leaning on the back bumper of his car in silence, when Tom Stone's Jeep screeched to a halt next to Sean McMullan's car. Tom leaped from the driver's seat and raced toward Katrina. "Are you OK?" he asked.

"Yeah, I'm OK."

Kimberly and Alexis slipped up behind Tom. "Hi, Katrina," Kimberly said softly.

"Hey, Kim," Katrina said, without looking up.

"I'm—I'm really sorry this happened to you," Kimberly said.

"So am I." The voice was Lexi's.

Katrina went to her daughter, and Alexis stood still to allow Katrina to hug her tightly.

"So, what's the plan?" Katrina asked then. "Geez, I feel like such an invalid here."

Tom chuckled slightly. "Well, it's about time you let someone take care of you for once, even if it's just to give you a damn ride home. Give me your keys."

Gilman produced them from his pocket. "We found them on the path near where you were attacked," he said.

"Kim is going to take you and Lexi to your house in my Jeep, and I'm going to follow in your car," Tom said. "Simple as pie. I'll even trot over to the gliderport to get your car... you don't even have to give me a lift."

"How'd you know my car was at the gliderport?" Katrina asked.

"Because I was married to you for nine years, dummy." He stuck out his tongue and jogged off.

Sitting in the passenger seat of Tom's Jeep, Katrina looked wordlessly out the window. Lexi and Kimberly were silent as well.

Katrina finally spoke. "I think there's something I need to tell you."

"Who?" Kimberly asked.

"Actually, both of you."

"What?" Alexis leaned forward over the back of Katrina's seat.

Katrina sighed and turned sideways in her seat in order to be able to face both of the other women. "I think we—I—well, maybe you too—might be in serious danger. I'm not convinced that this attack was random."

"I don't understand," Kimberly said. "I thought the terror threat was over. I thought now it's just a matter of you finishing whatever you're doing, and then the government will take it and move on. I thought everything is fine now."

Katrina shook her head. "It's not over. Something is still going on. My postdoc recently had his apartment broken into, and I'm wondering if this is related. I'm not saying you need to be paranoid. I'm just saying that you—all of us—should watch our backs. I don't know. Maybe *I'm* being paranoid. But better safe than sorry."

Kimberly took her eyes off the road long enough to give Katrina a hard glare, and then reverted to staring directly in front of her. "That job of yours is going to be the death of us all. You're like an alcoholic, too wrapped up in your own situation to see the effect it's having on you and everyone around you."

"Look, Kimberly," Katrina said. "I didn't say that I know for certain that there is anything to worry about. I'm just trying to give you a heads up in case there is. And anyway, it's not my fault. I'm doing the best I can. And it really has been a rough night for me. So cut me some slack, OK?"

Kimberly looked back over at her, but her face had softened. "I'm sorry," she said. "I know you've had a shitty, scary night and I shouldn't have said that. We'll talk about it later."

A moment passed in silence. "OK," Katrina said at last.

When she turned to address Lexi, who had been wordless throughout the exchange, her daughter was looking out the window. *I hope she is even listening,* Katrina thought. *If you never listen to me about anything ever again, just this one time, please, Lexi.*

"Alexis?" Katrina said.

The girl's face snapped forward, away from the window, and her eyes bored into her mother. What Katrina saw there was pure rage.

A prison guard opened a door to the visiting room, and Chuck Morales stepped inside. His twin was already waiting.

"Thanks for coming, *hermanito*," Oscar said. He was smiling.

"It's a long fuckin' drive from San Diego." Chuck was not smiling.

"I know it is, bro. I really appreciate it. Besides, it will be worth your while, I promise." He gave his brother a grin.

"So what's up now?"

Oscar leaned forward and whispered, "Give me some skin." He raised a hand toward Chuck. Chuck brought up a hand to claps his brother's and a look of shock crossed his face. "Ssh... " Oscar hissed. His eyes were darting past Chuck to the security guard, who did not seem to be looking.

Chuck had been expecting money. When he glanced into his hand before dropping it into his pocket, he instead saw two small, sealed glass vials. Each vial contained an off-white powder. Chuck began to tremble. *"What is this?"*

"Don't touch it. Don't eat it, and definitely don't fucking snort it. Understand?"

"*What the fuck are you trying to get me into!*" he snarled.

"Look, brother. Don't worry. I promise, I'll walk you through everything you need to know. You trust me, right?"

Chuck only glared.

"Right?" Oscar repeated.

"Yeah, I trust you," Chuck finally said, looking down.

"Good, man, I've never steered you wrong, have I?"

Chuck looked away for a moment. When he looked back into his twin's eyes, he shook his head. "No, man, you've never steered me wrong."

Oscar smiled. "I'm the one who's in *here*," he said lovingly. "And you're the one who's out *there*. I took the hit and did the time for both of us, you know."

"Yeah, I know. So what's the plan?"

Oscar looked over at the guard one last time. "You know I'm up for parole next year, don't you? I'm going to set us up, brother. We'll be in style for the rest of our lives. First of all, did you take care of the bitch in San Diego?"

"Not yet," Chuck said. "She got away. But I know where she lives and where she works. She won't get away again."

"Good. When are you going back?"

"Soon as we're done here, I guess. I gotta stop by the apartment first. At least this time I can plan to leave town."

"Okay," said Oscar. "But hurry up, 'cause we've got shit to take care of in L.A. now."

"Like what?"

Oscar paused. "I've got a plan, bro. But I need your help one more time. Do you remember Tony Ortiz?"

"Yeah, he's the motherfucker who got you put away," Chuck said.

"Right. He fuckin' set me up. Well, now he's running the biggest operation in L.A. based on *my* clientele. Yours too, bro. We're going to take him out of the loop. And while we're at it, we're going to monopolize the business."

"How's that?"

"Turns out blackmail is lucrative, brother. I've had a thing going on here for a while with that bitch you're going to get rid of shortly. Seems she doesn't want anyone to know she killed sixty-eight people, even if they were just death row inmates. She's been more than happy to fund our future endeavors.

"I've been laying low here. I think I'll get out on parole this time. And when I do, we'll have the business to ourselves, because nobody's going anywhere else. See, I've taken some of that money and I've put it to good use. I've got people on a fuckin' cherry payroll. I've got people who have infiltrated all of the major players in L.A.

"Those two vials I just gave you are enough to poison the entire narcotics supply from all of our competitors combined. All you need to do is divide it up into five smaller containers, and then I'm going to give you the names of five people. I'll set up meetings for you with the other guys, and they'll take care of the rest. A couple people will make the wrong deal, and everyone else will stop making deals with those fucks at all.

"The customers know me, though. They know I've got high quality product for them. They trust me. When they hear I'm getting out, and that people buying elsewhere are sick and dying, they'll come running back. They'll be scared shitless not to.

"Not everyone knows I have a twin. Let them see you. Let the word get out on the street. Let them think I'm out already. By the time I get paroled, you and I will be million-aires within a year. And nobody will be turning our asses in this time, because they'll be out of the picture. Starting with Tony Motherfuckin' Ortiz."

Oscar had expected Chuck to be impressed and excited about the plan. Instead, Chuck looked down and did not answer. Oscar ducked his head, trying to catch his brother's eye. "What's wrong, bro?" he asked.

"Why do you need me to do this?" Chuck asked. "Why not just wait until you get out, and then you take care of it. You know how to handle this shit. I don't. I get some of this on me, and that's it. You think I don't know that?"

"Look, *hermanito*. Like I said, I'll walk you through it. You'll be fine, I promise. But we can't wait until I get out. We need to set it up now. The funding for this is about to dry up, remember? Besides, the longer I hold on to those vials in here, the more likely someone will find them. And then, we're fucked. Mostly me, but you're fucked too because you won't have a big brother to take care of you anymore.

"They've been tossing cells here and questioning people—mostly Mexicans. It's only a matter of time before they come after me. You don't get life for this kind of shit. If they find those vials in my mattress, I'm ridin' the lightning. That's why I need you to do it now."

The Muslim robe and headscarf were gone. The dark face makeup was gone. The wig and long dress were gone. Today, it was jeans and a T-shirt.

"You did not go to the prison this weekend," the Doctor said.

"I didn't have time," came the response. "I'm going next weekend. But I need more money before I go. You know I can't afford to keep up the payments."

The Doctor stood quietly for a moment. Oscar Morales was almost finished. The prison guards were methodically searching cells. It was only a matter of time before Oscar would be found. And culpability would end there. Oscar would only be connected to a single regular visitor who would by then be dead.

The Doctor reached into a pocket and withdrew not a billfold, but a pistol. "Then I'm afraid you are no longer of use to me."

As he embarked on the long drive between San Francisco

and San Diego for a second time, Chuck Morales was sick and fucking tired of being Oscar's *hermanito*.

Oscar still wanted him to take the Bitch out. *Good thing*, he thought, remembering the night he had spent in the Pacific Ocean after she had kicked him in the nuts. *I ain't about to let that shit go.*

But then, when that was done, he was supposed to divide up two vials of anthrax and distribute it. The thought of opening even one of those vials filled Chuck with absolute, merciless, paralyzing fear.

Do I really need to do this for him? he wondered. *Maybe not. Maybe it's time I just did my own thing. Maybe I can use these two vials any way I decide. Maybe I don't even need to open them.*

As Chuck pulled onto the Interstate 5, he began to grin. It could be done his own way. There was a way to kill two birds with one stone. Or better said, one Stone with one vial.

Remember, Oscar had told him. *She knows my face. Your face.*

The Bitch knew who Oscar was. She had seen him every Sunday for months. But there was no way she had any idea he had an identical twin. And Oscar had stupidly revealed to Chuck that most of their customers didn't know either.

Maybe Chuck didn't need Oscar anymore, after all. Maybe he could get rid of her himself with just one unopened vial. And maybe he could just take his brother's advice and become visible on the street. Let everyone think Oscar was out. Approach his contacts in the other networks—and take over the business himself.

And Oscar could do nothing about it from where he sat.

"*Hermanito?*" Chuck said aloud as he drove. "*Not anymore, bro.*"

"Wait! I can still help you!"

The Doctor moved in and placed the barrel of the pistol against a sweat-glistening temple, and smiled. "Perhaps you can. I think I would like to employ your beautiful penmanship one more time. Generate two more copies of the same greeting card, and I will meet with you again."

"I don't understand. I've used up my entire knowledge of the Arabic language. Do you speak it?"

"These cards will be written in English," the Doctor said. "Now go."

Ever since Christmas Day, the activity at the lab had steadily waned. By the beginning of February, the security guard's job had been downright boring. Today, before he could wish for boring, he would be dead.

It was late afternoon, and most of the building's occupants had gone home. Professor Katrina Stone, the woman whose safekeeping was the guard's main objective, was always among the last to call it a day. He stood watch outside of her laboratory door wishing she would wrap it up and leave.

When a man stepped off of the elevator, the guard barely took notice, until he recognized the face as someone with whom he had previously argued. But before he could reach for his firearm, the man had closed the short gap between the elevator and the laboratory door.

The short, stubby barrel of a pistol jutted obscenely from the inner flap of the dark man's jacket like a rude, steel penis.

The guard gasped.

"Not a word," the intruder said quietly. "Open the fuckin' door and step into the room."

The guard fumbled for his keys and did as the man with the gun had instructed, raising one hand while opening the door with the other, and then leaving the keys hanging from the lock to raise that hand as well. As he stepped inside, he momentarily felt the hot breath of his assailant down the back of his neck. Then he saw a brief flash of steel as the pistol crossed over the front of him, followed by a massive right arm snaking across his face.

⠟⠺

Without dropping the gun, Chuck held his victim immobile with one arm for the brief moment it took to unsheathe his butterfly knife and slit the guard's throat. With a near silent gurgle, the guard slumped to the floor, and then he was no longer a concern.

For a moment, Chuck only stared down at the body. It was the same guard who had previously turned him away from the lab with condescending rudeness. Chuck smiled, closed the door behind him, and stepped over the dead guard.

Once inside the laboratory, Chuck cast his eyes around the room's interior, to familiarize himself with the new surroundings as much as to look for additional human obstacles. The main laboratory space was square, with additional doors around its edges. Chuck assumed that most of them probably led to office spaces. The opposite wall broke into what appeared to be a corridor. Chuck thought the connecting passageway looked cleaner and more freshly painted—perhaps newer than the rest of the lab. He walked past the whirring machines and cluttered workbenches of the lab, through the corridor, and around the bend into the adjacent room.

And no more than ten feet in front of him, there she was.

Roger Gilman removed his glasses and set them upside down on the page in front of him. He closed his eyes and massaged his temples in a feeble attempt to quell the headache that had been coming on for the last hour. Then he sat back to roll his aching shoulders back and forth for a moment.

Over the last few minutes, he had finally begun to admit to himself that he was no longer retaining the information he was reading. Confronted with a stack of two thousand abbreviated biographies, all incarcerated Hispanic males, Gilman was beginning to feel as if he had been examining the same biography two thousand times.

He glanced up at the hotel room alarm clock and was reminded that he couldn't read it. Over its face, Gilman himself had taped a computer printout. On it was the puzzle that sliced away at his nerves, day in and day out, and would stifle all meaning of time until he could solve it.

Taped over the alarm clock was the text from the White House greeting card. It was not the message that had been written in Arabic, which made no sense even to speakers of the language, but the English trace picked up by Teresa Wood's ESDA analysis.

WHO1315

DR1630

AL1800

The text still meant nothing to Roger Gilman. And right now, he just wanted to know what time it was. He tipped back a shirtsleeve and glanced at his watch.

It was 6:15 p.m. in San Diego. Dawn would still be awake. Gilman picked up the receiver of his hotel room phone and made the call. Dawn's voice was like heaven.

"Hi, honey," Gilman said when she answered the phone. "How are things?"

"Oh, the usual around here," Dawn said cheerfully. "We miss you to pieces, but I'm sure that isn't news. How's sunny So Cal?"

"It's overrated," Gilman said, but he was smiling. "Tell me what's going on at home. I want to hear something normal."

"The cable bill went up this month," Dawn said. "That's normal. I called the company to complain, but they said it's a standard price increase. The crooks!" She laughed, and he laughed with her.

"Oh yeah, that reminds me," Gilman said. "I talked to Bill Richards a few days ago, and he said he had just mailed us an invitation for his daughter's wedding. I forget the date. Did you get it yet?"

"Um, no," she said. "But now that you mention it, I don't think I've picked up the mail today. I'll check it out. But for now, I have to go. If I don't put the little ones to bed soon it's going to be a problematic day tomorrow."

Gilman smiled. "OK, sweetie. I'll call you soon."

"I know," Dawn said. "I love you."

Dawn put the children to bed, and they were excited to hear that Daddy had just called to say he loved them and would be home soon. The older ones knew that "soon" was poorly defined, and they had learned to accept that.

To the youngest, five-year-old old James and three-and-a-half year old Mary, time was a bit more wobbly. When Gilman finally arrived home, they would not really seem to have noticed that he had been gone at all.

After putting the kids to bed, Dawn reminded herself to get the mail before she could make a cup of tea and settle in with the novel that was her current guilty pleasure. She stepped out to the curb and pulled the stack from the mailbox, sorting as she reentered the house. Junk, bills, stuff worth reading.

There was a card, as her husband had thought there would be. Dawn opened the envelope and frowned.

The image on the front of the card was unlike any wedding invitation she had ever seen, but Dawn was not thinking about this as she flipped the card open to read what she thought would be the wedding date.

And then she was just confused. And after a moment, a bit uneasy.

The Bitch caught his movement out of the corner of her eye, and when she turned to look, it was obvious to Chuck that she recognized him. For a moment, the two stood immobile, only staring at one another.

She was standing next to a countertop on which stood a computer and a piece of equipment Chuck could not identify. She had a rack full of test tubes and had been feeding them into the machine. Behind her, on massive workspaces that stood detached from each other in the center of the room, several huge machines hummed with activity as their moving arms picked up items and relocated them, while other arms transferred liquids from one plastic container to another.

Slowly, she took a step backward, and then another. And then she ran.

Chuck aimed his pistol toward the fleeing target, but then hesitated. The laboratory was a 360-degree funhouse of unidentifiable equipment, and he knew that the Bitch worked with live anthrax. There was no telling what a bullet could set in motion.

Chuck pocketed the pistol and bolted forward. The Bitch sprinted behind a central island containing a large machine with moving robotic arms. And then they were at a standoff.

From the opposite side of the island, Chuck instinctively weighed his options. He could not leap over the island without colliding with the machine, and who knew what the machine was handling. Like a basketball player trying to anticipate an opponent's next move, he watched for signs of body language that would tell him whether she would duck to the left, back toward the main lab, or to the right, and into another space. Chuck guessed that the room on the right would lead back into the hallway.

The Bitch's eyes were locked on his, her blue-gray stare burning into his coal black one, and Chuck was briefly reminded of the same terrified fire in her eyes upon their first encounter on the hill near the ocean. But this time, there was something else behind them. It was rage.

Chuck glared into that rage and realized that he had used up his one opportunity to benefit from the element of surprise.

The woman's eyes flashed away from his for a moment. When he glanced in the direction they had gone to determine what she could be looking at, he found himself staring at a computer monitor connected to the machine between them. On it scrolled a continuous collection of mathematical and written instructions that Chuck could not decipher. The woman's eyes darted once, and then again a moment later, between Chuck and the computer screen. And he realized that she was waiting for something specific to appear on the screen.

Chuck ducked quickly to the left, as if to circumvent the island between them and catch her. She followed suit and ducked away as rapidly, and then snatched a final glance at the computer screen. Her breathing escalated and a labored moan escaped her lips as she dropped quickly downward to the floor, and out of Chuck's field of view with the island between them.

Without pausing to consider the machine, he stepped forward to locate her again. And at that moment, the robotic arm swung rapidly around behind him and smashed into the back of Chuck's head. And then locked.

The force of the blow was sufficient to throw dancing spots before Chuck's eyes, and he was distantly aware of blood trickling down the back of his shirt. But even worse, he was now trapped between the metal claw and the bulk of the machine, and the grip was tightening.

The airy, whirring noise characteristic of computer malfunction arose next to him as the robotic arm pushed stubbornly to follow its pre-programmed path, but it was hindered by the presence of Chuck's cranium where an empty space belonged. He felt his head being squeezed as if in a vice, and wondered what it would feel like when his skull popped open and his brains were squeezed out from the top like a pimple.

But just before it happened, the arm let go.

As if nothing had gone wrong, the robot continued its tireless repetitions. At the moment Chuck realized he was free from its grip, the woman bolted back toward the corridor to the main lab. He tore away from the machine and chased after her.

As she ran, she passed a bench containing two bottles of clear liquid. Both were uncapped. With lightning speed, and without slowing the pace of her dash across the lab, her right arm thrust outward and she quickly gripped one of the bottles, which she then carried with her like an intercepted football as she ran.

This is bad, Chuck had time to realize when she whirled mid-stride and threw the contents of the bottle in his direction like a priest exorcising a demon with holy water. And like the proverbial demon under holy water, Chuck began to flail and thrash about as the highly concentrated acid began to devour the flesh on his face.

Chuck began to scream, and his hands flew instinctively toward the source of the torture. He began clawing at his own skin, as if he could wipe off the acid that was searing him. It was the wrong instinct. There had initially been only a minor splash to his left eye, but the sudden hand movement smeared the liquid quickly and indiscriminately. Chuck realized, too late, that he had just blinded himself. Probably for life.

Katrina fought the burning sensation that was growing over her right thumb and the inner part of her first finger while she watched her assailant flailing before her. When his hands struck his face, and she watched him smear the acid into his eyes, she knew she was safe.

She raced to the sink and began the process of flushing the liquid from her skin. The golden rule was fifteen minutes of uninterrupted flow of cool, clear water to quench an acid burn. Fifteen minutes was not going to happen here today. But Katrina was confident, as her attacker squirmed and writhed on the floor before her, that she at least had time to rinse her hand for a moment.

Since the inception of the Stone lab at San Diego State University, Katrina had been constantly chastising her staff for leaving the caps off of the acids and bases that resided next to the pH meter. Today, she was grateful for her staff's lack of attention to safety. The acid had just saved her life with the help of Octopus, the lab's original liquid handling robot. Like an old friend.

With her right hand still under the running faucet, Katrina pulled the cell phone out of her pocket with her left and dialed 911. After a moment of reconsideration, she hung up and then speed dialed Sean McMullan instead. A final glance at the man writhing on the ground led her to conclude that she probably had time to wait for police assistance, but she was not interested in risking it. She had struggled with this man once before. He was exceptionally strong.

Katrina turned off the faucet and walked through the corridor toward the main lab space, still holding the ringing cell phone to her ear with her uninjured hand. At the moment Sean McMullan answered, Katrina's eyes fell onto the floor just inside the main laboratory door. She let out an ear-shattering scream into the phone, and then dropped it.

9:46 P.M. EST

Dawn Gilman stood in the living room of her Washington, D.C. home and read the greeting card in front of her for a third time. At first merely silly, its tone became increasingly disturbing to Dawn, who was accustomed to being on the alert for suspicious findings as a side effect of her husband's career. This was one of those findings. It read:

> Mr. Gilman -
>
> How unfortunate that you do not speak my language.
>
> The Doctor

After only a momentary hesitation, Dawn picked up the phone and called her husband back.

"Hello, this is Roger Gilman."

"*ROGER! Get to the Stone lab! Right now!*" a man's voice shouted.

"Huh?" Gilman asked. "McMullan?"

"Yeah, it's me!" McMullan answered. "There's been a murder at Katrina Stone's lab. Someone killed the guard and then went after her. Katrina burned the dude's face off with some kind of acid. She says it's the same guy that attacked her on the beach.

"He's still in the lab, but she doesn't know when he'll pull it together enough to get away. Far as I'm concerned, he *won't* get away again. I'm on my way and I'm hauling ass, but I'm coming from La Jolla. Where are you?"

While McMullan spoke, Gilman picked up the pants he had just removed a moment earlier and pulled them back on, holding the phone to an ear with his shoulder while he fastened his belt. The pants were still warm.

"I'm at the hotel. I was about to get in the shower—"

Gilman's sentence was broken by the soft beep of his call waiting signal. He paused, mid-sentence, to glance at the caller ID on the phone. It was Dawn. His plans for attending his friend's daughter's wedding would have to wait. "I'll be there as soon as I can," Gilman said, and hung up.

He tossed the cell phone onto the bed while he located the shirt he had worn that day, turned it right side out, and then hastily pulled it on. After double-checking that his wallet and keys were still in the pockets of his pants, Gilman rushed out of the hotel room to his car.

As he started the ignition, the cellular phone still lying on the bed in his hotel room rang again.

✖

The second time he did not answer his phone, Dawn assumed that her husband was really indisposed, even for an emergency. A wife's emergency didn't usually equal an FBI emergency, and Dawn had been OK with that for a long time. But this time, she was sure her emergency was important enough for her to keep calling.

When he didn't answer again, she left an urgent message and then sat down at the kitchen table, the card still in one hand. She was now shaking with adrenaline.

After a moment of thought, Dawn stood from the table. She pulled a ziplock bag out of a kitchen drawer and locked the card, and its envelope, inside. And then called her husband a third time. And again, he did not pick up.

B y the time Sean McMullan arrived, a large pool of blood had flowed out into the hallway from beneath the laboratory door. Students and faculty members stood encircling it, stepping backward periodically to avoid the soaking of their shoes as the puddle continued to grow. One of them had called 911, and two police officers followed McMullan off the elevator and toward the scene. McMullan flashed his badge to let the policemen know he was in charge.

The slain guard's keys were still dangling from the closed door.

"Has anyone gone in or come out of there?" McMullan asked of the crowd that had accumulated.

"No," said an older man with a mustache. "I haven't let the students enter, and nobody has come out since I've been standing here. I've heard noises from inside, however."

McMullan paled. "And how long have you been standing there?"

"About five minutes."

McMullan turned back to the officers. "You're on crowd control," he said firmly and then turned the key to open the door.

When he entered the room, McMullan glanced down at the body on the floor. There was no reason to take a pulse, nor would it have even been possible at the neck. The guard's throat was neatly flayed open from ear to ear, his face a ghastly white and frozen in a contorted expression of fear. The cleanliness with which the carotid artery and jugular vein had been severed indicated to McMullan that the man had never had time to feel pain. He made a mental note to relay this as gently as he could to the guard's family.

There was no way to enter the laboratory without walking through the pool of blood that surrounded the guard. McMullan treaded carefully to avoid slipping on the wet linoleum, stepping through the blood, over the fallen guard, and toward the dry floor inside the room. When he reached the clean space, he stomped on the linoleum a few times in different places to clear the bottoms of his shoes. As he did, he heard a soft moaning coming from beyond a gap in the wall to his right. McMullan quickly approached the source of the sound.

At first, McMullan was grateful to see Katrina standing upright and apparently unhurt. His relief was quickly replaced with anger as he realized that she had willfully disregarded his instruction to get out of the lab and as far away from the scene as possible.

Katrina stood over a large man, who lay on the floor covering his face with his hands. The flesh on both of the man's hands had corroded to the bone. Beneath, McMullan could somewhat make out the hideous molten mass that had been his face.

As McMullan stood taking in the scene before him, the man moaned again and wriggled slightly. Katrina kicked him—hard—in the back, and he quieted back down and was still again. When she looked up and saw McMullan, she was not smiling. There was no relief in her eyes.

"OK, McMullan," she said authoritatively. "It's time you fill me in on the details of this story that I haven't been told. And I don't give a fuck how classified your information is."

"Who are you?"

Hours after the attack in the lab, Katrina whispered to the man in the hospital bed beside her. Of course, he could not answer. The patient would remain unconscious for at least the remainder of this night, his face grafted with someone else's skin and encased in cotton gauze, his breathing labored through a tube in his nose and another in his mouth. His hands were also heavily bandaged. They would never produce a viable fingerprint again.

The steady beep of the man's heart monitor clashed with the ticking of the wall clock beside the hospital bed. The two noises synched up for a moment and then staggered again, two reminders that time would not stand still for Katrina to solve the mystery before her. A mystery that clearly held her future, if not her life.

Katrina tore her eyes away from the man who had now attacked her twice, and glanced up at the wall clock. From the first moment she had stared into his dark eyes in the lab, she had known that this was the man from Black's Beach. Confirmation of this, in the thickness of his body and the style of his movements as he chased her through the lab, had been redundant.

The man's DNA had already been fast-tracked at FBI Forensics, but Katrina was not hopeful. She hated the idea that his identification relied on the possibility that he would already be in the database. That he had to have a criminal record. That she had so little control over the situation. In her head, Katrina heard Tom calling her a control freak.

So what? she said to herself. *It's my own life I'm trying to control.*

Katrina looked up from her thoughts when the door opened, and the two armed guards beside it parted to allow Roger Gilman and Sean McMullan into the room. McMullan held a thick file and an expression of concern. He dismissed the two police officers, and they stepped out and closed the door without asking questions.

"What's that?" Katrina asked.

"It's the information you want," he said. "And you are *not* about to see this file. Understood?" His eyes locked on hers for a moment, and Katrina could see the struggle within Sean McMullan as he handed her the Manila envelope.

"There's something else that isn't in there yet," Gilman said. "The DNA results have come back."

Katrina was shocked. The PCR analysis had obviously been performed with amazing speed, and for the analysis to already have reached a conclusion, they must have found the man in the database.

"Great!" she said. "So who is he?"

"Well, there's a problem," Gilman continued. "We think we need to do the analysis again. Part of the reason we're here right now is to obtain another blood sample."

"Why?"

"Because according to the DNA evidence, this man is currently incarcerated and has been for the last eight years solid. I don't suppose you want to guess where."

𝕏

The clock and the heart monitor synched again, and then staggered. Katrina's vision blurred as she stared absently at the rise and fall of the unconscious man's chest.

Then she blinked and looked up. "Do you have a mug shot of the San Quentin inmate?" Gilman reached into his briefcase and removed an eight-by-ten black-and-white photograph. He handed it to Katrina. "Yep, that's him all right," she said, exasperated.

For a brief instant, she struggled with the question of how the man could have been in two places at once, and then suddenly, understanding dawned. Katrina looked again at the photograph and her eyes narrowed, but then, she was smiling.

The scar. The scar over the man's eye in the photograph. It was subtle. But it had not been there in the laboratory.

Quietly, Katrina began to chuckle to herself. The two other investigators exchanged a confused glance, and then they, too, began to laugh.

"How could we have missed it?" Gilman asked.

"Because we weren't looking for it," McMullan answered. "In fact, I bet they've been masquerading as one man for a long time."

In his shared minimum-security cell at San Quentin, Oscar Morales lay awake in a rare state of insomnia.

Two hours earlier, it had been a dream that awakened him. In his dream, Chuck had been at the prison. Oscar had handed his brother two vials of anthrax across the table of the visitation room. And with a smile, Chuck had opened one of the vials and swallowed its contents like a shot of whiskey. Oscar had been powerless to stop him.

Chuck's grin quickly decayed from sweet into freakish as an eruption of black sores obscured the flesh of his face. As Oscar watched, helpless, the sores grew together and began bursting, leaving behind a blackened, bloody nightmare of devoured flesh. Chuck raised his hands—also corroding—to his face and began to scream.

But the scream that awoke Oscar was his own.

"*Shut the fuck up!*" his cellmate shouted, and Oscar snapped out of the dream.

⋈

Still sitting beside the hospital bed, Katrina looked down at the thick file in her hands. McMullan and Gilman had left the room to retrieve the personal belongings of the man in the bed, the identical twin brother of a San Quentin inmate named Oscar Morales.

Katrina was examining Roger Gilman's Venn diagram of suspects in Operation Death Row. She was at the center. She could understand why. The data before her was circumstantial, but it pointed repeatedly to her. Her preliminary inhibitor data from the original grant application. A witness' claim that a female had ransacked Jason's apartment. A lab coat fiber located in the greeting card. The card itself, bearing the same crystal structure she had posted on her office wall.

Katrina flipped through the pages of the file and saw a photocopy of the White House greeting card. For a moment, she studied the crystal structure of the anthrax toxins interacting with the host cell. There were no alterations to the structure; it was indeed identical to the image printed in the 2004 issue of *Nature*.

She opened the card and stared at the Arabic text, and then found the English translation on a subsequent page in the file.

Dear Mr. President,

Your nation of puppets will soon know at last the price of fighting against our Islamic State. Those of you who survive Allah's justice will reflect upon 11 September of 2001 and consider that date insignificant.

A small taste of the pain we promise has already been put to course. Make no mistake

*that the blood that will flow is on your hands.
Let it paint for you an image of our strength
and resolve. Let it serve as a reminder that you
cannot defeat Islam.*

*You will stand powerless and witness this small
shedding of blood, and you will then have the
privilege of living in fear for two months, as
our faithful brothers and sisters have lived in
fear of your Christian Crusaders.*

*And finally, on your Christmas Day of this
year, there will begin a cleansing of your
country unlike any you can possibly imagine.
It will blanket your nation and no man,
woman, or child will be safe. Only Allah will
decide who may be spared.*

*Our Muslim brothers and sisters have been
imprisoned by the western leaders for too
long. The world will now see that you are
the prisoners, and Allah will praise the final
victory of ISIL.*

Katrina reviewed the text several times. *A small taste of the pain we promise has already been put to course. Imprisoned. Prisoners. It will blanket your nation. Christmas Day. This year. ISIL.* But Christmas had come and gone, and there had been nothing. *Why?* Katrina began committing the text to memory.

Her concentration was broken when the door opened and Gilman and McMullan re-entered the hospital room. Both looked pale. In McMullan's hand was a ziplock bag, which he held out to her with trembling fingers. "We've been through this man's personal effects," he said. "These were in his pocket."

Katrina took the bag from Sean McMullan and gripped one of the two sealed glass vials through the plastic. In contrast to those of the FBI agent, her hands were steady as she shook the vial gently to observe the movement of the powder inside. "You haven't opened this, have you?" she asked calmly.

"*Oh, hell no!*" McMullan said.

"Good. What about the hospital staff?"

"We asked," Gilman said. "They say they haven't either."

"I bet you a million to one I know the exact molecular composition of what's in these vials," Katrina said. "Leave the analysis to me and I'll confirm it. It can be done with PCR by late morning."

"Absolutely not," Gilman said. "We've already gone out on a limb by *not* giving you the file that you're *not* looking at right now. There's no way we're letting you take over the forensic analysis of this investigation."

"I have no interest in taking over the forensic analysis of the investigation, but I can have this done before the San Diego FBI wakes up for the day. This is what I do, all the time."

"Forget it, Katrina—" Gilman began to say, but she cut him off.

"Seriously, Roger! What are you afraid of? That I'll use the anthrax to poison someone? Do you not realize I could have done that at any time over the last several years? Do you not realize that even if you take these vials with you, I can go to my lab right now and take out another?"

"Oh, for Pete's sake," Gilman said finally. As he said it, he looked at his watch. It was now 4:33 a.m. and the three of them had been at the hospital since Katrina's attacker had been admitted the previous evening. "I have to go get some sleep. If you can really finish that analysis by tomorrow morning—or *this* morning, I guess it really is—be my guest. But I want the other vial for our forensics team to confirm whatever you find."

"Of course," Katrina agreed.

Gilman looked to McMullan, who nodded approval. "I'm going to sleep too, Katrina," McMullan said. "You OK?"

"Yeah, I'm fine," she said, but there were heavy bags under her eyes. "I'll harvest the DNA in BSL-3 and then the rest can be done in BSL-2. All I have to do is set up the PCR, take a nap while the machine runs, and then run the gel. It will only take about twenty minutes after that. I'll have the data by the time you guys wake up. Then it's my turn to sleep."

Katrina pulled one of the vials from the ziplock bag, resealed the bag and returned it to Sean McMullan. With a final nod, the two FBI agents left the hospital room. Katrina gathered her belongings and the FBI file and left for the BSL-3 facility.

5:23 A.M. PST

As soon as Roger Gilman arrived back at the hotel room that had now been his home for several months, his cell phone chimed. Exhausted, he picked up the phone and looked at the caller ID. Dawn had called seven times.

Gilman's state of sleep deprivation began to feel like a break with reality as he listened to the multiple voice mail messages from his wife. In the first, a hint of concern was reflected in Dawn's voice. Subsequently: conviction, trepidation, and anger. With each reading of the card, Dawn had become increasingly aware of its implications. The card was a threat. Mailed to their home. Where seven children were sleeping.

"... *creepy greeting card... funny looking flowers... how unfortunate... speak my language... The Doctor...* "

Creepy greeting card. Funny looking flowers. Gilman sat down, hard, on the bed, and began to breathe deeply. For a moment, he thought he might faint. Then he called his home in Washington, D.C.

Dawn answered on the first ring.

"Where is the card now?" he asked immediately.

"In a ziplock bag, sitting on the kitchen table in front of me."

"Describe the 'funny flowers' to me," he said, and she did.

"Dawn, leave the card right where it is. Gather up the kids and get them out of the house. Take enough stuff for a few days and go to your mother's. There might be no real cause for concern, but I'm not taking any chances. There will be FBI investigators at the house within the hour to remove the card. Don't touch it again."

Dawn began to weep softly, and Gilman sat quietly on the phone to allow it to pass. After a brief breakdown, Dawn cleared her throat. "OK then," she said. "I know you can't tell me what's going on, but I trust you. I'll do as you say. But Roger, please come home when you can. I need you."

"I'm already on my way."

It took four phone calls for Gilman to secure a flight from San Diego to Washington, D.C. He made the calls in the car on the way to the airport. Once the flight was scheduled, he made two additional calls.

The first was to Guofu Wong, the CDC epidemiologist heading Operation Death Row. Wong assured Gilman that there would be special agents and a HazMat team at the Gilman house in twenty minutes. And that, as soon as he could, he would personally join them from Atlanta.

The second call was to Sean McMullan's cell phone.

"Hello?" McMullan said groggily.

"McMullan, wake up!" Gilman practically shouted.

"Oh, God, now what?"

"Who gets your mail when you're out of town?"

"Come again?"

"Where is your mail for today?"

"My personal mail?"

"*Yes!*"

"It's being forwarded to me here in San Diego. It, ah, comes to a P.O. box. I pick it up every three or four days."

"When was the last time you picked it up?"

"A couple days ago. Roger, what are you talking about?"

"I got a greeting card. At home. My wife opened it. It's got a bouquet on it and a weird message. From Dawn's description, the bouquet sounds like the same one from the other card. The bouquet that's really the molecular structure of anthrax."

Sean McMullan paused. "You mean the writing was in English?" he asked, bewildered.

"Well my wife doesn't speak Arabic, as far as I know."

"Why do you think I'd have something in my mail just because you did?" McMullan asked.

"Because whoever wrote that card knows I'm the investigator on this case. And you're the other one. So if you don't have something similar in your mailbox, then I'm obviously being personally targeted. And our number one suspect clearly likes you a hell of a lot more than she likes me." And with that, Gilman hung up.

Katrina purified the DNA out of the anthrax in the vial at her BSL-3 facility in Sorrento Valley. Once the infectious material from the bacteria was removed, the DNA itself was harmless. So she returned to her lab at SDSU, which was en route to her house and the bed she so longed for.

For the first time in months, there was no guard at the laboratory door. The guard that should have been on duty was currently at the morgue. A chalk outline had been traced where he had fallen, and the door was locked and blockaded off with police tape. Katrina yanked it aside and stepped into her lab, her shoes sticking in the blood that had now become tacky.

Katrina took the reagents she needed from a freezer and rubbed the vials between her fingers to thaw them. It only took a few minutes to set up the PCR reaction.

One of the most widely used techniques in modern molecular biology, PCR is nothing more than a succession of repeated cycles of precisely controlled temperature fluctuations. Once, researchers were required to submerge the reaction by hand, one step at a time, into a series of water baths to alter the temperature manually. Today, the process is automated.

The scientist merely places a reaction tube into a machine and dictates the temperature changes and timing on the machine's computer. And then waits.

Once Katrina had programmed the PCR machine, she had a two hour and forty minute wait for the reaction to reach completion before she could look at the results on a DNA gel. She pressed the start button and sat down at the lab bench beside the machine, finally succumbing to her exhaustion.

As she began to fall asleep, Katrina tipped sideways off of the chair she was sitting on and then quickly jerked awake. Her mind dazed, she glanced up and saw a puddle of clear liquid on the floor between the main lab and the robot room. She recognized the liquid as the portion of hydrochloric acid that had missed her attacker's face. The puddle reminded Katrina of a series of events that couldn't possibly have taken place in this room just the evening before. The prospect of sleep was suddenly over.

She stood up and began wandering through the lab, retracing her steps and those of her attacker, whose first name she still did not know. Morales. Something Morales. Twin brother to Oscar Morales. The Oscar Morales at San Quentin.

Except for the mess at the front door, and a few smears of Something Morales' blood and facial tissues on the floor where he had fallen, the lab looked remarkably innocuous. Like the other robots, Octopus was still working away as if totally disinterested in murders, murderers, or Katrina's self-defense tactics with his jerky robot movements and concentrated hydrochloric acids.

As Katrina walked past the robot room and into the room beyond, her eyes fell upon the liquid nitrogen tank, and something dawned. The activator data was still in there. She and Jason had hidden the data months ago, and she had never had a chance to dig it back out. The lab had always been guarded. Until today.

Katrina shook her head rapidly from side to side for a moment in an attempt to clear the fogginess of sleep deprivation. She needed the capacity to think.

There had now been a murder in the lab. If the activator data had been a threat before, it was an even bigger threat now. Perhaps it was time to destroy it for good. And this might be her only window, her only chance with no guard at the lab. And besides, she no longer needed it.

Katrina glanced around momentarily, as if she might see someone else in the room. Of course, she did not.

She found the stool used to reach the top of the tank and the blue cryo-gloves required to touch its contents. Then she reached into a closet to retrieve the item she had purchased from the humane society where Alexis worked.

Over the course of the last few months, Katrina's lab had become the most sophisticated infectious disease laboratory in the world. Within it, the shiny new Pooper Scooper looked ridiculous. But with its stainless steel arms, long reach, and plastic handles, it was the perfect tool for retrieving something from the bottom of a tank held at one hundred ninety-six degrees below zero.

Katrina raised the lid of the tank and stood back to allow the initial cloud of sublimation to puff out. Then she waved away as much of the residual vapor as possible with a blue glove. She removed the four towers that she and Jason had placed atop the cryogenic bag containing the data and set them onto the floor. Then she fished out the bag with the Pooper Scooper and dropped it onto the linoleum.

After replacing the towers and closing the lid, Katrina used a gloved hand to pick up the still frozen bag. And as she did, she heard a door close.

Katrina raced to the nearest laboratory island and opened

a top drawer. She dropped the bag containing the data, still smoking with sublimation, inside the drawer and slammed it shut, and then took off the gloves and dropped them onto the table. She crammed the Pooper Scooper back into its closet, just as an exhausted-looking Sean McMullan rounded the corner into the room.

Katrina could feel herself flushing. "Oh, you scared me," she said. "What are you doing here?" As she spoke, Katrina walked away from the closet and back toward the robot room.

With a quizzical look on his face, McMullan followed. "I was just stopping by on my way out of town. Roger and I have an emergency and we have to go back to D.C. He already left. I wanted to make sure everything was OK here before I followed him."

"Yeah," she said too quickly. "Everything's fine. I did the DNA extraction, and the PCR is running right now. I just need to run the gel in a little bit."

"Good, I'll see you soon then."

He followed her out of the room and back into the main lab. Behind them, a thin ghost of sublimation vapor was still creeping upward from the drawer next to the liquid nitrogen tank.

At the local FBI branch office in San Diego, a special agent was observing a series of video monitors. As Sean McMullan and Katrina Stone were stepping away from the liquid nitrogen tank in Stone's lab, the guard leaned forward toward his controls to digitally rewind the video that had just captured his interest. He watched again as she pulled an object out of the tank and then hastily shoved it into a drawer upon the arrival of McMullan.

"*Gotcha*," the agent said under his breath and picked up the receiver of his telephone.

4:35 P.M. EST

By the time Sean McMullan arrived at his partner's home outside of Washington, D.C., the majority of FBI, USPIS, and HazMat officials had already cleared out. Roger Gilman was sitting at his kitchen table with Teresa Wood, James Johnson, and Guofu Wong. Teresa, wearing white latex gloves, was delicately touching the sides of the greeting card on the table while reading its text.

McMullan did not need to see his partner's card. He had an identical copy in his back pocket, pulled out of his own San Diego post office box that morning before boarding his plane. As he approached the other inspectors, he wordlessly removed it and tossed it onto the table next to the other copy.

Guofu Wong was the first to speak. "At least there's nothing hazardous on them," he said.

"Of course there isn't," Teresa answered.

"Can I get an 'amen' for e-beam irradiation," McMullan added. As he spoke, his cell phone buzzed in his pocket. McMullan looked down and silenced it.

"Perhaps you overreacted in sending our entire task force

and HazMat team to respond to this," Johnson suggested coldly to Gilman.

Gilman's eyes blazed. "And what would you have done, Dr. Johnson, if it was *your* wife and seven children in here?"

The eyes of the two men locked and a terse silence followed. Then Johnson broke Gilman's gaze and looked down. "I don't know," he said quietly.

"Mr. Gilman," Wong said, "Dr. Johnson's *one* child died of leukemia forty years ago, and his wife passed away just last year."

"I'm sorry," Gilman said. "I didn't know."

Johnson ignored the brief revelation of his personal life. "Well, we have a more current issue to address," he said. "Obviously, this Doctor character knows a lot more about this case than he should."

"Agreed," said Wong. "He knows who is on this case, and he knows your home addresses—two pieces of information that were never available outside of the FBI."

"Which means that he—*or she*—is either *in* the FBI, has infiltrated, or has gotten to someone else." The comment was from Teresa. As she spoke, her eyes darted rapidly from one of the four men at the table to the next. Although she had not said it, her point was understood. All four of them were now suspects as far as the USPIS was concerned. "With that being said," Teresa continued, "I'm afraid I have to raise a really awkward issue at this point."

"You can't be serious!" Gilman interrupted. "And if us, why not you?"

"Well, first of all," Teresa said. "I'm not in the FBI. I do not have access to the two pieces of information we just discussed. The only way I knew how to get here, in case you don't remember an hour ago, was by getting directions from you."

"I'm not in the FBI either," Guofu Wong pointed out.

"No, you're not," Teresa conceded, "but I think you and I should both cooperate as well. I will happily offer my DNA, a handwriting analysis, pap smear, and whatever else you fellows need. And I expect that the FBI will put its forensics people on this analysis to corroborate whatever I find in my investigation. But you can bet that *my* investigation will be thorough."

Another cell phone rang. Each of the inspectors checked his or her phone, and Gilman announced, "It's mine." He pressed the button to silence the phone.

"We're done here, anyway," Teresa said. And then, glaring at Gilman, "... provided I can collect a hair sample from each of you on our way out the door."

She turned to Johnson, whose head was totally bald. "Dr. Johnson, I can use hair from any body part of your choice, as long as I get to pluck it. Or, I can come by your office this afternoon and take an oral swab."

Johnson loosened his tie and unbuttoned the top two buttons of his shirt, revealing a chest speckled with white hair. "As much fun as that oral thing sounds... be my guest."

Katrina awoke from a fitful sleep and pulled a robe over her naked body before stepping out of the bedroom. Her hair was still wet from the shower that had failed to wash off her most recent encounter with "Something Morales."

The house was silent. Katrina knocked on Lexi's door and then poked her head into her daughter's room. Alexis was not home. Katrina looked at her watch. It was almost four thirty in the afternoon.

Katrina walked out into the kitchen and brewed a pot of coffee. Then she sat down on the living room couch with a fresh cup and the FBI file. She found the spot where she had left off at the hospital and resumed her reading.

A thick forensic analysis from the United States Postal Inspection Service confronted her. Scanning quickly for relevant information, Katrina read through reports detailing Crimescope analyses, hair fibers, lab coat fragments, and ESDA analyses. The majority of lab tests were similar to assays Katrina herself had used religiously for years, and it was easy reading.

Then she saw an image that made her pause. It was the scanned image of the writing from the greeting card. The text that had been picked up by the ESDA trace analysis.

WHO1315

DR1630

AL1800

Katrina stared at the text for a moment longer. Then she leapt from the couch, spilling coffee onto her robe as she did. "*Shit!*" she shouted as the liquid seared her leg, but she did not stop moving.

Katrina raced into the bedroom to quickly dress, brush her teeth, and pull her long hair back into a clip at the nape of her neck. Then she darted into the guest room that doubled as a home office and switched on her computer.

Eagerly, Katrina clicked into the start menu of her computer to confirm what she already knew. She clasped a hand over her mouth and sat for a moment, thinking. And then, with trembling hands, Katrina opened her Internet browser, where she pulled up an online road map function.

Abell over the door jingled softly as Alexis Stone stepped into the Army surplus store on University Avenue. She flashed a smile at a man dressed in full camouflage behind the counter.

Alexis walked past the shelves of miscellaneous items and through a narrow hallway leading to the restrooms. She passed both restroom doors and knocked softly on a third, unmarked door at the back of the hall.

"Yeah?" came a voice from inside.

"Code word Lincoln," Lexi said softly, after checking over her shoulder for unwanted company. Lincoln. Freer of slaves. It could not have been more appropriate for the Animal Liberation Front.

The door opened and Alexis stepped in, then locked the door behind her. Scattered around the room were a variety of mismatched, tattered chairs and couches, a refrigerator, a television, and several tables.

On the walls was a collection of posters. In one, an anonymous person held a white rabbit closely, protectively to his or her face, which was covered with a black ski mask. The caption read "If not you, who? If not now, when?"

Several people were seated at a table and sprawled on the couches. They greeted Alexis with nods and hand-waves when she entered the room. Lexi walked over to a teenage boy sitting on a loveseat, leaned down and kissed him with tongue, mindless of the others in the room.

"Hey, babe," he said casually, and sat up to allow room on the loveseat for her. She sat next to him and draped one leg across his lap. The boy began to rub her calf.

"So what's the latest?" Alexis asked.

"Finalizing strategy for the biotechnology convention next week," said an older man. "Sounds like we're going to have quite a turnout."

"Good," Lexi said. "How many?"

"Well over a thousand, according to my estimation," said the same man. "But we're counting on you to be at the forefront. Since your mom is the keynote speaker, you can really call attention to us. Grab the press. Make sure they know who you are, and make sure they know you don't support your mother's work. The press goes crazy when it comes to conflict within families, so you are in a really strong position to discredit your mother."

"You bet," she said. And then with a giggle, "I'm going to be grounded for the rest of my life."

The room erupted with snickers and a few more boisterous laughs.

"And how many people *won't* be at the convention," Lexi asked with a mischievous grin.

"We have three teams of seven targeting the Salk Institute, Scripps Research, and UCSD. We've got contacts to let us in, and we're taking the animals out in vans. It's just mice and rats, so they'll be easy to handle. We've narrowed it down to the best three labs for the operation, based on the fact that all of the major players from those labs will be at the convention."

"Cool," Alexis said, and popped the gum in her mouth. "Well, sorry, but I can't stay tonight. Just stopping by on my way home." She turned to the boy on the loveseat rubbing her leg. "Coming over? I'm sure my mom will be gone half the night as usual."

"Yeah," he said. "I just have a few things to catch up on at home. I'll meet you there in a bit."

Alexis stood to leave, and the boy slapped her backside as she walked away. She turned and hit him playfully on the arm, but as she left the room, she was smiling.

With the girl gone, the older man turned his attention to the boy on the loveseat.

"Are you sure everything's OK with her?" he asked.

"Oh yeah, she's cool. We'll be down at the convention, remember?"

"Just as long as you're sure that's where she'll be. I don't want anyone getting in the way. I know you say she's cool, but it *is* the girl's mother we're talking about here. Girls are surprisingly protective of their mothers even when they pretend to hate them."

"I know," the boy said, "but it's under control. Katrina Stone will be speaking at the convention, and I'll keep Alexis out of the way. If she wants to leave the convention, I'll take her back to her house. That's good for at least an hour, hour and a half." He was smiling.

"Yeah right, try ten seconds," said a girl across the room, and laughed.

"Shut up," the boy said. "Anyway, Lexi isn't a problem. You guys just get into the BSL-3 facility like we planned. Do you have the floor plan?"

The older man nodded, and the boy continued. "Good. Focus on the monkeys. According to my contact there, the infected monkeys are kept quarantined away from the un-infected ones. It's too late to save the infected ones, but my contact says that there are currently six monkeys that have not yet been infected. Make sure you know which ones they are. If you get the wrong monkeys, the world has a seri-ous problem."

Sean McMullan and Roger Gilman had deplaned in San Diego and were walking across the Skywalk to the airport parking lot when Gilman remembered to switch his cell phone back on. A message chimed immediately when he did.

Without slowing his pace across the Skywalk, Gilman listened to the message and then closed the phone. He grabbed McMullan's arm casually and began trotting toward the parking lot. "We have a situation," he said.

McMullan easily kept up at a slow jog. "I'm parked right over here."

"Good." Gilman was already running out of breath. "You drive."

Once in the passenger seat of Sean McMullan's sedan, Gilman dialed the San Diego Branch of the FBI while McMullan navigated his way out of the parking lot of San Diego International Airport.

The agent who picked up the phone immediately yelled, "I've been trying to get a hold of you guys all day!"

"We've been dealing with an emergency," Gilman said defensively. "On the east coast time, by the way. We just got back. What?"

Gilman listened while his contact relayed his observation

from the surveillance video of Katrina Stone's lab. *She was hiding something in a tank all this time,* Gilman thought. *What was it?* "How big was the thing she pulled out?" he asked.

"Not much bigger than a book or something," the agent said.

McMullan was driving while glancing at his partner every few moments in an effort to deduce information from the one-sided conversation he was hearing. "Roger, where am I going?" he finally asked.

"San Diego FBI headquarters," Gilman answered.

"Wait," said the agent on the phone. "I haven't told you the rest. While she was getting the stuff out of the tank, McMullan showed up and she immediately hid it in a drawer. She looked guilty as hell. If I were you, I'd pick up Stone first. You can look at the video later."

Gilman hung up the phone and grabbed the steering wheel, jerking McMullan's car into a rapidly approaching turn lane. Another car entering the same lane almost hit the swerving sedan from the side.

"*What the fuck?*" McMullan said, shoving his partner away and regaining control.

"Turn!" Gilman said, and McMullan did.

"Change of plan," Gilman said. "Get to Stone's house. Right now."

It was unnecessary for the two agents to kick in the front door to Katrina Stone's house. The door was unlocked. Guns drawn, McMullan and Gilman burst through the door but then stalled.

Sitting at the kitchen table was a young man. Lying across the table was Alexis Stone. Both of them were stark naked, and the boy was holding a can of whipped cream over a small mound of strawberries and raspberries, arranged delicately on the girl's stomach. When the door opened and the two agents came in, both teenagers looked up.

After her initial start, Alexis scrambled off the table and hastily tried to hide her naked body behind her boyfriend.

McMullan and Gilman exchanged a confused glance and then bolted past the two teenagers and up the stairs. "Get some clothes on," Gilman mumbled as he passed.

Given the scene in the kitchen, neither agent was surprised to find Stone's bedroom empty. She should have been in bed, finally sleeping after the eventful last twenty-four hours. Instead, her bedroom was disheveled, clothing thrown haphazardly across the bed, along with a small array of toiletries. A small collection of luggage had been thrown out of the closet and was still strewn across the floor.

"Shit!" McMullan said.

Gilman stepped out to sweep the rest of the house, avoiding the front area where two embarrassed, horny, and sticky teenagers were dressing.

McMullan stepped into the bedroom and rifled through the mess on the bed, and then through the adjacent bathroom, looking for evidence of where she might have gone. *Katrina, this can't really be you.* He withdrew his cell phone and speed-dialed San Diego FBI headquarters.

"Now what?" the agent asked.

"She's leaving the country," he said. "Alert TSA."

"*Sean!*" Gilman's voice rang through from the next room.

McMullan stabbed at his phone to end the call, cutting off the other agent's voice. Following the direction of his partner's shouting, he raced into another bedroom, where Gilman was looking at a computer monitor. McMullan stepped up behind him and stared for a moment.

On the screen was an electronic calendar. The month

displayed was July of the previous year. It was obviously Katrina Stone's schedule. The calendar was filled with dates and times of seminars, lectures, and experimental timelines— next to each, the name of one of Katrina's students or her postdoc. Lab meetings. Departmental meetings. And days with Alexis, versus days that Alexis was to be at Tom's house.

McMullan studied the calendar for a moment, seeing nothing of interest. Confused, he looked at Gilman, and Gilman pointed to a specific date.

"Recognize this section?" Gilman asked.

"No."

The area to which Gilman was pointing read:

```
Seminar: World Health Organization: 1:15
Hosting Dan Russel: Pick up at 4:30
Pick up Alexis: 6:00
```

"I give up," McMullan said. "What?"

"You didn't obsess with that piece of paper like I did," Gilman said, and picked up a pen off the desk.

On a yellow Post-It note in front of him, replicating the handwriting on the ESDA trace the best he could, Gilman scrawled:

WHO1315

DR1630

AL1800

"The first greeting card from the White House. The ESDA trace. It was a section of Katrina Stone's schedule." Gilman looked up from the computer monitor and into his partner's dumbfounded gaze. "You still think your girl didn't do it?"

Oscar Morales was pleasantly surprised when he saw the woman who was there to see him. He had not been expecting anyone, not today, and was annoyed at having to leave his cell in the first place. At least this chick was a looker. *Damn, she's hot*, he thought as she approached.

The woman was in jeans and a T-shirt and was holding a file. She didn't look very happy.

"Who the fuck are you?" Oscar asked.

"Who the fuck are *you*?" the woman snapped in return.

"Don't jerk me off, bitch... you came here to see me."

"What do you want with me?"

"Lady, I don't even know you, so fuck off," Oscar said and stood up from the visiting table to leave. As he turned and began walking away, she asked, "Recognize this person?"

Just like that, the nightmare returned to the forefront of Oscar's mind. His heart was in his throat as he turned around.

Suddenly, Oscar felt like he was in a movie—the kind of movie where a cop comes to someone's door and shows that person a photograph, and then says that the person in the photograph is dead. Oscar stepped toward the woman and looked at the page in her hand.

The person in the image was unidentifiable, lying in a hospital bed with his or her face completely covered in a fluffy white envelope of gauze. "How the fuck am I supposed to recognize that person?" Oscar asked. His heart was still in his throat.

"How about now?" the woman asked casually, and showed another picture. In this one, beneath the gauze, the camera had caught the upper half of the hospital bed. A bare chest was exposed, and the large tattoo across it was still intact.

MORALES

"*You fucking bitch!*" Oscar screamed and lunged at the woman. She ducked quickly away and Oscar crashed across another of the visiting room's tables.

The guard on duty rushed forward, reaching for his nightstick.

"*What did you do to him?*" Oscar demanded, whirling around to face the guard instead of the woman. He managed to land a forceful blow upon the guard's jaw, but the nightstick still collided with his knee and sent him to the floor.

"Your brother did this to himself," the woman shouted through the commotion. "*What did he want with me?*"

"*I don't know!*" Oscar yelled. He stood again and lunged toward her, but then there were three more guards upon him.

✖

Katrina stood immobile as the guards subdued Oscar Morales. Each of the four men pinned a powerful limb to the floor, and then one of them withdrew a needle and syringe.

The guard uncapped the needle and plunged it through the prisoner's pant leg into his massive upper thigh. With all four guards still holding tightly, the inmate began to relax, and then he was quiet. They picked him up by the limbs and carried him out of the room.

Katrina sat down heavily at the visiting room table once again. *He really did not know who I was*, she thought, and the connection she thought she had made—between the twins, herself, and the anthrax attack at the prison—was broken.

DNA

Katrina was still sitting in the visiting room, staring absently at the floor in front of her, when the door opened. She did not turn around to see Sean McMullan and Roger Gilman approach her from behind. When McMullan placed a hand lightly on her shoulder, she jerked and then looked up into his face, dazed. "I'm fine," she said. "You guys didn't need to come here."

"Actually," Gilman said quietly, "we're not here to help you."

Katrina looked from one agent to the other, questioning.

Gilman and McMullan glanced at each other and Gilman nodded to McMullan. "Go ahead," he said firmly.

McMullan sighed. "Dr. Katrina Stone," he said. "You're under arrest for sixty-eight murders in the first degree. You have the right to remain silent... " And as he rattled off the Miranda monologue as if in a trance, Sean McMullan took out his handcuffs.

"How can you possibly think I killed all those inmates?" Katrina asked on the plane back to San Diego.

"How can we possibly think you didn't?" Gilman replied. "We found your schedule on the greeting card."

"I sort of figured," she said, remembering how, in her haste leaving the house, she had stupidly left her calendar app open on her computer. "Obviously, I'm being framed. I had nothing to do with that card." Her eyes bored into McMullan, and he looked at the floor of the airplane. For a moment, Katrina thought it was embarrassment on his face.

"Actually Katrina," he said, "that's not all we found."

"What, then?"

"Well," McMullan continued with an air of reluctance, "you knew we were monitoring you when we started this investigation. You were amply forewarned, and your staff was amply forewarned. You all signed agreements acknowledging this."

"Yeah? So?"

Gilman interrupted. "In fact, the grandiose salary

increases you all received were negotiated because of your so-called endangerment and the privacy loss you willingly accepted. So the government was operating completely within our rights."

"What are you *talking* about?" Katrina asked.

"You knew we had placed guards around your lab," Gilman continued, "and that these guards were there to monitor the activities in the lab as well as to protect you and your staff. What you weren't told is that there were also bugs placed throughout your facility. We knew that if there were guards most of the time, you'd be lulled into thinking that the guards were your only surveillance. The guards were a decoy."

"*Oh my god,*" Katrina said quietly.

"Katrina," McMullan said, "our San Diego agents have been to your lab and they have collected the bag of notes that you fished out of your liquid nitrogen tank. Our specialists have read those notes. And they agree that those pages describe in detail the discovery of the molecular activator that comprises the Death Row Complex."

In the main forensics laboratory at USPIS headquarters in Dulles, Virginia, Teresa Wood shook her head as she viewed the results of her initial PCR analysis. This time, she was not looking for a suspect. She was looking for evidence against Katrina Stone; she was looking for the data package that would put the rogue scientist away forever. And two more pieces of data had just been provided. Two new greeting cards.

As Teresa had suspected, there was no infectious material present on the greeting card from Roger Gilman's house or the one from Sean McMullan's post office box. *Same result, same MO*, she thought to herself, reflecting on the similar result—or lack thereof—that had been obtained from the original card mailed to the White House.

Teresa stared blindly at the fluorescent pink bands for a moment before switching off the UV light that allowed them to show through the DNA gel in front of her. *She's playing with us*, she thought.

Until last Friday, Teresa had felt a certain kinship toward

Katrina Stone. Both women were laboratory researchers, both immersed in the constant uphill battle to succeed in male-dominated fields. Both women supervised several other people, stepping into the lab themselves occasionally to don gloves as required by the current situation.

But that kinship was shattered last Friday, when Roger Gilman discovered that the ESDA trace was a snapshot of Stone's online calendar, and when Stone was caught red-handed hiding the data that led to the Death Row anthrax strain.

Teresa closed her eyes and envisioned Stone's office desk, which she had never actually seen but could imagine well enough. In Teresa's mind, the desk resembled her own workspace three floors above where she now sat. In the postal inspector's vision, Stone sat at her desk in San Diego doing similar work to that done daily by Teresa in Dulles. Reviewing the data of her subordinates. Reading the scientific literature. And like Teresa's own desk, she saw Stone's desk piled with raw notes, loose reports, data-stuffed notebooks, and scientific journals.

But there was one discrepancy. In Teresa's vision, there was an item on Stone's desk that should never have been there. Beneath a stack of pages in front of Stone, there was a greeting card with a computer graphic on the front, the graphic copied from one of the scientific journals on the shelves above the desk. A card with a threatening message written in Arabic. A card that had not yet been mailed to the White House.

Teresa pictured Katrina Stone going through her daily activities. She saw Stone glancing from her computer screen down to the pages she was reading at the moment. She saw her clicking into her computer to bring up her schedule. She saw her making a note on a piece of paper to remind herself of her obligations that afternoon. She saw her pen making indentations through the page being written on, indentations into the card that lay beneath.

History repeats itself, Teresa thought, and made a decision. She threw the DNA gel in front of her into the trash and removed her gloves. The next assay she performed on the new greeting cards would be the ESDA.

8:36 A.M. PST

The San Diego County jail system is currently comprised of seven facilities. Male inmates are generally booked at San Diego Central downtown, where they may be held or transferred to one of the others. Female inmates are typically taken to the Las Colinas Detention Facility in Santee.

In response to a truly surreal phone call from his post-doctoral advisor, Jason Fischer had only to drive four blocks from his Santee apartment to visit Katrina at the Las Colinas facility. More than an hour after his arrival, Katrina was finally brought out to see him.

Jason was shocked at her appearance.

Like Jason himself, Katrina had always excelled under pressure. The two had collaborated brilliantly from Jason's first day in the lab. Without ever needing to try, they understood each other. Both worked hard at all times, but it took a deadline to bring both Jason and Katrina to top form. When a grant was due, when a revised paper was due, or when a milestone was approaching, Jason and Katrina functioned as one mind. More than her postdoc, Jason was her colleague, ally, and good friend.

It was obvious to Jason that right now, Katrina was at her breaking point. The inmate uniform covering her body was way too large, and in it, her diminutive size was accentuated. In looking so small, she also looked exceptionally vulnerable. Her thick auburn waves, streaked with the occasional gray strand, were tangled and unkempt. Several frizzy, unruly strands sprang outward from her face in a crazed, electric halo. Her normally animated blue-gray eyes were swallowed in deep black cavities. The look on Katrina's face was madness.

And the biotechnology convention was eminent. The opening keynote speech was scheduled for the next morning. The scheduled keynote speaker was Katrina Stone.

"What's going on?" Jason asked.

"Jason, it's a long story," Katrina said nervously. "In a nutshell, the FBI found the activator data, along with some other stuff that gave them reason to think I was the person who released the anthrax at San Quentin and killed the whole death row wing."

Jason was immobile.

"I need to ask two favors of you," Katrina continued. "You're the only person I can trust right now."

Without hesitation, Jason asked, "What do you need?"

"First, I need you to give my keynote speech at the convention tomorrow. Obviously, I can't be there. Obviously, the fact that I won't be there because I am in *jail* is going to put a minor wrinkle in my credibility and my career as a scientist. I'm trying like hell to negotiate a release, but it's not looking good. So if I can't be there, I want you to be there. My talk is on the desktop of my computer. If the FBI has confiscated that, you can still find the presentation in the Cloud. You know the password. Give the talk, and do the best you can to control the damage when people start asking questions about why I'm not there. I don't know if it's going to be public by tomorrow that I'm in jail. So far, I don't think the press has caught wind of it."

Katrina paused. "I know this is a lot to ask," she said. "If word gets out about where I am, I'll be crucified at the convention. And you'll be crucified based solely your association with me. So I'm begging you—just do what you can."

To Katrina's surprise, Jason smiled. "Dr. Stone," he said, feigning formality, "as the resident death-metal-head of the SDSU biology department, I'm no stranger to being judged out of context. I'm also no stranger to conflict. I look forward to the convention." His smile widened when he saw the look of gratitude on Katrina's face, and the tear that streaked down her cheek. She gently wiped it away with one forefinger.

"What is the other thing I can do for you?" he asked.

"I need you to look into someone. His name is Oscar Morales. He is a prisoner at San Quentin. The man who attacked me—twice—was his monozygotic twin. I don't know the twin's first name but he had a vial of the Death Row strain of anthrax *on him* when he came after me in the lab.

"I think he was in the lab to poison me with it or just kick my ass, whichever became more convenient. I also think that Oscar had to have been the one on the inside who released the bug in the prison. If you can find out Oscar's story, and who gave it to him, and why, you might be able to save my reputation. And by association, your own."

"My reputation's beyond salvation," Jason said, "but I'll see what I can do."

As Jason was leaving the visiting area of Las Colinas Detention Facility, an FBI forensics researcher at the San Diego headquarters was confirming what Jason had just been told by Katrina. The vial found in Chuck Morales' pocket had been filled with the Death Row anthrax strain.

10:02 A.M. PST

Mr. Gilman -

How unfortunate that you do not speak my language.

The Doctor

In an office of the San Diego FBI headquarters, Sean McMullan and Roger Gilman stared at the Xeroxed copy of the card that had been inadvertently opened by Gilman's wife. And at the copy of a nearly identical version, addressed instead to a "Mr. McMullan," and sent to his personal mailbox.

The original cards were in Dulles, Virginia in the hands of the United States Postal Inspection Service. The fact that the agents had not heard a word from Teresa Wood suggested to them that nothing of value had been found on either card. And Katrina Stone was confessing to nothing.

The image on the front of both cards was the same image as that on the original card that had been mailed to the White House just before the Death Row anthrax attack. It was the crystal structure of anthrax infiltrating a mammalian cell. But the text of the latter cards was not like that of the first. It was written in English, not Arabic.

"*How unfortunate that you do not speak my language,*" Gilman said under his breath, "written in English, as if to make the point. Just when I was starting to think that ISIL was off the hook."

"Maybe it's not ISIL," McMullan said. "Maybe it's another terrorist organization. But what the hell is the connection between *any* terrorist organization and Katrina Stone?"

"I'll give you that," Gilman said. "There most definitely isn't one. If there was, she would never have worked with live anthrax in the first place. She started her own lab after 9/11, which she never could have done with any red flags in place. So if she's made friends with ISIL, she has done it so discreetly that the FBI and Homeland Security had no clue."

A moment later, McMullan changed the subject. "And who the hell is the Doctor?"

Gilman shrugged his shoulders. "Katrina Stone is a doctor."

"Yeah, I realize that. But as you just pointed out, she couldn't possibly have been involved with ISIL, and I'm fairly certain she doesn't speak Arabic."

"*I know!*" Gilman yelled, picking up a paperweight off the desk and throwing it across the office. The paperweight smashed into the wall clock, breaking its face, and then landed with a thud on the thin, worn carpet.

McMullan let out an exasperated sigh, and Gilman sat back down. "Sorry," he said.

McMullan didn't hear. His mind was elsewhere. "Maybe you're onto something, Gilman. Maybe it is a scientist. Maybe it's a doctor. Maybe it's not Stone."

"You *really* want it to not be Stone, don't you?" Gilman said.

"Admittedly, I just don't feel the pieces fit with her, even though they increasingly seem to. But... do you remember what Guofu Wong said a while back? About Johnson."

Gilman looked into his partner's face. "Johnson thought that Stone plagiarized his data," he recalled.

"So he could have motive to frame her," McMullan said.

"But like this? By terrorizing a prison?"

"He, too, is a doctor. And there's something else that fits as well. Johnson is in the FBI. He leads the infectious disease division. He has access to personal information for other agents, and he knows that you and I are the two agents on the case. Johnson has all of the information necessary to be running this show. Katrina Stone doesn't."

Gilman was unconvinced. "With that logic, anyone at the FBI—especially any doctor, could be *this* Doctor."

"Correct," McMullan said, "but not everyone at the FBI has motive to go after Stone."

"So I ask you again, why do you think Johnson would do any of this in the first place? Just to frame Stone? There are a million other things he could do to get even with her besides the anthrax prison attack. Things that would have been a lot simpler. He *is* in the FBI, after all."

McMullan thought for a moment. "Do you remember that first meeting we had about this case? Do you remember how he and Guofu Wong argued about her?"

Gilman cast his mind back to the FBI meeting. "Wong wanted to fund her research and Johnson didn't."

"Yeah, but there was a bigger issue. Wong wanted to fund Stone's research because he thought she could bring some really cutting-edge science to the forefront. Johnson was against the idea just like you were, and for similar reasons.

He believed that scientists needed more time to earn their stripes than she had put in, but like you, he was also really old-fashioned in his thinking. Remember, this is a guy who has been in science since before there were computers. He probably chiseled his Ph.D. thesis on stone tablets. I think that Johnson didn't want Katrina's research to go forward for reasons *other* than just a lack of national funding."

Gilman looked skeptically at his partner's face, which had acquired a renewed enthusiasm as he spoke. "What do you mean?"

"I think," McMullan continued, "that he didn't want her technologies in the mainstream at all. I think he was afraid of what could happen if those technologies became commonplace and fell into the wrong hands.

"So maybe he released the Death Row strain in order to warn us. To show us what her work—those molecular screens she does—can produce. Maybe he knew from her preliminary data that those kinds of activators would be found in those molecular screens. In fact, maybe she even mentioned them in the grant proposal. Maybe he thought he could punish her, *and* stop the technology from going forward at the same time. Maybe he thought the release of the strain was a necessary way to show the world how catastrophic it could be."

10:35 A.M. PST

In the back room of an Army Surplus Store, an Animal Liberation Front officer stopped talking upon hearing a knock on the door. He cast a questioning look around the table. It was met by equally confused glances. The officers were not expecting anyone else. The knock on the door came again, this time, more loudly.

"Yeah?" shouted the officer from inside.

A female voice came through the door. "Code word Lincoln."

"*Shit*," the officer muttered under his breath. And then to the table, "It's Lexi! Cover this shit up!"

The five officers hurried to conceal a floor plan of Katrina Stone's BSL-3 facility. After a cursory glance around the room to confirm that nothing was out of place, the speaker nodded to the boy nearest the door. The boy opened the door, and Alexis Stone entered the room. She was beaming.

"Hi!" Alexis said cheerily to the boy and tried to kiss him.

He pulled away, scowling. "What are you doing here? You know this meeting is officers only."

"You won't be mad when you hear what I'm about to say,"

she said. She was still smiling but now there was hurt behind her eyes.

"OK then," said the leader. "What do you have for us?"

Alexis popped her gum and grinned again. "So I was at my dad's house a while ago, and I was supposed to go back to my mom's tonight. My dad calls me into his bedroom to talk to me. He's all serious. My step-mom is in there, too. They're both, like, totally upset." Another gum pop.

"Cut to the point, Lexi," the leader said.

Alexis sighed. "Fine! OK, so, my dad tells me I can't go back to my mom's house tonight. *Guess why!*"

"I give up," said her annoyed boyfriend.

"Because my mom is in *jail!* She got arrested because they found something on her computer the other day when those FBI guys busted into our house. I don't know what she did, but it must be pretty bad, because I'm supposed to stay at my dad's house, like, sort of indefinitely right now. I think it's something having to do with her work. So maybe she won't be able to finish the monkey studies she's been doing! Maybe she'll have to let the monkeys go!"

The leader exchanged a glance with Alexis' boyfriend and then asked, "Aren't you the least bit worried about your mom?"

"Oh, God no," she said. "Whatever my mom did, it's her own fault! Besides, she's a heartless, hard-assed bitch! I'm sure she'll be fine! It's the monkeys I'm worried about! *They're* the ones who can't defend themselves!"

For a moment, nobody spoke. Finally, the lead officer said, "Lexi, can you give us a moment to talk amongst ourselves?"

Alexis looked thrilled to have been asked, rather than ordered out of the room. "Sure!" she said and skipped out the door.

"I told you we can trust her," the boyfriend said when she was gone.

"I'm inclined to agree with young Kevin here," the leader concurred. The others agreed. And there was so much more that Alexis could do for them. When Alexis re-entered the room, the leader sat her down. "We weren't going to tell you this because we weren't sure you could be trusted. No offense, but it *is* your mom. Anyway, what you just told us gave us confidence that we can let you in on the rest of our plans. When you and Kevin are at the biotech convention tomorrow, there will be a group breaking into Katrina's BSL-3 facility. We're going to free the uninfected monkeys. You and Kevin will be keeping the press and the scientists occupied in the meantime, and drumming up a bit of controversy over your mom's work."

Alexis thought for a moment, and then looked accusingly at Kevin. "I can't believe you didn't think you could trust me with that! Of *course* I'm happy to help you free the monkeys! Then, we just carry on with the plans like we said?"

Kevin looked at her warily, but felt relieved. She would get over her offense at his lack of faith in her. And, more importantly, she was on board. "Yeah, you and I just go down there like we planned," he said. "These guys have everything else taken care of already."

"So, really, it doesn't even matter that she's in jail," Alexis said with disappointment.

"Oh, yes it does," said the leader, smiling. He turned to Kevin, and said, "Call the media."

McMullan walked into a private consultation room, and Katrina glared when she saw him.

"If I wasn't in handcuffs, I'd punch you," she said.

McMullan dismissed the jail guard with a gesture and a flash of his FBI badge. Before the guard left the room, McMullan confiscated his keys. Then, he removed Katrina's cuffs.

She struck him in the jaw—hard—with a closed fist.

McMullan took the blow. "Fair enough." An angry, swelling welt began rising. He ran his tongue over his teeth and the inner lip. "But now, start talking."

"You've got to get me out of here. I'm supposed to be talking at the biotechnology convention tomorrow, first thing in the morning. If I'm not there because I'm in jail, my career is over. You know this. You know how hard I've worked for this career. You know that without it, I have nothing. And you also know that I'm innocent."

"What makes you say that?"

"Because you're here."

McMullan sighed. "I can't possibly get you out of here," he said. "The evidence against you is too strong. So it's irrelevant what I think." He paused. "Explain something to me in lay terms, Katrina. How and *why* did you make that activator? And why in God's name did you *hide* it from us? From *me*? What was your role? What was Jason Fischer's role? We've already gathered that the data was from his notes."

"OK," she said. "Listen, McMullan. I wish you had your infectious disease experts here right now. They would back up the science of what I'm saying."

"Well, then you won't mind my recording this conversation and playing it back for them?" he said and clicked into the voice-recording app on his cell phone.

"Jason and I *did* make the activator."

McMullan stared at her without speaking.

"It was an accident," Katrina said. "Look McMullan, you know that my research involves screening for inhibitors of anthrax lethal factor. We have a very simple enzymatic assay. We program the robots, and the robots run hundreds of thousands of molecules through that assay. Inhibitors are found because the assay produces a fluorescent signal. When an inhibitor is in the mix, the signal is decreased. That's all there is to it.

"Sometimes the assay can pick up activators as well. It's not like we are looking for them—they just pop up. We see them in our data because all of a sudden, there's an *increase* in the fluorescence produced by the assay when that particular molecule is tested.

"Activators are rare. But yeah, in hundreds of thousands of molecules screened, we do find a few. Jason found one a while back that was exceptionally good. He brought the data to me and asked me what to do with it. I told him to just hang on to it."

"Why?" McMullan asked. "Why would you want to keep it, and more importantly, why did you try to hide it from us only to dig it out later?"

"I kept it because activators of an enzyme can be changed to convert them into an inhibitor. And I convinced Jason to help me hide the data because I knew that an activated strain of anthrax had been discovered. And we wanted to avoid this exact scenario—our lab being linked to that strain. And I dug it out to get rid of it when I didn't think we needed it anymore.

"There are monkeys in our BSL-3 facility being inoculated as we speak. Those monkeys will be given the drug that we've redesigned since Christmas. I'm confident that it will work this time—so confident, in fact, that I've already scaled up the production of it. We've got a shitload of this drug. It's the right one. I know it is."

McMullan smiled. Even with her career and life falling apart around her, she was still focused on the cure. But then his smile faded. "I want to believe you," he said. "But we still have a problem, Katrina. The DNA sequence is the same. The Death Row strain of anthrax doesn't just have an activator in it. It has *your* activator in it."

PART III: CON SCIENCE

Jason Fischer stepped into Katrina Stone's SDSU laboratory on the first day of the biotechnology convention. He had expected the lab to be abandoned, all of its normal occupants already en route to the convention. Instead, he was greeted by Joshua Attle, who was working frantically at a lab bench. "Hey, what are you still doing here?" Jason asked.

"I'm just getting an experiment going, and then I'm getting down to the convention," Josh said. "What are *you* doing here?"

"I've got to get something off Katrina's computer." Jason walked through the main laboratory space and into Katrina's office. He jumped when he saw Roger Gilman sitting behind her desk. "Jesus Christ, you scared the shit out of me."

"A little jumpy, Dr. Fischer?" Gilman asked.

Jason ignored him. "Look, dude," he said. "I need to get on that computer. So you mind moving your pudgy ass out of my way for a minute?"

"Actually, I do," said Gilman. "I'm taking this computer. Sorry." He feigned a sad face.

"I can get what I need off the Cloud, douchebag, so why don't you just make it easier and move?"

Gilman scoffed. "Fine." He stood from the desk and moved to a chair across the office. Then he changed the subject. "You and your advisor have a pretty close relationship, don't you, Jason?"

Jason sat down at the computer monitor and began browsing. "Um, yeah," he responded absently. "I guess so... we've been working together for years." He found the file of Katrina's presentation on her computer desktop and opened it, then scrolled quickly through the slides. Satisfied that the presentation was intact, he closed the file again and saved it to a portable memory stick, which he popped out and dropped into his pocket.

As he stood up, Jason was overwhelmed by a dizzy spell. He placed both hands onto the desk and stood quietly for a moment until it passed. A fever was coming on. Again. When he was certain he could walk normally, he brushed past Roger Gilman and walked out into the hall.

Gilman followed. "You're looking a little unwell," he said loudly as he walked closely behind Jason out of the office and toward the door to exit the laboratory. "Another impending herpes outbreak? You gotta watch out for those groupies, you know." Gilman clicked his tongue and turned to Josh as he spoke, who had looked up at the goading remarks and was now gaping, slack-jawed, back at Gilman. Gilman grinned at him, and Josh shook his head and returned to his work.

Jason stopped walking and turned. He walked back

toward Gilman and stood inches from his face, his chest puffed out, his jaw working, his fists coiled.

Josh slipped quietly out of the laboratory.

Gilman recoiled as if preparing for a blow.

Jason only smiled. "Have you figured out yet that Oscar Morales spent six months as a research assistant in biology?" he asked.

Gilman paled. *"What? Where? When?"*

Jason stepped backward. Still smiling, he ignored Gilman's question and turned to glance at his own reflection in the glass of one of the laboratory's cold cabinets. He reached into the pocket of his pants and found a small band, with which he tied back his shoulder-length hair, smoothing the sides and the top until he was satisfied with it. "How do I look?" he asked, batting his eyelashes dramatically.

The truth was that he looked strikingly handsome and unusually professional. In contrast to his normal attire of ragged blue jeans, black t-shirts with band logos, and combat boots, Jason was currently dressed in a suit and tie. His loafers looked as if they had never before been worn. The fever Jason was battling lent a hint of color to his normally vampire-pale cheeks. The result was a healthy-looking glow on a face that rarely saw daylight. With his jet-black hair clean, combed, and now tied back at the nape of his neck, Jason looked every bit the respectable scientist.

Gilman only stared.

"Huh?" Jason said then. "Oh, yeah, that! Morales. Research assistant. Biology. Yeah." Another long pause. "He was at UCLA in the lab of Qiang Zhao ten years ago. Even got himself co-authored on a paper once. He was fourth author, but still—it was him! His job was to make solutions and reagents, clean glassware, do literature searches for people, maintain cell lines, that sort of thing. He would have learned how to sustain a culture of bacteria, and he would have learned sterile technique. And those are the exact skills one would need to contain and distribute anthrax.

"But then I guess he decided that dealing drugs was a better way to make money. And frankly, he's right. This career pays for shit. Morales must be smarter than I am."

Gilman had lost his spunk. "How do you know all that?" he asked miserably.

"Because one of us is actually a competent investigator. And let me give you *another* hint, Gilman. It's not you." Jason turned on the heels of his polished loafers and trotted cheerfully out of the lab.

10:42 A.M. EST

On the other side of the country, Teresa Wood was preparing an ESDA analysis. This time, the experiment would be performed on two greeting cards instead of one.

With gloved hands, she pulled both cards from their respective sealed envelopes and placed them onto the vacuum. She laid a clear, thin film over each card and watched the vacuum suck it down. She held the corona wire over each card independently to deposit the appropriate negative charge to its surface. And in the same order, to maintain her time frame, she filled the indentations with the tiny, toner-covered glass beads. The hand-written text intensified. And then, the traces became visible.

The procedure was one Teresa had performed a thousand times. She was always pleased to find a hidden indentation of some kind in a piece of mail. Usually, it was just a fragment of something. The circle of a keychain, adjacent to a partial indentation from a key itself. A dent from a piece of jewelry or a button from an article of clothing. A change in depth or pressure in a line of text, indicating that the document had been altered after its initial generation. When an ESDA trace produced a new writing, the task was even more cryptic, and even more rewarding to solve. Rarely were more than a few words revealed—a fragment of text copied onto another piece of paper over the questioned document.

This time, Teresa could barely process the information that came to light as each tiny bead occupied its own cavity in the two greeting cards. As the trace became increasingly visible, Teresa's breath caught in her throat and she began to shiver. It was unlike anything she had ever seen before in an ESDA.

One card was devoid of trace indentations. The other contained an entirely new text. The writing was in English. It was as clear as the original text on the surface. It had obviously been etched deliberately for the ESDA trace to reveal. And it was addressed to Teresa by name.

7:58 A.M. PST

The crowd that greeted Jason Fischer in downtown San Diego was wildly larger than he had imagined it would be. And it was hostile. Even though the convention center was still several blocks away, clashing lines of biotechnology supporters and protesters stretched down 4th Avenue and spilled into the horizon of Horton Plaza to the right of Jason's ancient, struggling car. *Damn, I wish my band could draw like this*, Jason thought as he turned left onto 4th Avenue off of F Street.

Jason stopped at a red light and offered a distracted middle finger to a college-aged group dressed as monarch butterflies and bearing signs that read "Biotech is Murder" and "Kill the NIH." As he did, one of the protestors leaped onto the hood of his car. It occurred to the young scientist that the gradually unraveling Darwin fish on his bumper would probably not be very popular among some here.

"You people are destroying the earth!" the man on the windshield screamed, and a fine spray of spittle splattered from his mouth onto the glass directly in front of Jason. Without breaking the man's rabid gaze, Jason smiled sweetly

and turned on his windshield wipers, smearing dirt and saliva onto his attacker's waiting hand, which was promptly retracted.

Before Jason could decide what to do about the angry tree-hugger beating at his windshield, a peace officer in full SWAT attire parted the human wall lining the street and jerked the youngster by the shirt collar. The pair pulled free of Jason's car just as the light turned green, and Jason crept into the grid-locked intersection. He watched as the cop gripped the protestor by the nape of the neck and roughly pulled him away from the crowd.

Inching forward, Jason turned right onto Market Street off of 4th Avenue, and the pedestrian traffic thickened. As he turned left onto Front Street and again onto Harbor Drive, it became asphyxiating. Harbor Drive ran parallel to the San Diego Bay. And over the bay hovered the San Diego Convention Center.

As Jason pulled parallel to the complex, his mouth ran dry and he sucked air in abruptly. The reflex launched a short but violent coughing fit, and the fever that Jason had been fighting all morning felt as if it had intensified instantaneously. It had just become clear that the public was, indeed, aware of Katrina Stone's arrest.

No less than a thousand of the protestors lining Harbor Drive were dressed identically, in black-and-white-striped "prisoner" Halloween costumes. Behind them, a long banner stretching down Harbor Drive read "This is the Ethics of Science." Several of the individuals held smaller signs with a simpler message: "Stone Stone."

The protestors were feverishly chanting, and out of morbid curiosity, Jason cracked his window in order to make out the words. "Eye for eye! Bone for bone! Execute Katrina Stone!"

Interspersed among the sea of black and white stripes were representatives from every television network Jason had ever heard of. As he continued his slow progress down the street in unison with the other cars, he could catch fragments of the interviews that were being conducted with bystanders.

"... serves her right! These scientists think they're God... "

"... nothing short of a self-righteous, over-educated, home-grown terrorist!"

"I say she's a hero!"

Jason slammed on his brakes when he heard the surprising last statement. He rolled his window the rest of the way down and then engaged his parking brake. Then he shoved his head out the window, scanning the crowd to look for the speaker.

"How many times have we all wanted to do the same thing?" the voice continued, and Jason located a tall, good-looking young man speaking into a microphone with a large square announcing "News 10" on its handle. A cameraman faithfully recorded.

"I say it's about time the scientists stopped doing research on helpless, innocent animals, and started letting convicted murderers and rapists finally make a positive contribution to society," the boy continued. "It's the ideal justice. The killers on death row have had their chance at life, liberty, and the pursuit of happiness. They chose to give up that chance when they chose to commit whatever hideous crime landed them on death row. There are too many of them, and they're living like kings on our money.

"Did you know that prison inmates are not allowed generic prescriptions? Brand name only. Does your HMO have that rule? I didn't think so. It's high time our death row prisoners *earn* those prescriptions and help science to develop the drugs that benefit them. Let's stop paying those people to avoid the death sentence that has already been handed down to them. Let's instead use that death sentence to free the innocent animals."

The shocked reporter stammered a bit as he said, "thank—thank you very much for that, uh, interesting, piece of insight, Mr... "

"Stein," the boy said calmly. "Kevin Stein."

Beside him, a petite girl with auburn hair stood beaming, her arm laced through his. Her deep maroon suit contrasted sharply with the wall of black and white behind her. Jason recognized the suit; it was one Katrina had worn to several conferences in the past. And there was no mistaking the relation between this girl and Jason's postdoctoral advisor.

"And you, miss?" the reporter asked, pressing the microphone toward the girl's small chin.

"Alexis Stone," she said, smiling. "Dr. Katrina Stone is my mother."

The revelation turned other heads in her direction and in a quick commotion, additional microphones were thrust forward to join that of the 10 News reporter. Several questions were blurted out at once at the girl.

"Is your mother guilty?"

"How much do you know about Dr. Stone's illegal activities?"

"What do you think of your mother's decision to disregard the law and conduct scientific research according to her own personal code of ethics?"

"Or lack thereof?"

The cars behind Jason's Honda Accord had begun to honk loudly, but he paid them no attention as he strained to lean forward in anticipation. Katrina's smile. Katrina's eyes. Clearly, Katrina's intelligence. All shone through as she glanced patiently from one reporter to the next. She had them in the palm of her hand, and she knew it. They would wait all night to hear what Katrina's daughter had to say.

"I don't know if she did it or not," Alexis finally said, and a collective, frustrated sigh resounded from the other side of the cameras. "But I hope she did."

The sighs changed to gasps.

"All my life," she explained, "I have considered my mother a mass murderer. Hundreds—*thousands*—of mice, rats, and even *monkeys* have been tortured and killed to further her work and the work of other scientists. They have excused this practice by swearing that there was *no other way*.

"If my mother did what she is currently being charged for, then I couldn't be prouder. Because she *found* another way, and she had the guts to show it to the rest of the world regardless of what it would do to her own career. If she did this, she martyred herself for the world's most noble cause. I just hope the scientific and legal communities will follow her lead."

"And what if she didn't do it?" shouted a reporter.

The smile on Lexi's face morphed into a cynical smirk. "Well, then, she's just an animal killer without any justifiable cause."

Alexis looked to her boyfriend, and he nodded his approval. The interviewers continued to shout questions, but Kevin waved them away. He wrapped an arm protectively around Alexis. It was clear that he considered the interview over for the both of them.

Jason rolled up his window and disengaged his emergency brake, and then rolled forward.

For the first time ever, Teresa felt stifled and claustrophobic in her office at the United States Postal Inspection Service national headquarters. And for the first time that the brassy Navy veteran could recall, she was trembling in terror as she examined the printout in front of her.

An identical visual was on the monitor of Teresa's computer, scanned from the ESDA trace she had just performed in the lab. Just as the message had, in fact, predicted, Teresa was holding a phone to her ear, desperately wishing for someone to pick up at the other end.

The handwritten text was tiny. It completely covered both inner surfaces of a folded greeting card. Even so, the message barely fit. The Doctor had a great deal to say.

Shame on you, Teresa, for you have failed.
The convention has begun, and sadly, I must
explain myself. From my vantage point within
Operation Death Row, I see clearly that my

message might never be deciphered. And your
time for deciphering it has expired.

As you read this, thousands at the convention
collaborate for a common cause. These efforts
will make them thirsty, and they will drink
water to quench that thirst. Later, they will
realize that they are the chosen prophets.
They will writhe and moan and eventually
understand. They will see the short-sightedness
of their actions. They will beg forgiveness.
When this dirty business has run its course,
and I have been martyred for a cause you
can never appreciate any other way, you will
thank me. Because the path of our society, so
wrongly paved, will finally be corrected.

I have given you more than sufficient
time. As I had predicted, you wasted that
time. Fascinating that none of you could
understand the Doctor.

Very shortly, McMullan and Gilman will
receive frantic phone calls from you, Teresa.
They will race to the convention center. Like
you, they have already failed. You all share
a common fatal flaw. You do not speak my
language. Shame on you. The Doctor

When Sean McMullan cleared security and entered her cellblock at Las Colinas Detention Facility, Katrina was pacing her cell like a caged animal. Her surprise to see him quickly turned to shock as he approached. Beneath his leathery tan, McMullan's face was a ghastly, bloodless shade of whitish yellow.

"What are you doing here?" she asked through the bars of the cell. Wordlessly, he reached into his pocket and removed a key ring, found the appropriate key, and unlocked the cell door.

She only looked at him questioningly. She stood dumbfounded while he entered the cell and produced his handcuffs, linking them around her wrists, but leaving them loose enough to be comfortable.

Neither spoke as McMullan led Katrina through the cellblock, her hands cuffed behind her back. He signed the appropriate transfer paperwork and collected her belongings, and then she was free.

As they drove away from the county jail, he unclipped the handcuff key from his key chain and handed it to her. She unlocked the cuffs and dropped them into the center console of McMullan's sedan.

✖

"Well?" Katrina said at last.

McMullan took a moment to carefully select his words. It would take approximately twenty minutes to get downtown to the convention. Not much time to bring Katrina up to speed. And to find out what else she had been lying about. "Explain something to me," he finally asked. "How could your inhibitors block the Death Row strain of anthrax without being designed against it?"

"Because they block both normal and Death Row anthrax. My team designed the inhibitors against normal anthrax. It's a fortunate coincidence that they bind the Death Row strain. The original inhibitors that were in my grant application provided the starting point that I used in designing the final antidote."

Her explanation was consistent with the opinions of Johnson and Wong. But McMullan was still not reassured of her innocence. "Have you ever reviewed an NIH grant written by a researcher named James Johnson?" he asked then.

"No," she answered without hesitating.

"How can you be so sure?"

Katrina looked sideways at McMullan. His eyes were straight ahead as he drove. "Johnson is a legend in the field of infectious diseases," she said. "I would remember reviewing one of his grants."

McMullan hoped his frustration was not showing through to the woman next to him. Her answers were only raising more questions. If she was lying, she *could* be guilty of plagiarizing Johnson's data. If she was telling the truth, then

Johnson's motive for framing Katrina in the Death Row anthrax attacks was an illusion.

He took another approach. "I have to ask you a hypothetical question about research grants. What would happen if a reviewer got an idea for work he wanted to do by reading someone else's grant application? Could the reviewer steal the idea?"

Katrina took a moment to respond. "Well, to alter one's entire research program based on something you've read in a grant application is probably pretty stupid. For one thing, the researcher proposing the studies in an application would already be set up to conduct those studies. Frequently, he would have already begun and completed some of the work, but he would have held off on including information that is still too preliminary in a grant application. So, if you tried to beat him to the punch, you'd lose—especially if he was well funded and you were not."

Why did she say that? Why did she even think *of that?* McMullan took a deep breath. "But what if you got the funding and the other researcher didn't?" he asked. "Or, what if you *were* already set up to do the work, and you could just alter your program slightly based on his idea?"

She shrugged. "I guess if you were already funded and set up, you could scoop someone else's idea. And then it would come down to 'first-to-file' law: whoever files the patent first gets the intellectual property, regardless of whose idea it really was. Why? What are you getting at?"

"Never mind."

"No!" she snapped. "You're asking me these questions for a reason, and I want to know what it is!"

McMullan sighed. He had just broken a federal prisoner out of jail under a false pretense—without the approval, or even the knowledge, of his partner on the case. But he could no longer trust Gilman. Gilman had his own agenda. He could no longer trust Johnson. Johnson, most certainly, had his own agenda. He didn't even know for certain that he could trust Wong or Wood. McMullan was out of allies in the FBI.

But he needed Katrina for his next move, and one thing was certain. If the Doctor was telling the truth—if the water supply at the biotechnology convention had really been poisoned—Katrina Stone was the *one* person who could not have done it. She had been in jail the entire time.

"Ah, hell," he said, and pulled a folded, two-sided sheet of paper from his pocket. He handed it to her, and while he drove, Katrina began to read.

"The front of that page is the Xerox of a *second* greeting card from our perp," McMullan said. "I got one copy and Gilman got one copy. The back side is the trace writing that was picked up by the ESDA trace our postal inspector did. It seems to be a message from the person who is orchestrating this whole thing."

She read the text on the front of the page, flipped it over, and read the reverse. "Oh my god!" she yelled suddenly. "They're going to poison the water supply at the convention!"

"I know, we've gotten that much," he said. "The rest is still a bit of a mystery."

"You don't understand!" Katrina shrieked. *"My daughter is down there!"*

The press had finally given up and moved on. Kevin picked Alexis up by the waist and swung her around in the crowd. Alexis burst into giggles.

"You did *awesome*, baby!" He planted a hard kiss on her mouth.

"Damn, that felt great," she said. "Talk about finally getting to speak my mind about my mother's work!"

Around them, several Animal Liberation Front members in black-and-white-striped costumes cheered and slapped high fives. Occasionally, someone would lean in to pat Alexis or Kevin on the back and offer congratulations.

"I'm glad we went with the jailbird angle," Alexis said, trying to calm down a little. "I think it really got their attention."

"I have to concur," Kevin said jovially. "Hey, I'm going to call our people at the labs and see how everyone is doing."

"OK," Lexi said. "I have to pee. Too much excitement!"

"Use the bathroom in the convention center," Kevin ordered. "And when you're inside, listen up to whatever conversations you can catch. I want to know if everything going on out here is being brought in there."

"Cool," Lexi said. "Be right back! And while I'm in there, maybe I'll pepper spray some scientists!" She sprang toward him for one last kiss before dashing off into the crowd.

𝕏

Alexis was still smiling from ear to ear as she trotted toward the entrance of the convention center off of Harbor Avenue. Her smile faded when she was stopped.

"Badge?" the convention attendant asked curtly.

Alexis looked around. At that moment, she realized that everyone entering the convention center had an ID Badge pinned to his or her chest. *Shit*, she thought. *I should have known.* "Oh," she said aloud, "I left my badge with one of my colleagues inside. Maybe I can just pop in and grab her?"

"Sorry ma'am. You can't get in without it. It costs hundreds of dollars to attend this event. We can't just let anyone in off the street."

"Look at me!" Alexis argued. "Do I look like just anyone off the street?"

"No ma'am," the man said. "Nonetheless, I'm sorry. I can't let you through. Perhaps you can phone your colleague inside?"

Lexi's face lit up as an idea came to her. "I've tried calling," she said. "Unfortunately, my colleague's cell phone isn't getting signal with all the activity at the convention." *Thanks, Mom, for being so perpetually hard to get a hold of.*

𝕏

The convention attendant looked the young woman up and down for a moment. It was true; people were constantly complaining about that problem. Nobody's phone ever picked up reception in the convention center. Still, the boss would have his hide if he started letting people in without

320

badges. And this girl, while dressed professionally, looked to be about sixteen years old. What was she doing here?

While the attendant was debating whether or not to bend the rule, a man in a navy blue suit approached. Unlike the young woman in front of him, this man was clearly old enough to have business here. More importantly, he bore the required badge.

"Did you leave your pass inside again, Doctor?" the man asked the girl.

She looked up at him and smiled. "Yes, and I don't know what to do," she said. Then she leaned in and lowered her voice to say, "and to be honest with you, I *really* have to use the restroom!"

The man looked toward the attendant and said, "Sir, surely you can let my colleague use the restroom and retrieve her badge. She really is a well-known scientist at this event. I will promise to take responsibility for her."

The conference attendant shook his head and took one more glance at the man's badge before waving them through.

Oscar Morales stepped into a room and sat down behind a metal barrier. His privilege to use the open visiting room had now been revoked, ever since he attacked a young woman inside it and had to be forcibly subdued.

"Who the fuck are you?" he asked. It was becoming a familiar greeting for Oscar, who, as of late had been visited by a number of strangers, each with his or her own questions. This time, it was a squat, balding man in a wrinkled pair of slacks. The man's button-down shirt was unbuttoned at the top, his tie loosely hanging from his neck. He looked exhausted and cross.

"Federal Agent Roger Gilman," Oscar's visitor replied and flashed an FBI badge.

Oscar stood to leave the room. "I'm not talking to you pigs," he said over his shoulder.

"Don't you want to know how your brother is doing?" Gilman shouted after him.

Oscar turned back around. He sat down and glared at

the FBI agent through the barrier. "You're keeping tabs on my brother?"

"Yes sir," Gilman responded. "And on the woman who burned your brother's face off. And, as a matter of fact, on you. A fledgling biologist turned imprisoned bioterrorist? Yes sir, Mr. Morales, you are someone we now have a great deal of interest in."

"I'm still not talking to you. Show me that Chuck is OK."

"He's fine. Feeling pretty good, actually. Morphine can do wonders for one's mood. But I'm sure you know that, given your long and lustrous career as a drug dealer." Gilman shook his head dramatically. "You know, Morales, I'd love to say you should have stuck to biology. But as it turns out, you might still have ended up here. Looks like some of your former colleagues in the field certainly will."

"What do you want with me?" Oscar asked.

"Like I said, your brother is feeling pretty nice these days. He's awake, and of course he's stoned on morphine pretty constantly. It's made him remarkably talkative. Chuck says you carried out the biological terror attack that took place in this prison back in October. He says you orchestrated the whole thing from inside here.

"Your brother also says you're now responsible for a second attack that's in progress in San Diego even as we speak. To be frank, Mr. Morales, your brother's gab is about to land you on death row. So I'm just here to get your side of the story."

Oscar listened intently to the smug agent in front of him. *Second attack?* "My brother wouldn't rat on me," he said calmly. "And as for a second attack, I don't know anything about it. Obviously, I didn't do it. I'm in here."

"Sound logic," Gilman said, "except that we have two

vials of the anthrax you gave your brother." He paused and grinned, as if for effect. "Guess what I learned today, Oscar? I just learned today that identical twins don't have identical fingerprints, even though they have identical DNA. It was your prints on the vials, my friend. Not Chuck's. Yours."

Oscar slammed his fists against the metal barrier. *"Chuck was the one you caught with the anthrax!"* he roared. "Fuckin' baby never could take care of himself!"

He paused to think before saying, now calmly, "If my prints are on those vials, there was probably something else in them when I had my hands on them. I don't know what the fuck my brother did. I'm only in here in the first place because of Chuck. I took the fall for him years ago, and now he's expecting me to do it again. Well, not this time. Fuck him. I'll give him up. I'll tell you everything you want to know. But I want my sentence reduced in return."

"Can I get that in writing?" Gilman asked with a smile.

"Hell, yeah."

But instead of producing a pen and paper, Gilman shouted back over his shoulder. "Did you catch all that, Chuck?"

"It's so obvious," Katrina said.

McMullan braked to slow his sedan as the eastbound 94 freeway came to a dead end in downtown San Diego. "What's so obvious?" For the last five minutes, neither he nor Katrina had spoken. She had been reading and re-reading the second greeting card.

"The language he keeps referring to," she said, "the language that none of you speak."

"We thought at first it was Arabic. Remember, the first card was written in Arabic. We were looking at ISIL and some of the other Arabic terrorist organizations. Nothing panned out."

"It's not Arabic," Katrina said. "It's science. This man is a scientist. He's frustrated that you aren't fluent in science."

"What makes you say that?" McMullan asked.

"The fact that he put a crystal structure on all three of these cards. He handed you the fact that anthrax was the weapon of choice. He knew from the beginning that the image on the front was the only definitive link between the greeting card and the attack at San Quentin.

"He was making a point that you missed the significance of the image and wasted time because you don't 'speak' science. To drive it home, the second cards say, 'it's unfortunate that you don't speak my language.' And, I gotta hand it to the Doctor. He's right. If you're still looking at Arabic, your heads are up your asses. The language is science."

Katrina took a breath and continued. "He chastises you again for not understanding him. Again, heads up your asses. No offense."

"None taken," McMullan said, but he could feel himself flushing slightly. "But why would he carry out the attack on a prison?"

"He wanted to see if his weapon would work. And, truth being told, that was really the best way, from a scientific point of view. There is only so much we can decipher from animal studies. The only way to really measure the effects of a drug—or a biological weapon, for that matter—on humans, is to test it in humans. He wanted to test his weapon on humans, and he thought the prison was a good place for the experiment to be conducted. I assume he reasoned that the only loss of life was sixty-eight inmates who had already been condemned to die anyway."

"Creepy, but logical," McMullan said and then hastily, "put that away!"

Katrina shoved the computer printout into the glove compartment as McMullan's black sedan rolled into the circus surrounding the convention center.

"OK then, Doctor, here's another dumb question," McMullan said. "Why in the *hell*, if he's a scientist, would he come out here and poison a bunch of other scientists?"

Katrina shook her head. "To eliminate the competition

for funding?" She half chuckled, expecting McMullan to do the same.

Instead, he jerked toward her, eyes blazing. "*I think you're right!*" he yelled.

"Sean, that's insane," Katrina said. "I was kidding."

"Yeah, but you don't know the whole story! This is the reason for all the questions I was asking you earlier. You didn't answer the *real* question, but then again, I didn't exactly ask it." He slammed on the emergency brake and turned in his bucket seat to look Katrina directly in the eye. Then he took both of her wrists into his hand to monitor her pulse as he spoke.

"Katrina, I want to know the truth. Did you, or did you not, plagiarize the grant application of James Johnson? And before you answer, remember I'm an FBI agent. I know liars. Even good ones."

Katrina looked shocked. "*No!*" she said. "What are you *talking* about?"

"James Johnson is an NIH funded anthrax researcher, as you know. He's also one of the FBI infectious disease specialists on this case. Guofu Wong, the other one, says that Johnson has accused you of plagiarizing his research for your own work. Moreover, Johnson is very old-school. He's very much against the technology that you are bringing to the forefront. Wong is in favor of it. He wanted to fund your application a year ago, the one that was rejected by the NIH. In fact, it was rejected largely because of Johnson's influence on the reviewing committee.

"The message from the Doctor says that our society is 'short-sighted.' That we are heading down the wrong path. That these attacks are the only way for us to realize this, and that he—the Doctor himself—will be a martyr for this cause.

"I think that Johnson is responsible for these attacks. I think he poisoned those prisoners as a test run, and I think he's poisoning the scientists at the convention today to punish modern biotechnology as an institution and to lead 'us,' society, down what he considers the 'right path'—that path being his way, the old-school way. I think he set you up as a scapegoat to punish *you* for plagiarizing his work, because you represent the modern. And I think the attacks on you by Chuck Morales were also his doing.

"And yes, I think you're innocent. But do me a favor, Katrina, and help me prove it. Because otherwise, to be honest, I'm just as fucked as you are."

Katrina listened to McMullan's hypothesis, taking in each statement in sequence. He was right. It all made sense. Every piece of the puzzle fit with Johnson. She suddenly felt carsick.

She rolled down the sedan's passenger window, and the car was flooded with screaming from the chaos in the street. As her eyes scanned the crowd, she remembered Alexis and began scanning for her. It was like looking for a needle in a haystack. A short needle. She might never find her here.

"Where are Johnson and Wong now?" she asked weakly.

"Actually," McMullan said, as if realizing it for the first time, "they're here. Both of them registered months ago to attend the convention."

9:01 A.M. PST

As her new friend led her past the convention attendant and into the main foyer, Alexis nonchalantly asked, "So who are you?"

"I'm a friend of your mother's," he said with a smile. "Glad you could join us today. I'm sure she'll be happy to have your support."

Alexis looked up into his face. He was smiling kindly. *He has no idea*, she thought.

"Well, thank you for getting me in," she said. "I'll have to get my badge from my mom as soon as I hit the ladies' room."

"This way," he led, pointing to a sign marking the nearest restroom. "I think I'll head to the little boys' room myself."

As she reached for the door to the women's room, and the stranger started into the men's room, Alexis thanked him again and half-waved. Once inside, she let the door swing shut behind her and approached the nearest stall.

As she pushed the stall door open and turned around to close it behind her, Alexis barely had time to process the blurred image in the bathroom mirror.

A staccato scream escaped her throat, and then he was on top of her.

In a no-contact visiting area of San Quentin State Correctional Facility, an FBI agent whom Oscar Morales had just met opened the door behind him. Oscar suddenly felt weak and sick when a freakish remnant of a human being shuffled into the room.

Chuck's face was halfway covered with tattered gauze bandages caked with dried blood. Visions of the areas still exposed would haunt his brother for the rest of his life.

The skin that had been smooth and brown was now a patchwork of various blacks and reds. It was thick and hard and just beginning to twist into the creased, plastic shell of the severely burned. Chuck's single exposed eye cavity was empty; the eye had been seared inward, and remnants of vitreous humor were glued within the cavity in a molten mass. It looked like a charred egg white.

When the FBI agent reached forward and guided Chuck into the room by one elbow, Oscar realized that his brother would require such assistance forever. Chuck was blind.

In sharp contrast to his disfigured face, Chuck's body was relatively intact. A noteworthy exception was a walking cast on one leg that extended from the foot upward to Chuck's knee. With one hand, Chuck carefully maneuvered a cane, repositioning it with each slow step to minimize the weight endured by the leg that had been kicked hard enough by a woman in a lab to fracture the tibia.

Gently, almost tenderly, the FBI agent helped Chuck to ease into the chair across from Oscar. At close range, Oscar could see that it was a struggle for Chuck to breathe through nostrils that were melted shut and a mouth that was barely recognizable. The sickly, labored rhythm was the only sound in the room until Chuck spoke to his brother.

With considerable effort, he whispered, *"You're dead."*

✹

Roger Gilman pulled up a chair next to the now-less-attractive twin and watched the exchange between the brothers with amused interest. *Go ahead, string each other up*, he thought.

Chuck turned to Gilman and motioned as if he was writing, and Gilman realized that speaking was too difficult for him. "You want something to write with?" he asked. "Sure, let's see here... " He rifled through his briefcase and found a pen and his own notepad, half filled with messages to himself. He found a section of blank pages and tore a few of them out. He placed the paper and pen on the small table in front of Chuck.

"OSCARS A FUCKIN LIAR," Chuck wrote in large block lettering, and then picked up the page and slammed it up against the chain link divider for his brother to see.

"*Hermanito*," Oscar said quietly. "I can't believe what that bitch did to you. She'll pay for this if it's the last thing I do."

But Chuck did not even answer. Instead, he leaned forward and scribbled frantically while the two other men patiently waited. When he was finished, he groped to his side until he located Roger Gilman, and then shoved the page toward him. When Gilman took the page, Chuck stood, leaning heavily on his cane, and turned to walk back in the direction he had come. He found the wall, felt alongside it for the door, and left the room without another gesture in the direction of his brother.

Gilman watched him go, and then looked down at the page in his hands. It read: "I wasnt even ever here b4 the attak. Oscar planed it with the bitch. He called me later. He paid me to kill her. Chek the vidios. I wasnt here."

Gilman looked up from the note and smiled through the barrier at Oscar.

"Your brother says San Quentin surveillance will clear this whole thing up," he said casually.

9:04 A.M. PST

In a private room at the San Diego Convention Center, two scientists were engaged in a heated argument. One of them was young Jason Fischer. The other was the red-faced chair of the first session of the biotechnology convention.

"Just who do you think you are, you *narcissistic, arrogant ass!*" Jason was saying. "You can't *forbid* me to speak! You're a *mediator!* You're not a policeman and you're not God or even the pope, and you have no more authority here than my *mother.*"

"Look, son," said the chair with aggravation. "I arrived here this morning with a predetermined agenda. On that agenda was an introduction for the keynote speaker. The keynote speaker was Katrina Stone.

"I have a lovely—highly complimentary, I must say—breakdown of her scientific career committed to memory, waiting patiently for me to relay it to the audience. Nowhere in the woman's curriculum vitae does it say that she can't come to the podium because she's locked up in the slammer. To introduce another scientist on her behalf at this moment is impossible. It would turn this entire event into a bigger freak show than it already is, and I won't have a mockery made of this convention. Not to mention that *you,* Dr. Fischer, will be crucified. You should thank me for putting my foot down."

"Thank you?!" Jason shouted incredulously. "Are you listening to yourself, you self-righteous fuck? You're *not* doing me any favors—I *have* to speak. It's the only chance I have to defend myself—and Katrina—and to point out the fact that she has not been convicted of *anything,* since some of you seem to have already lost sight of that.

"If Katrina simply shrinks away apologetically, she might as well be pleading guilty to the absolutely ludicrous charges against her. Her career will be ruined. My career will be ruined as well, and the careers of several other bright young scientists under her training. You are not only stopping the *careers* of these young scientists, you are also damaging the future of science itself by taking *several* of its promising rising stars out of the equation."

"Now who is being arrogant?" asked the chair. "Young man, legitimate science has been communicated in this forum among legitimate scientists since before you *or* your twelve-year-old colleagues were even born. And when today is finally over, this tradition will continue without any of you.

"No, sir, I think the best course of action is to simply announce Dr. Stone's cancellation due to personal reasons and leave it at that. My concern here is damage control—not to your career, I'm sorry to say, but to this convention and to the reputations of the scientists in it who are *not* felons. You can plead your case in front of a court of law like everybody else. That's the end of it. Now if you'll excuse me, I'm already ten minutes late, and the natives are getting restless."

The older man turned and stepped out of the room,

slamming the door behind him. After he was gone, Jason let out an exasperated sigh. Then he reached up to wipe a fresh outpouring of sweat from his brow.

><

Out in the hallway, the session chair stopped for a moment to take a few deep breaths. Afterward, he felt calmer.

He smoothed his suit and stole a glance at his reflection in a large, blue glass flowerpot decorating the hallway. He straightened his tie. Satisfied with his appearance, he stepped through another door and onto the stage of an auditorium, where tens of thousands of scientists, vendors, investors, and members of the press were rapidly growing impatient.

"I'm sorry for the delay," the chair said when he reached the podium. "We've obviously had a bit of excitement this morning, but I would like to urge us all to continue with the convention as professionals. There is a great deal of equally exciting *science* to be discussed over the next five days."

The chair paused briefly, and someone in the audience began to applaud. As if following a cue, the auditorium erupted with a lengthy standing ovation.

The chair smiled gratefully. He could feel himself reddening all over again as he waited for the applause to die down, but this time, he didn't mind that he was blushing. "Thank you," he finally said. "Welcome to the International Biotechnology Convention and Exhibition. I'm James Johnson, and I'm honored to be chairing this morning's first session."

S
ean McMullan and Katrina Stone were arguing as McMullan's black sedan crawled through the mobbed streets of downtown San Diego.

"We can't just go in there and raise a big stink," Katrina said. "First of all, these people are too logical—trust me. If *I* was in there and someone came in and said there was a biological terror attack on the convention, I'd do anything but take his word for it. I'd run through every possibility of how the alleged attacker could or could not have done such a thing, weigh the different scenarios to decide which I thought was the most likely, and then decide for myself. And if Ockham's razor told me it was probably a hoax, then I'd sit back down and listen to the next lecture without giving it another thought.

"And anyway, if they *did* believe you, they'd kill each other stampeding out of here, you'd never catch who did it, and then they'd all be gone before we can do anything about it. I guarantee you that they've *already* been drinking the water."

"Well, what do *you* want to do, then?" McMullan asked. "And what happens when some of these people leave for lunch and then don't come back afterward. Does that ever happen?"

"Actually," she conceded, "you're right. We are all prone to playing hooky during sessions that are less relevant to us. And the weather this week is mighty nice, and a lot of the attendees are from out of town."

"What do you suggest then? That we jog over to Sea World and the zoo and round them all up when this turns out to be for real?"

"First of all, the precedent suggests that it will *not* be for real. We've already been duped by this guy once. Nothing happened on Christmas. I'd say it's equally likely that nothing will happen today, and when it doesn't, then we've made the FBI and the scientific community look like a bunch of total idiots. So why don't we proceed with caution and decide how likely it is that the Doctor could have done anything. My experience at conferences is that the water comes in sealed plastic bottles, every time.

"So let's check it out and play it by ear, OK? There is so much press around here that we will have no trouble at all getting the word out if there really is cause for panic. And at that time, if it comes to that, we can make an *informed* announcement over the air along with explicit instructions for what people are to do, so there won't end up being a rumor mill that will get people killed. It's much better that way."

"OK, I'll go along with that. But if I think for a moment that all of these people are in real danger, I'm blowing the whistle. And if any of these Ockham's Razor Blade people don't believe me—well, I guess there's nothing I can do about that. You can lead a horse to water but you can't make him believe that it's poisonous."

McMullan's black sedan turned off of Front Street onto

Harbor Drive as he approached the San Diego Convention Center. "*Get down!*" he shouted, and Katrina obliged.

She had seen it as well. The sea of black and white clad protestors.

"*Oh my god!*" she exclaimed as she dropped as low in her seat as she could manage. "Well, now what?"

"I don't know. I assume that everyone inside will know your face?"

"Not everyone, but too many of them. I can't go in there. Once one person recognizes me the jig will be up, and I'll be swarmed. And what we need right now is to blend in. *Damn it!*"

"Well, I *have* to go in," McMullan said. "Someone needs to scope out the situation with the water. I haven't really come up with a plan after that, and to be honest, any vague plan I had so far included your being there to tell me what to do."

"You'll be in the right place to ask your questions," she said sarcastically. Poking her head between the two bucket seats, Katrina scanned the back seat of McMullan's sedan until she saw his gym bag.

"What are you doing?" he asked.

"Ugh, don't you ever wash this stuff?" she asked as she pulled out a musty sweatshirt and baseball cap.

"Well *now* I will," he said.

Katrina pulled the sweatshirt over her head and knotted the excessive length at her waist. Beneath it, the light blue pants of her prison uniform resembled hospital scrubs or, potentially, regular pants to a person not paying attention. She tucked her hair under the baseball cap and pulled it low over her forehead.

"Your cell phone won't work in the convention center," she said, "but keep it on and keep stepping outside to check for messages from me. Call me if you need to ask questions about anthrax—but I don't know what to tell you about crowd control in emergency situations, so you're going to have to play that one out by yourself."

"Where are you going?" he asked as she opened the door and stepped out of the car.

"To find my daughter."

Katrina's daughter was only a hundred feet away. She was being led by the arm by a pleasant-faced man who smiled and nodded at people they passed. A man who had a concealed gun pointed at her back. A man who, moments before, had assaulted her in the ladies' room and injected something into Alexis' right arm.

Now, she winced as the man's grip on the same arm tightened and the gun was forced deeper into her back. They stepped through the main entrance of the convention center and onto Harbor Drive. The San Diego sunlight was blinding, and without thinking, Lexi moved her hand to reach for her sunglasses.

"Don't even think about it," the man said, and Lexi realized that her pepper spray would have been a better thing to reach for.

"I was just trying to get my sunglasses," she said softly. "It's too bright out here. Can I get them? They're right here in my jacket."

"Keep your hands right where they are." He smiled and nodded at another passerby.

Shit. Alexis scanned the crowd, not knowing what she was looking for, hoping that the answer would come when she saw it. And then, she did.

Standing a few yards away was a figure in light blue pants and a black sweatshirt. A baseball cap was tucked tightly over the small person's face, but Alexis recognized her. Her mother was looking in her direction.

Oh God, Mom, please see me. And please don't say any-thing. Alexis shook her head, barely perceptibly, side to side, unaware if her mother could see the motion. "*No,*" she mouthed.

Katrina turned away and faced into the crowd, and Alexis and her captor passed by so closely that she could have reached out and touched her mother. And then, they were walking away from her.

After a flash of his badge to clear security, Sean McMullan entered the San Diego Convention Center. He thought for a moment and then found an information booth.

"Excuse me," he said to the middle-aged woman at the booth. "I am new to this event, and I'm terribly thirsty. Can you tell me where I might find a drink of water?"

"There's an entire buffet set up down the hall," she said and unfolded a map of the convention center. "You can find a number of goodies there." With one finger, she traced a line to the room she spoke of. "There are also drinking fountains, but that's San Diego tap water. You're better off with the bottled stuff at the buffet." She looked up and smiled.

"Thank you, ma'am." McMullan headed over to the room she had indicated and peered inside. Several tables piled with food and beverages were being attended to by a catering staff. The drinks were all in bottles. Sealed water bottles, just as Katrina had said.

McMullan approached one of the bartenders and asked for a bottle of water. "On second thought," he corrected a moment later, "can I get two of them? I'm really thirsty, and I'd hate to miss the next lecture to have to come back here."

"Of course," said the bartender with a nod. He handed McMullan two of the small bottles.

After leaving the room, McMullan made a beeline for the nearest restroom, where he promptly emptied one of the bottles into the sink, taking care not to touch its contents. From there, he found the nearest drinking fountain and refilled the empty bottle. Again, he did not allow the water to come into contact with his skin. *I guess that about covers the data collection*, he thought and maneuvered his way back toward the entrance.

"Um, Mister?" Alexis said, as they crossed Harbor Avenue and started up Fifth.

"What?"

"You never did let me pee at the convention center."

"So what's your point?"

"Just that I really did have to go, and now I have to go more. And I'm not exactly un-scared, and frankly... don't you think it would draw a bit of attention to the both of us if I pissed myself right here walking down Fifth Avenue? Because I think I might."

"All right, fine," he said, "but if you try anything at all, I'll put a bullet in your back and walk away. And don't think I can't get away with it." The door to The Strip Club was open, and the man shoved Alexis inside, his gun still buried in her back.

As she passed through the door, Alexis braved a glance over her shoulder. The small figure in blue pants and a sweatshirt was still trailing behind them.

"Remember what I said," her kidnapper said under his breath.

"We're closed," said a woman wiping down tables.

"I'm terribly sorry," said Lexi's kidnapper in a polite, apologetic voice. "My niece really has to use the restroom, and I could use one myself. Would it be too much trouble? You won't even know we were here."

"OK, hurry up," the woman said, and motioned behind her. "They're over there."

The pair walked past the waitress and into a narrow hallway, where they found a swinging door announcing the women's room. As Alexis pushed it open, her kidnapper did not leave her side.

"Oh, come *on*," she said. "Can't you let me pee in peace?" He glared at her for a moment, but to Lexi, it looked as if he was weighing his options. "What, do you think I hid a gun in the stall just in case this was going to happen? Give me a break... "

The man pushed the door open and scanned the walls of the ladies' restroom. There were no windows. He glanced back toward the waitress. She was around a corner, out of sight.

"Hands up," he said.

Oh God, he's going to shoot me right here. Alexis raised both hands slowly while watching the hand with the gun. She could feel the weight of her pepper spray in her pocket.

But the hand with the gun remained still. Instead, her captor casually reached for her with his other hand. Feeling up and down. Frisking her. He took her pepper spray. And then her cell phone. And both of Lexi's plans for escape were destroyed.

As soon as he stepped outside of the convention center, the chime on his cell phone indicated that he had a voice mail, and McMullan remembered Katrina's warning about the phone not working inside the convention center. He pulled the phone from his pocket and played back the message. It was from Katrina, and it was frantic.

"*Sean!*" Katrina was practically screaming. "You've got to get out here! Alexis is being kidnapped! She's being led by a strange man! I'm pretty sure he has a gun at her back! I'm following them, but I'm afraid if he sees me, he'll kill her! *Oh, God, Sean, please hurry!*"

McMullan slammed the message off and picked up a dial tone to return the call to her cell phone, but then reconsidered. *If she's tailing them, her phone might be within his earshot.* He glanced around him in all directions, but saw neither Katrina nor her daughter. So he took the chance that she had silenced her phone and texted her: "Where are u"

Katrina's response came through almost immediately: "Strip Club."

McMullan bolted out into the Harbor Drive traffic without looking.

"Now hurry up," the kidnapper said and thrust Alexis into the bathroom. As the door swung closed, she could see him concealing his pistol. She raced into the stall and arranged herself over the toilet. While she sat urinating, she struggled with tears. There wasn't much time to devise a new strategy.

When she reached to flush the toilet, a jolt of pain shot through the crook of her arm. Sucking in her breath, she pulled up the sleeve of her mother's jacket and located the small puncture wound in her vein. The spot where her kidnapper had injected her. *What did he give me?* It had bled a little bit, but was now clotting.

And then a new plan came to her.

The bathroom stall door was metal. Its edges were sharp.

She clicked open the door and slid a fingertip along its lock, a sliver of metal that slid into a bracket. She traced it delicately, feeling for the roughest corner, and then gripped the metal tightly with one hand. Then she bit into her lip to avoid crying out as she thrust her arm upon it, gouging the metal deeply into her clotting puncture wound.

✕

The Doctor began to lose patience as he waited outside of the women's room for Katrina Stone's daughter. *Is she even worth all this?* His job was done. The rest would certainly take care of itself. The abduction of the girl, once she had serendipitously revealed her identity to the press right in front of him, had been spontaneous.

It is *worth it*, the Doctor decided after all. *Imagine the publicity when they find her body. The woman's very* daughter. *Nobody is safe. Nobody is immune. I could not have planned a more perfect end.*

But where is she? She should be finished in there by now. The Doctor reached forward and began to push the swinging restroom door inward when a force blocked its movement. He withdrew his hand and the girl swung the door outward and toward him. "It's about time," he said.

The girl did not answer. Through the dark maroon of her suit jacket, the Doctor could make out a circle of a different red color. The injection site was bleeding. No matter. With one hand, he reached forward to take her arm as before. The other held the pistol, jutting outward toward her through the pocket of his coat. As the Doctor reached toward her with his one free hand, her leg swung upward, and before he realized what was happening his groin was on fire.

✕

"*Take that, fucker!*" Alexis shouted as she kneed her kidnapper between the legs. He let out an agonized yelp. She bolted past him and out of the narrow hallway of the Strip Club, racing toward the door and the daylight beyond it. Behind her, she heard a gunshot. And then a blood-curdling scream.

A vague sensation of pain came over her, and the sunlight before her faded as her vision began darkening from the edges inward. And Alexis realized that the scream she had heard might have been her own.

9:25 A.M. PST

Inside the Strip Club, Katrina was crouching behind the bar, fervently hoping that Sean McMullan received her text message in time, when Alexis came running toward her. But then the shot rang out, and Katrina's worst nightmare was realized for the second time in her life.

A murky waitress raised her hands to her face in slow motion, and the bar swirled around Katrina like the cabin of a ship on a choppy sea. She felt herself falling to the floor behind the bar. She heard the crash of breaking glass, and then everything faded to black.

It is the week before Katrina's scheduled qualifying exam. She is in her bedroom, sitting on the bed she will no longer be sharing with Tom. She is crying.

She hears the crash of breaking glass.

She runs to the living room.

She screams.

The front room window is shattered and Christopher is lying on the floor in front of it. Next to him, his favorite plastic cup lies on its side, and the carpet is soaked with the water he had gotten up for. The yellow racecar on the front of his cotton pajamas is now stamped with a spreading, bright red ellipse.

As Katrina races to him, she stumbles on a toy and almost falls on top of her son. She lands on her knees next to Christopher and tenderly pulls his pajama top up to look at the small wound on the upper part of his chest. Sobbing, she lifts his limp body to a sitting position, and then she sees that the bullet has gone all the way through her son's body. Blood is spreading across Christopher's pajamas from a ragged exit wound.

Oh God, please, no, please, no, God! Oh God!

Christopher is awake and looking at her. Large, blond curls spring out haphazardly from the left side of his head; on the right, the locks are damp and one is stuck to his rosy cheek from the peaceful slumber he was in just moments ago. The soft skin beneath the curls is creased in several places from his pillow.

Christopher's wide, bright blue eyes shine with fear and pain. A tear spills from the corner of each, leaving two clear, wet tracks down the sides of his nose and over his mouth. His full, pink lower lip trembles, and he blinks several times. He reaches for Katrina's hand, still on his chest, and wraps a soft, chubby fist around her index finger. He gasps for breath and quietly mouths a single word: "Mommy."

Sean McMullan ran through the door of the Strip Club with his pistol drawn. At first, the restaurant looked abandoned. Confused, McMullan glanced from side to side. And then he saw them.

Jutting out from behind the bar was pair of legs. He recognized the loose, blue pants that enveloped them.

Katrina was unconscious, but alive, lying on top of a pile of broken glass. Her cuts from the bar glasses she had fallen onto appeared to be superficial. McMullan lightly tapped the sides of her face. Katrina's eyes rolled, and then slowly opened. For a moment, she only looked at him, appearing dazed. Then her eyes widened and she struggled to stand up.

"Stay still," he said authoritatively. But when a woman's shriek rang out from the back of the bar, Katrina jerked past him to a standing position.

Together, they followed the sound. As they reached the narrow back hallway, the door of the women's restroom swung open, and the bar's waitress emerged. She was crying, and a small trickle of vomit was still on her chin. "I think you need to see this," she said and led them into the bathroom.

It was clear which stall the waitress had just lost her breakfast in. But McMullan wondered why he needed to see it, until the waitress pointed to the door of the adjacent stall. Its lock, a jutting sliver of metal, was covered in blood.

Katrina pushed past McMullan and reached for the door, looking it up and down, and then quickly opened it.

Her daughter's message was scrawled in blood on the wall tile near the toilet: "*Yuppie Ant Farm.*"

✂

Alexis shoved tourists aside as she ran up Fifth Avenue, gripping the bleeding arm that had been grazed by a bullet. Occasionally, she looked over her shoulder to confirm that she was still being chased. When another shot rang out from behind her and through the crowded street, Alexis knew that the Doctor would now stop at nothing to kill her.

✂

A police cruiser pulled away from its post at the biotechnology convention to respond to the frantic 911 call of a waitress. To clear the crowd from the streets before them, the officers inside the cruiser activated their lights and sirens. And as the black and white car pulled off Harbor Drive and onto Fifth Avenue, several news vans followed.

R oger Gilman opened a door and entered a small closet-like room at San Quentin. A brief glance around the room revealed three walls lined with video monitors, each projecting its own scene from within the prison. On the fourth wall was a built-in bookshelf containing rows upon rows of videodiscs.

Two boys who looked no older than eighteen were at a table playing checkers. They looked up, startled, when Gilman entered without knocking. One reached for a gun.

"Agent Roger Gilman, FBI," Gilman said, preemptively, and flashed his badge. The youth's hand fell away from the pistol at his side. "You scared the crap out of me," he said. "Thanks for knocking. What can we do for you?"

"I need to see all of the surveillance you have that pertains to the visitation of one of your minimum-security prisoners. His name is Oscar Morales."

The two boys exchanged a glance. One of them shrugged. "What are the dates you want? All of our visitation videos are dated, but they're not catalogued by name of the prisoner. You should be able to get records of when each prisoner had visitors though. That'll be logged elsewhere. We just do the AV stuff."

"I see," Gilman said. "Then I'll be back shortly."

><

Fifteen minutes later, Gilman returned with a list of dates and times and a borrowed wall calendar. He was surprised to have learned that for months, Oscar Morales had been visited every Sunday morning like clockwork.

When he stepped into the AV room for the second time, only one of the teenagers was in the room. The boy looked up at Gilman and slammed shut a Penthouse magazine, then dropped the magazine into a drawer.

"Where's your partner?" Gilman asked.

"He had to take a piss."

Gilman shook his head and sat at the table across from the boy, shoving aside the forgotten game of checkers. He handed the list to the boy and said, "These are the dates and times I need to see the visitation videos for."

The boy scanned the list. "I can get you the later ones right now, but the ones that are more than three months old are in the archives. You'll have to fill out a request form and it takes a week or so to get those out."

"I don't have a week," Gilman said. "Show me what you can."

The boy picked up the list. "We'll start with the most recent then," he said, and selected a disc from the wall. As he popped the disc into a player and cued up the appropriate time, Gilman leaned in to scrutinize the monitor. He let his breath out quickly when he realized he had been holding it. The disc began to play. There was no sound.

"Don't you have sound on these things?" Gilman asked.

"No, these are visual only."

Gilman did not recognize the prisoner that was in the field of view. In frustration, he reached for the control pad and began a fast forward scan. Then he located Oscar Morales. And across from him, Katrina Stone.

Gilman quickly flipped the wall calendar to look at the date. It was the day he and McMullan had found her schedule on her computer and her daughter having sex on the kitchen table. The day he already knew she had been here. This information was redundant.

"Do you remember seeing this woman?" he asked the guard.

The boy started to laugh. "Actually, I don't know the woman, but now that I see the video I *totally* know the dude. For months he had the same chick come visit him every single weekend. Not the chick you're looking at, though. The other chick was a *scary* ass bitch! Looked about like a bag full of smashed assholes! My partner and I used to sit there and crack up when we saw them talking. Even the prisoner looked a little grossed out.

"Then one day, he starts getting visits by a twin brother. We freaked out at first because we saw the brother coming in and thought it was the same guy. We thought he'd gotten paroled or something, till we saw them together and figured out it was twins. And then, out of nowhere, *this* chick." He pointed to the monitor and shrugged. "I guess he finally dumped the ugly chick when he got a hotter one."

Gilman was shocked. If the boy's memory was correct, he had just corroborated Chuck Morales' story verbatim. "I'm going to need a written statement from you reiterating exactly what you just said," Gilman said. "But first, I need to see one of the earlier videos. One of the ones with the other woman. Do you have some of them here, or are they too old?"

The boy squinted and looked past Gilman, as if searching his memory. "Um, no, I think she was here pretty recently. Let me try to find one of the CDs." Consulting the list of dates again, he selected another disc from the wall and popped it in. He scanned until he located Oscar. The visitor in the video was Chuck. "Nope," he said, and pulled the disc out to search another.

It took several tries to locate a disc with the visitor of interest. And when they did, Gilman became even more confused. And even more frustrated.

He couldn't see the woman's face. Thick, black ropes of hair hung along both sides, blocking her countenance. And her face was carefully positioned at all times. She avoided eye contact with the guards. She avoided looking toward the cameras. She looked sideways. She looked down. She hid her face carefully at all times.

Moreover, Gilman couldn't make out much of her body. A chunky, shapeless, turtleneck sweater pulled over an ankle-length skirt covered any trace of a form. But she was tall. Taller than Oscar.

As Gilman watched, she reached forward and placed her hand across the visiting room table. Oscar reached forward and brought his hand up to meet hers. Then the woman pulled away.

"*Wait! Go back!*" Gilman shouted excitedly, already reaching forward to rewind the video. As he played it back a second time, he paused when the woman pulled her hand away from Oscar's. Oscar's hand remained for just a moment longer. And there was something in it. It might have been money. "Do you see that?" Gilman asked accusingly.

"Yeah," said the guard. "I guess I never noticed before."

"You must have been too busy monitoring Oscar's love

life instead of doing your job!" Gilman snapped. "How did she get in here with something to give him? Don't you guys frisk visitors?"

"We frisk them but we don't strip search them," the boy said, a bit defensively. "And we don't do cavity searches on visitors, for God's sake. They could hide something small in their—well, lots of places."

Gilman's mind was racing. "Let me see the video from the week before!"

The boy produced it. When they got to the segment showing Oscar and his visitor, Gilman was not surprised. Same woman. Same procedure. Gilman quickly looked at a third disc, and then a fourth. All four videos showed an identical pattern. This woman had been paying Oscar every weekend for months.

Gilman looked again at the printout of Oscar's visitation dates. They had begun before the death row attack and continued ever since. Without stopping the fourth video, Gilman stood to leave the room. In his distraction, he almost did not see the movement of the woman on the screen. But it was enough to catch his eye.

"*There!*" he said, and sat back down on his thin chair hard enough to hear a cracking sound from beneath him. He quickly rewound the disc again, and then watched eagerly as the scene replayed. At the precise moment of interest, he paused the disc.

There was just a moment. Just a partial view. But the woman's face was showing, at least, most of it. The angle afforded a three-quarter view, and a lock of hair in front of her shoulder obscured her from the mouth down. But it was enough. Gilman squinted to make out the image in front of him. *I know that face.*

His mind scanned through vision after vision of the female suspects in Operation Death Row like a video montage—the women he had been obsessing about for months. Their faces were all blending together. Katrina Stone. Her daughter, Alexis Stone. Her ex-husband's new wife, Kimberly Stone. Oxana Kosova, Stone's Russian student. Li Fung, Stone's Chinese student.

The guard's laughter interrupted Gilman's thoughts. "See, I told you!" he said. "Uglier 'n homemade soup, that chick!"

Gilman paid no attention as he continued to think. Angela Fischer, Jason Fischer's ex-wife. Lisa Goldstein, his vapid, violent groupie. Gilman shook his head, blinked his eyes, and looked again. And then he felt the color drain from his face as he realized who he was looking at. He turned to face the boy before leaving the room. "It's not a chick," he said.

Katrina and McMullan ran quickly and steadily up Fifth Avenue toward Horton Plaza. Neither spoke. Except for their clothing—Katrina in a blue prison uniform with a much-too-large sweatshirt and carrying a purse, McMullan in a navy blue suit—they might have been a couple out for a mid-morning jog. A couple out for a mid-morning jog with several news vans intently tracking their workout.

When Katrina reached into her purse and retrieved her cell phone, McMullan asked in a husky, slightly winded voice, "Who on earth... would you possibly... be calling right now?"

"My ex... " Katrina panted. "He deserves... to know... what's going on... with his daughter."

When Tom answered his phone, Katrina realized she had neither the time nor the energy to sugar coat what she had to say. And she could not afford to waste the breath. "Lexi... has been kidnapped... " she said. "She's somewhere... at Horton Plaza... "

"*What?*" Tom shouted.

"Can't talk... " Katrina said and hung up her phone. The

phone began to ring, and she tucked it back into her purse without shutting it off.

McMullan looked at her in disbelief and she shrugged. "I told him... " Katrina began to run faster, and McMullan sped up to keep pace with her.

"Horton... Plaza?" McMullan asked.

"It... was brilliant... " Katrina said. "She knows... the place... like the back of her hand... and it's otherwise... impossible to navigate... she was leveling... the playing field... "

When they reached the corner of Fifth Avenue and E Street, they turned left and followed E to the dead end at Horton Plaza. A large escalator ran upward from the street. Without slowing, Katrina began trotting up the escalator stairs two at a time, absently pushing people out of her way as she ran.

DXI

They reached the top of the escalator and Katrina bolted forward across a narrow catwalk. McMullan followed, gaping with exasperation at the architecture in front of him. This place, at this moment, was his worst nightmare. He finally understood Alexis' joke.

Stepping into Horton Plaza really *was* like entering a giant human ant farm. Or an M.C. Escher print.

To McMullan's right, the balcony overlooked a large traffic circle at street level, three floors below. To his left loomed the most bizarre construction he had ever seen.

In his field of vision were several additional catwalks crossing an open center, around which various levels of the mall layered across each other. Staircases of varying lengths and heights interrupted the walkways and broke each floor up into multiple elevations. He could make out a few more escalators, jutting forward at angles that appeared totally random. The escalators had no counterparts moving in the opposite direction, so the flow of traffic between floors was restricted in a way that seemed totally without reason. In the open center of the building was a ponderous, pale blue stucco structure stretching across the mall in several step-wise fragments. As shoppers passed between its cylindrical support poles and walls into small openings between them, they became visible, then obstructed, and then visible again, sometimes on another level.

We might never find her here, McMullan thought, *and even if we do, we might never get to her.*

Katrina leaned out over the railing and scanned the crowd. McMullan joined her, his eyes sifting through couples holding hands, families, and groups of women or teenagers giggling and clutching bags from the various retailers. There was no sign of Alexis.

Abandoning their present vantage point, McMullan and Katrina stepped away from the railing and ran forward on the catwalk, passing the large, blue structure that linked the two sides of the mall. As they passed, McMullan looked down the corridor within it.

Inside were two staircases separated by a foot-thick wall. The staircase on the left led downward from where they were standing, and the one on the right upward. Neither was steep enough to actually provide access to a different level of the mall. McMullan could not tell what they connected to or where. *What a zoo.*

Katrina was now leaning over another balcony. In front of her was a threatening triangular structure, painted an odd, geometric pattern of black, white and red. An esca-lator disappeared upward into it from ground level. There was no corresponding down escalator at the same level, but

McMullan could make out one at a distance. It did not, however, connect the same two floors.

The triangular structure was punctuated with arches through which McMullan could see more shoppers as they passed, and others that appeared to be sitting or standing still. Two more catwalks connected the structure to the floor McMullan and Katrina were on, or so he thought.

Next to McMullan and Katrina, a booth attendant talked boisterously on the phone. A siren approached, momentarily drowning out the constant hum of multiple conversations surrounding them, and then faded. A shriek cut through the din.

"*Mom!*"

McMullan and Katrina looked in unison toward the source of the sound and saw Alexis through an arch in the triangular structure looming before them. She was on a level not quite an entire floor above them. McMullan raced to the nearest catwalk that appeared to connect with the triangle. As he crossed it, he realized he had taken the wrong path. The catwalk led to a staircase heading to a lower level.

He turned back around to see two gently graded wheelchair ramps, one leading up and the other down, both leading toward unknown and different destinations. There was also an escalator between the floor he was on and the one where he thought Alexis had been. It ran in the wrong direction.

Katrina had already disregarded the intended direction of the escalator and leaped onto it, running against its flow and past surprised tourists. Slowly and laboriously, she began to overtake its movement. McMullan followed.

The path led to a food court stretching along one side of the mall. The mixed scents of international cuisines blended with the unmistakable aromas of hot dogs, popcorn, and cinnamon. Extending into the triangular structure they had seen from the other side was a small, shaded outdoor café, where patrons of the various eateries sat at tables enjoying their meals. Some of them looked a bit startled. Alexis was gone.

"*Lexi, where are you?!*" Katrina shouted into the crowd as McMullan caught up to her in the food court. When he stopped running, he felt a light tug at his pant leg and looked down.

A small boy of perhaps four years was looking up at him. "She went through there, mister," the child said softly and pointed to another staircase heading upward.

McMullan smiled kindly and thanked the boy, then ran up the stairs with Katrina at his side. Another catwalk came to a T on the opposite side of the mall, one floor—a true floor—above the spot they had started from.

"*Which way!?*" Katrina shouted rhetorically, glancing feverishly to her left and right. To the right was a long, shaded corridor. To the left, a shorter one extended through a sunny patch into another triangle. Alexis answered the question.

"*Mom!*" she shouted again, and McMullan and Katrina followed the sound.

✖

Katrina's eyes flashed when she saw her daughter.

Alexis stood atop a protruding square balcony lined with flowers. The balcony was a true top level, and through the brilliant blue sky Alexis was exposed and vulnerable. Her arm was bleeding heavily from two sources: one at the shoulder, the other, the inner crook of her elbow. And there was also something else wrong with her, something that only Katrina could see. Her daughter was not well.

Katrina had always known instinctively when one of her

children was falling ill. She knew even before they knew. It was in the color of their skin, the glint in their eyes, even the smell of their breath. When Christopher had died, the ability to detect illness in Alexis had intensified within Katrina.

Her need to reach Lexi was suddenly the strongest she had ever felt in her life. But then she saw a shadow loom over her daughter.

The Doctor grabbed Alexis again from behind, his arm over her neck, his gun again pressed firmly into her back. She jumped and a shriek escaped her lips.

Beside Katrina, McMullan shouted, *"You!"* And Katrina realized that he recognized Lexi's kidnapper. Katrina did not.

McMullan raised his pistol, but then hesitated. As if reading his thoughts, Katrina shouted, *"No! You'll hit her!"*

The Doctor had no such concerns. He aimed his pistol toward Katrina and a shot rang out. And backward she fell, crashing to the floor behind the waist-high stucco wall. *I'm dead.*

The only pain she could feel was in the back of her head where it had hit the concrete floor, but the world was swimming, the carnival of Horton Plaza around her a backdrop for the confusion that threatened to drown away her consciousness. But then slowly, her vision stabilized and she came to realize that it was not the gunshot that had knocked her down. It was the two hundred pound Navy Corpsman on top of her. *Tom.*

Katrina struggled to speak.

Her ex-husband was faster. *"Are you hit?"* he demanded, rolling off of Katrina to examine her horizontal body.

Katrina looked over Tom's shoulder for Sean McMullan. He was gone. In his place, a portly, unfortunate tourist lay on the concrete a few feet away, each puff of his chest spewing a geyser of brilliant red like the blowhole of a whale harpooned through the lung. Mall patrons scattered, screaming.

Tom poked his head up to assess the balcony where Alexis and the Doctor had been standing, and then immediately dropped back down as a second bullet whizzed past and crashed into the glass window of the store behind them.

Tom reached into his waistband and withdrew a pistol—the same pistol over which he and Katrina had fought constantly while they were married. Because Katrina was afraid for the children.

Together, the former couple raced along the walkway, alternately popping up to catch a glimpse of Alexis and then dropping back down to avoid the Doctor's bullets. But the Doctor held Lexi close, and Tom still had no shot.

Directly across from the balcony on which her daughter was held, Katrina dropped down behind the wall beside a bench.

Tom fell in beside her. "I can't get a shot," he said. "I might hit her."

"I'll get you one," Katrina said. "When you get it, take it."

Before Tom could ask where she was going, Katrina jumped back up and began running across the walkway. This time, she was not ducking under the gunfire. As if on cue, the Doctor fired two shots. Remarkably, neither connected. But he did not let go of Alexis.

Katrina caught her daughter's eye and stopped running. Defiantly, she stood still in front of the Doctor, no more than twenty feet away as the crow flies, a moat of confusion separating them. *"Come on, you bastard!"* Katrina held her arms out beside her, surrendering, inviting her own death.

The Doctor pulled Alexis slightly off to one side and slowly took aim on Katrina. And as he did, a thin popping noise came from below. A small chunk at the back of the Doctor's head burst outward, and a thin, red river began pouring from his right eye.

Alexis screamed and dropped down out of Katrina's sight. The Doctor's intact left eye reflected bewilderment. His head tilted sideways like that of a dog trying to pick up a distant, high-pitched sound. Then his body followed, and gravity dragged him down.

The Doctor flipped forward over the balcony, that absurd, quizzical look still on his face. Three floors below, or what might have been four in the numerically devoid architecture of Horton Plaza, he smashed through a classic San Diego gaslamp before coming to a rest on a staircase.

Katrina turned backward to behold Tom, whose eyes moved from her to the man on the stairs. Tom shrugged. In answer to a question she had not yet posed, Tom shouted, "It wasn't me! I didn't shoot him!" Tom trotted over to join Katrina. Together, they scanned the crowd alongside and below them. And then they saw Sean McMullan, at ground level, walking slowly toward the Doctor's body and holstering his pistol.

"Holy shit," Tom said. He cast his eyes at the impossible angle and distance between McMullan and the balcony, on which the FBI agent had somehow managed to put a bullet into the Doctor's *eye* while avoiding his daughter. Tom looked toward Katrina, and the respect on his face was unmistakable.

✕

A frustrating five minutes later, Katrina and Tom finally made it to their daughter.

Alexis was sitting on the concrete of the balcony where the Doctor had lost his eye, her body slumped over, her mother's maroon suit filthy and torn. Her breathing was shallow and labored, her face pale. Katrina raised a hand to Alexis' forehead, while Tom examined the wounds on her arm.

"He stuck me with a needle," Alexis said quietly.

Katrina and Tom exchanged a look.

"When?" Katrina demanded. "How long ago?"

"Maybe an hour?" Lexi guessed.

As they processed the information, McMullan came running toward them, panting. Katrina was amazed that he had found them so quickly.

"Nice shot," Tom said.

"Hurry," McMullan panted, leaning forward momentarily to catch a breath. "He's still alive."

Behind a one-way mirror in a small room at San Quentin, a young inmate sat fidgeting in his chair. He was in way over his head. All this stuff with the cops, the FBI, and a bunch of lawyers babbling legal bullshit at him, and nobody would tell him anything about what was going on. But two things had been promised. If he told the truth, his own sentence would be reduced. And they'd keep him away from the guy he ratted on.

Several months earlier, the young prisoner had been serving kitchen duty. All he had to do was ration out a bunch of dinners for one of the death row wings. Some Mexican had paid him to take over the job for one night. And he wasn't about to argue about it or ask why. He took the money and went back to his cell.

Now, months later, he was supposed to point out the Mexican. He wasn't sure if he'd get the right one. It was a long time ago, and he hadn't been paying much attention. He didn't know what would happen if he picked the wrong guy. Maybe they already knew who the right guy was, and this was a test. Maybe his sentence would be even longer if he gave the wrong answer.

When eight dark-skinned and heavily tattooed men were lined up in front of him, he sighed with relief. Seven of them were men he had never spoken to before. He was sure.

"Number three," he said quickly.

"Are you sure?" the guard asked. "Take your time."

"I'm sure. It's number three. Can I go now?"

❎

In a temporary holding cell within the same building sat the blind, disfigured twin brother of the man who had just been identified. Chuck Morales was quietly tearing his shirt into thin strips and tying them together.

Katrina felt a wave of physical revulsion when she reached her daughter's would-be killer.

The Doctor looked peaceful as he lay on his back, a halo of shattered white glass surrounding him from the gaslamp he had fallen through. His body rested on the staircase, his head elevated on a higher stair, his legs spilling downward and jutting out at sickening angles. It was obvious that the legs had taken the brunt of his fall.

To Katrina's surprise, his one remaining eye was alert. When she reached him, he even smiled—a freakish smile that only graced half of his face, the other half paralyzed by the bullet that had passed through his brain.

"*Who are you?*" Katrina demanded.

"That's Guofu Wong," McMullan said quietly from beside her. "He's the scientist who wanted to fund your research from the very beginning. He's also the head of epidemiology from the CDC."

Katrina tore her hypnotized stare away from the man on the ground and looked at McMullan. *Why?* It was incomprehensible.

She stepped over the man on the stairs, straddling him, and leaned in, inches from his face. Her voice was trembling. *"Who gave you the Death Row strain of anthrax?"* she demanded.

The life in Guofu Wong's eye was fading, but his grotesque half-smile persisted. With considerable effort, he whispered, "You did, Dr. Stone. It was your activator." And then the light in his one remaining eye burned out.

The four San Quentin guards made quick work of tossing the cell of Oscar Morales—its contents were sparse. For the most part, the cell was devoid of contraband. Oscar's cellmate was removed for the event, and Oscar himself stood by, handcuffed and shackled.

The guards diligently checked the usual hiding places—under the inner rim of the toilet, within small cracks in the concrete floor, gaps in the walls. But it was a small slit in Oscar's mattress that revealed what they were looking for. A wad of cash amounting to almost sixteen thousand dollars. The final piece of evidence that would surely suffice in a reasonable court of law. Even without the testimony of his accomplice.

But the police and the FBI hoped to obtain that as well. Roger Gilman was already on his way to San Diego to try.

Money in hand, a lanky, pale guard approached the prisoner and waved the wad toward him. His accent was pure back-country Mississippi. "This worth it for ya, spic?" he asked. "Sixteen grand an' a woman who looks like first kin to a yak?"

"I can turn sixteen grand into six million, bitch," Oscar retorted.

The guard laughed. "Not now, ya can't. You're gettin' the needle, boy."

In the private holding cell where he had been detained for the last two hours, Chuck Morales finished his handiwork. Guided only by feel, he stood on his chair to grope along the ceiling, periodically stepping down to reposition his chair around the room, until he found an exposed rafter. He tested its strength with a half pull-up. Satisfied, he groped around again until he relocated the table on which he had laid the long, thin, knotted strand that had previously been his own shirt.

Quickly, Chuck tied one end of the make-shift rope to the rafter and the other to his own neck, and kicked the chair out from under himself. The shirt ripped in two from the weight of the thick man, but not before snapping his neck. And the remainder of Chuck Morales' miserable life was unceremoniously extinguished.

11:04 A.M. PST

When Katrina finally looked up from the dead man before her, she slowly realized that she was no longer alone with McMullan and the remnants of a family she had known in a former life. Until now, she had failed to notice the entourage of news anchors and cameramen gradually encircling them like a school of sharks. She looked helplessly toward McMullan.

"Don't say a word," he said. And then, to the press, "We have nothing to say at this time. Step aside or you're interfering with an official FBI investigation." McMullan flashed his badge and took Katrina's hand to lead her toward a nearby exit sign. Numb, Katrina remained quiet, grateful that he had taken control.

"This way," Tom corrected, and motioned toward another exit sign. "I'm driving."

Only then did Katrina realize that their mode of transportation—McMullan's sedan—was still parked at the convention center. She fell into step behind Tom. Alexis was still in Tom's arms. The reporters followed like stalking predators.

Tom laid his daughter gingerly into the passenger seat of

his Jeep, tipping the seat back to grant as much comfort for his daughter as he could. The teenager was looking increasingly ill.

Katrina and McMullan leaped into the Jeep behind Tom and Alexis.

"Hang on," Tom said as he started the Jeep's engine. Without further warning, he tore rapidly out of the parking space and began the downward spiral to exit the parking structure of Horton Plaza. The reporters who had escorted them to the Jeep were now meeting up with their respective vans, which waited like vultures at the 4th Avenue entrance to the structure. Tom did not seem concerned.

Pulling out of the parking structure, Tom surprised all of them by making a left onto 4th Avenue—the wrong way up a busy one-way street. Horns blaring, two oncoming cars parted to avoid crashing into the speeding Jeep, and Tom hit the gas hard to pass between them, then jerked the Jeep to the left to avoid a third car.

Several news vans were left behind, but two remained glued in caravan to his rear bumper, apparently trusting that if an accident occurred the Jeep would take the brunt of it. An even juicier scoop.

McMullan looked over to Katrina with one eyebrow raised. Looking surprisingly calm, she shrugged. "We used to fight about his driving all the time."

Tom jerked the Jeep to the right and narrowly missed one more car before crashing through a small barrier—the barrier designed to prevent traffic from entering C Street off of 4th Avenue. That stretch of C Street was closed off to automobiles—it was trafficked only by the Trolley, San Diego's public transit rail.

As Tom's Jeep straddled the set of Trolley tracks on the

right side of the street, the driver of the news van immediately on his tail evidently lost his nerve. The van swerved away and came to a halt, still facing the wrong direction on 4th Avenue. As Tom sped down the Trolley tracks, Katrina turned around to see the defeated news van making a three-point turn in an effort to find the correct flow of traffic. But the other van surged forward and assumed the alpha position behind the Jeep.

"*Watch out!*" McMullan yelled.

Immediately in front of them, an Orange Line Trolley was halted at the stop on the corner of 5th Avenue and C Street. Several cars long, the Trolley blocked the rail on the right side of the street, but it was the pedestrians who were in danger. Dozens of men, women, and children on both sides of the Trolley were crossing over the tracks to enter the waiting train. None of them seemed aware of the speeding Jeep bearing down on them.

Tom laid on his horn and swerved to the left to head down the opposing set of tracks. Startled pedestrians scurried out of the way. And as the Jeep cleared the rear car of the parked Trolley, the characteristic triangle of lights of another oncoming train came into view.

"*Jesus Christ!*" Tom yelled. "These things only come every fifteen minutes!" But as he said it, his foot was already pressed to the floor, a deft right hand slamming the Jeep into a lower gear for a burst of speed.

The screech of metal upon metal was hair-raising as the Trolley driver attempted to stop the train from ramming the Jeep speeding directly head-on toward it. A man on the northwest corner of 5th Avenue and C Street dove to the side as the Jeep cut over the sidewalk to turn left, heading northbound on 5th Avenue. A loud clank marked the collision of the train with the overhanging rear bumper of the Jeep, and the bumper was pulled clean off.

The Trolley came to a stop just inches from a halted news van, wide-eyed reporters staring up at the driver of the train. Tom's Jeep jetted up 5th Avenue, finally in accord with the flow of traffic, and finally clear of the press.

Tom weaved in and out of traffic to pass the cars heading northbound on Fifth Avenue, his three passengers silent. Finally, Katrina spoke. "Where are you going?"

"Where do you think? The hospital," he said grimly. "We've gotta get Lexi checked out, now."

"No," Katrina said and both Tom and McMullan swiveled in their seats to look at her. "Not the hospital." Katrina looked toward Tom. "Trust me. We have to get her to my lab first."

Tom visibly flinched, but made the necessary changes in direction to get to San Diego State University.

"How do you feel, Lexi?" Katrina asked then. Her voice was clinical but concerned.

"Like ass," the girl answered quietly. A moment later, Alexis added, "I saw him before."

"Who?" McMullan asked.

"The guy who kidnapped me. He was getting a drink of water."

McMullan and Katrina looked at each other and Katrina slapped a hand over her mouth in shock. McMullan began fidgeting with the pockets of his pants.

"Where?" Katrina demanded. "Inside the convention? How did you even get in? You would have needed a badge."

Alexis shook her head. "It wasn't inside the convention where I saw him. It was outside."

McMullan spoke up. "I don't know what you mean. I was inside the convention and I saw all the water they had for it. I actually collected some bottles"—this part was directed at Katrina—"but I guess I've dropped them. They're gone now." He paused, an expression of concern clouding his face. "Anyway, I thought all the water for the scientists was inside."

"Not for the scientists," Lexi said quietly. Her breathing was shallow and labored. "We had a bunch of carboys set up. The water was for the protestors. The only people who drank it were protestors... except for a few scientists who stopped by to ask us about our cause."

From his seat in the auditorium, recent Nobel laureate Jeffrey Wilson stood up in the middle of watching a presentation. The speaker droned on, but Jeff had lost interest, the growing sensations of fever and nausea distracting him. As quickly and quietly as possible, Jeff gathered his belongings and exited the lecture.

On a private plane from San Francisco to San Diego, Roger Gilman stared absently out the window and watched the sprawling California coastline slowly inch by. His brow was furrowed as he struggled to connect the pieces of a convoluted puzzle.

Oscar Morales had released the death row strain of anthrax into the rice in San Quentin's death row several months before. He had been sought out for his knowledge of safe laboratory practices and had turned the occasion into a lucrative blackmailing situation for himself—for a while. The unfortunate late Chuck Morales had been dragged in by his brother to dispose of Katrina Stone, because Stone was the one who had known of Oscar's involvement.

But it was *not* Stone who had involved Oscar. Nor was it Stone whom he had been blackmailing. The video was crystal clear proof of that. It was a member of her staff. A male member. And it was possible that he, or Stone, or *any* member of her staff, had actually planted the Death Row strain of anthrax on Chuck Morales in the lab.

How far would she go to manipulate them? Gilman

thought back to a conversation—could it really have happened that very same morning? *"You and your advisor have
a pretty close relationship, don't you, Jason?"*

*"Um, yeah. I guess so... we've been working together
for years."*

The train of thought brought Gilman's mind to McMullan—
another person with whom Stone seemed to have developed
a closeness over the last several months. Gilman had not
spoken to his partner all day, and not entirely because he
was too busy to call him. Gilman reached absently for the
small gold cross that hung around his neck from a thin
chain, a habitual gesture he employed when in the throes of
an ethical dilemma.

As the plane slowed and then came to a halt on the run-
way, Gilman pulled out his cell phone to call McMullan. And
then, for the third time that day, he decided against it.

11:21 A.M. PST

In the back of her ex-husband's Jeep, Katrina felt almost airborne as the Jeep flew eastbound on the 8 freeway at more than one hundred miles per hour. She had no idea if there would be highway patrol after them, and she didn't care. Her only concern was getting Alexis to the lab.

Sean McMullan broke a long silence abruptly. "Where in the *hell* does Guofu Wong get off being our killer?" he shouted. "All this time, I was sure it was Johnson."

Katrina looked at him. "Wong framed Johnson," she said. "He convinced you that I had plagiarized his data. That's why you thought it was him all along."

McMullan paused for a moment, and then mused, "Wong certainly had the resources to orchestrate the attack at the prison. But there's no way he worked alone. He had an accomplice." He turned to Katrina. "It had to have been someone from your lab who started this whole thing. I still can't imagine why."

"We were assuming he was going to poison the *scientists* at the convention," Katrina pointed out. "But Wong was going after the protestors. It does make sense. You told me

Wong wanted to fund my initial grant application a year ago because he was so in favor of biotechnology. He worked for the CDC and within the NIH. He knew how under-funded this type of research is. He knew how vulnerable to a biological attack our country really is, and how little is being done to promote the research that can stop one."

The Jeep approached the exchange for the 15 freeway, and a highway patrol car parked along the shoulder came into view. Tom quickly hit the brake to reduce his speed and then passed the officer, glancing into his rearview mirror. The highway patrolman did not follow.

"That's right," McMullan said. "In the greeting card, he wrote, 'when I have been martyred for a cause you can never appreciate any other way.' Wong considered himself some kind of warrior for science. And a long time ago, he told Gilman that the word conscience means literally 'with science.' He must have thought he was really doing the right thing—making a necessary sacrifice for the greater good."

"Something a jarhead can relate to," Tom chimed in.

"Me too," Katrina agreed. "Despite what Lexi thinks, I always felt that way about animal research."

Alexis had been staring through the window. Katrina had thought that she was not listening to the conversation, but when her name was mentioned, Lexi spoke up. "He said something else, too," Lexi said weakly. "He said to me, 'These fools down here, they're just ignorant. They'll get the cure and they'll learn. But *you* should have known better.'" Looking pained, Alexis turned her head slowly to look at her mother sitting behind her. "He was counting on you to save the other protestor's lives," she said weakly, "but not mine."

Katrina looked at her daughter and understood Wong's

strategy. The others had ingested the bacterium. Their illnesses would be slower to manifest. But Alexis had been injected. The distribution through her body had been immediate. Alexis had much less time.

11:26 A.M. PST

In 1954, Jonas Salk changed summertime forever.

Prior to the release of Salk's vaccine for poliovirus, parents of young children spent the season in a state of panic. Would their children come down with the crippling disease while they stood helplessly by, or would they escape it for another season?

As the vaccine became commonplace, the nation reveled in relief, and the summer season once again became a time of enjoyment for children and parents alike. Polio was all but eradicated.

A common myth is that Salk injected one of his children with the vaccine in order to prove its efficacy and safety to the public. The truth, however, is that he injected all three of his children. And his wife, his laboratory staff, and himself.

As Katrina opened the freezer in her laboratory space at San Diego State University, she was wishing for Jonas Salk's confidence. Despite the assurance she had offered McMullan at the jail just the previous day, and despite the fact that she had already stockpiled the formulation, Katrina was terrified.

The antidote had been developed way too quickly. There had been no time for proper trials—not even in primates. There was no way to know the drug's effectiveness, and there was certainly no way to know its long-term safety. The first human subject to test the antidote for the Death Row anthrax strain would be Katrina's only daughter. The only child she had left. Alexis would be the guinea pig.

Katrina reached into the freezer and pulled out a box, from which she removed a small glass vial. As if in a trance, she stepped away from the freezer, leaving the door open behind her. Ice-cold sublimation billowed outward.

Tom exchanged a glance with Sean McMullan, who wordlessly stepped to the freezer and closed the door.

Katrina walked to the cold room as if to a gallows. Once inside, she rummaged mindlessly through a shelf until she found an unopened bottle of solvent. She tore the protective wrapper from its cap and dropped it to the floor as she left the cold room. Again, the door left open. Again, McMullan behind her to close it.

Alexis was sitting on a lab bench with her head in her hand. She was shivering.

As she approached her daughter, Katrina reached into a cabinet and found a sterile needle and syringe, which she unwrapped and connected while walking. Standing in front of Alexis, Katrina brushed the condensation from the sides of the glass vial. It had finally begun to thaw.

For what seemed like hours, she rubbed the glass vial between her trembling hands to thaw its contents completely. Then she filled the needle. Her hand was cold as she reached for her daughter's arm.

Katrina brought the needle forward, but could not still the shaking of her own hands sufficiently to administer the injection. Her breathing shallow, she closed her eyes and swallowed hard, then stepped backward. A tear rolled down her cheek.

Tom reached forth and took the needle gently from his ex-wife. "IV or IM?" he asked softly.

Katrina's response was barely audible. "IV."

Tom turned Alexis' arm to reveal the soft inner flesh. He tapped the skin in the crook of her elbow to locate the vein. Tom's eyes met Lexi's and held for a moment as he took a deep breath and let it out slowly. After a final glance at Katrina, with the expert precision of an experienced combat medic, he pressed the needle into Lexi's vein as lovingly as possible and depressed the plunger.

Katrina could not look away.

A few moments later, the silence was broken by Sean McMullan. "We have to... " His voice cracked slightly, and he cleared his throat and began again. "We have to get you to the hospital," he said. "And I'll get a courier from the FBI to transport the rest of the antidote there, too."

As the three others began slowly guiding the weakened girl toward the door, Alexis shook her head gently. Then she reached over and laid an arm onto Katrina's as if to detain her. Katrina stopped walking and turned to face her, leaning in close to hear the feeble voice. "Go get the bastard who did this to me," Alexis whispered.

Katrina looked into her eyes, and then toward McMullan, and then Tom.

"I'll take her," Tom said. He put his arm around Lexi and scooped her up into his arms for the third time that day, then carried her out of the lab.

When McMullan turned back around, Katrina was gone.

11:28 A.M. PST

Katrina wandered through the empty office spaces adjacent to the lab, not knowing what she was looking for. In the absence of Tom and Christopher, her staff members had become like her family. She could not believe, could not *imagine* that any of them would have done this. But McMullan was right, and Gilman had been right all along. It had to have started here.

Guofu Wong's dying words rang through her mind once again. *It was your activator.* It was indeed.

Katrina walked into the office shared by Li, Oxana, and Jason and scanned the tall bookshelves and workspaces. Each of the desks was piled with its own stacks of loose journal papers. She walked over to Li's.

Li was the most organized person Katrina had ever known. The three-ring binders and lab notebooks on her bookshelf were clearly labeled and ordered, first by function and then by date. Except for one small picture of her husband and infant daughter in Beijing, Li's desk was devoid of personal effects. Katrina pulled Li's most recent notebook from the shelf and thumbed through. All of her data was scanned, her notes typed. Each experiment was clearly catalogued in a table of contents and detailed according to classic scientific method: objective, materials and methods, results, and conclusions.

No way, Katrina thought. *This is the most well-behaved girl on the planet.* She slid the notebook back into its slot and looked over at Jason's desk.

In sharp contrast to Li's meticulous style, Jason was, and had always been, a total pig. Katrina had never complained, as Jason's work itself was meticulous and he had always been an exceptionally prolific young scientist. Everyone seemed to agree that his promise was endless. His eccentricity reminded Katrina of Richard Hoffman, the chairman of biology at SDSU. Or Einstein.

In addition to the haphazard collection of unlabeled notebooks and creased, well-worn journals, Jason's bookshelf held CDs, empty liquor bottles, and dirty coffee cups. The wall above his desk was plastered with photos, mostly of large, rambunctious parties. A computer printout on the left wall next to his chair showed a smiling man holding a steaming beverage cup. The caption beneath read "How about a nice warm glass of shut the fuck up?"

Katrina pulled a notebook down from the shelf. A stack of loose paper, films, printer paper, and bar napkins with notes scrawled in Jason's barely legible writing fell out. Katrina flipped through some of the data, decided nothing looked out of the ordinary, and quickly gave up trying to decipher his madness. She stuffed the wad of information back into the binder and returned it to its spot.

As she shoved it between two other books on the shelf, an item fell onto the desk below. Jason's CD. She had seen it before. She had even been to a couple of Jason's shows over the years in the spirit of support, although she could not stand heavy metal.

The front of the CD case showed a topless, blindfolded woman. Her arms were raised and stretched as though she were being crucified. The album was self-titled, and the name "Lethal Factor" was displayed over the woman's bare breasts. Two years earlier, Katrina had laughed when Jason told her that he named his fledgling band after his work.

She picked up the CD to return it to its shelf, but then paused as a line of text on the back of the square case caught her eye. She looked again, and her breath caught in her chest.

Track Seven was entitled, "Message From a Terrorist," and in smaller lettering beneath, subtitled, "Dear Mr. President." Katrina quickly recalled the translation of the terrorist threat from the original greeting card, the one received at the White House all those lifetimes ago. It had begun exactly that way.

Katrina focused on her breathing to stay calm as she carried the CD out into the lab. With slightly trembling fingers, she turned on Jason's CD player and put in the CD, then skipped to Track Seven.

Distorted guitars and drums began their frenzied crashing at once. Katrina waited for the vocals to come in, trying to convince herself that she was just being paranoid, that the stress had finally gotten to her. Then the lyrics began, and she realized she could not have been more wrong.

Dear Mr. President,

Your nation of puppets will soon know at last the price of fighting against our Islamic

State. Those of you who survive Allah's justice
will reflect upon 11 September of 2001 and
consider that date insignificant...

It was the message from the card. Verbatim. Blinking
back frustrated, incredulous tears, Katrina started the track
over again, struggling to make out the screaming vocals over
the overbearing guitars. She could only catch some of it.

She clawed open the CD case and pulled out the sleeve,
unfolding it into its eight panels. The sleeve contained acknowledgements from the band collectively and from each
band member individually, production studio and artwork
information, equipment, and copyright information. She
flipped the sleeve over to look for the song lyrics.

Katrina's eyes were instantly drawn to the Track Seven
lyrics. They were written in Arabic script.

The CD was still playing when Katrina realized that Sean
McMullan was standing right next to her. He was looking
over her shoulder at the Arabic text. The cacophony had
become a soundtrack for a hell Katrina could no longer even
understand.

McMullan seemed to realize this, and he sounded almost
sorry when he said, "I think I have some questions for your
postdoc, Katrina."

"So do I." She looked at her watch. "He's at the convention."

"Oh, great," McMullan said. "The hardest place I can
think of to get to him, find him, and pick him up without
a problem."

Katrina sighed. "At this point, we won't even be able to
get in until the day's sessions are almost over. Jason could

already be gone anyway. We could get down there and run around looking for someone who has already gone home."

"Then we go to his apartment and wait for him there."

"OK," Katrina said, "except that we don't have a car. Yours is at the convention center and mine... in the parking lot at San Quentin, I think. I don't remember. But neither of our cars is at SDSU and we are. Call Gilman."

McMullan looked down and sighed. "I can't," he said. "I didn't exactly tell him that I was pulling you out of jail. We're on our own."

Both Katrina and McMullan fell silent, each of them engrossed in the latest roadblock. At first, neither noticed when the door to the lab quietly opened and closed. But then, someone laughed.

Katrina foggily looked up to see Josh Attle.

"You guys closet Lethal Factor fans?" Josh asked cheerily.

Katrina reached forward and turned off the CD. The silence was golden.

"I feel a little awkward saying this," Josh said, "but I thought you were in jail?" His face was clouded with concern, and Katrina sighed.

"Yeah, I got out," she said, without offering more.

"Good," he said. "I never doubted those guys were whacked for thinking you could have done anything wrong." Josh winked at Katrina.

She offered what she hoped to be a sincere smile and turned back to McMullan. As she did, Josh nodded and stepped past them toward his lab bench.

"We need your car," McMullan said abruptly.

Josh turned back around. "Huh?"

Katrina looked at McMullan and then at Josh. "I can't explain it," she said, "but soon enough, I promise you'll know what's going on. Please?" The "please" was a gesture. Katrina knew that McMullan could merely take the car, but she had no reason to cause problems with Josh. Or to believe that he would say no.

"I wasn't planning on being at the lab for very long," Josh protested. "I was planning on just doing something quick here and then going home. I'd rather not end up stranded."

"Take a taxi," McMullan said. "It's on the FBI. Where are your keys?" Josh reached into his pocket and produced them. McMullan took the keys and then reached forward to pop the CD out of the player. He returned the disc to its case and dropped the case into his own pocket.

Behind the wheel of Josh's decrepit car, Katrina sped inland toward Santee.

McMullan was staring blindly out the window. "I don't think anyone else heard," he finally said.

Katrina looked at him, not understanding. "Heard what?"

"I was right next to you when Wong died," McMullan said. "I heard what he said to you. That it was your activator. But he was barely whispering, and I think the press was too far away to catch it."

Katrina wondered where he was going with this. "Yeah?"

McMullan's eyes bored into her for a moment. "That's *good*, Katrina," he said. "If the press heard that, you're screwed. If they didn't hear, then maybe we can still contain this. Provided, of course, that we get to Jason and clear the rest of it up for good."

Katrina had not even been thinking about the ramifications of Jason's involvement with respect to her, but now, she gave McMullan a grateful look and then sighed. "Yeah, I guess you're right," she said.

The struggling motor of Josh's car protested when Katrina asked for a burst of speed to pass another car. As she approached the rural town of Santee, the ratio of full-sized trucks to passenger cars increased dramatically.

Katrina turned onto Jason's street and approached his apartment. A familiar beat-up car came into view, parked halfway onto the curb next to the apartment building. "That's Jason's car," she said. "He's home."

Wordlessly, the pair climbed the stairs to Jason's apartment. McMullan rapped on the door. They waited in silence for a moment, but there was no answer. McMullan knocked again, even harder than before. "Come on Jason," he said. "Let's not make this harder than it has to be."

Nothing.

"Jason, we just want to talk to you," Katrina shouted. "We know how things look, but I still can't believe you could have done this. So open up!" Still nothing.

Katrina exchanged a glance with McMullan and stepped back reluctantly. In one quick motion, McMullan fired a practiced foot forward to connect with the door. There was a brief cracking sound, and the door swung open.

Jason was not in sight.

McMullan drew his pistol as he stepped forward into the living room, and Katrina followed. Slowly, they stepped through the kitchen and toward the bedroom. At its closed door, Katrina looked toward McMullan, and their eyes locked. He nodded gently, and Katrina reached forward and opened the door. And there, on the bed, was Jason.

The frozen expression of agony on Jason's face was the same one that had brought Sean McMullan into Operation Death Row. The same expression that had been on the faces of sixty-eight condemned inmates at San Quentin. The cause of death was obvious from the characteristic black lesions covering Jason's body, the lesions for which anthrax—from the Greek for *coal*—had been named.

11:54 A.M. PST

Back behind the wheel of Josh's car, Katrina wiped a tear-stained cheek and sighed before starting the ancient engine again. But then she paused. She had no idea where to go. The discovery of Jason's poisoned body destroyed what she had thought was the last piece of the puzzle.

From the passenger seat, McMullan interrupted her thoughts. "Does Jason speak Arabic?"

"Good point," Katrina said. "Not on your life."

"Then someone else was involved with this."

Katrina thought for a moment and then said, "Let me see the CD again." McMullan produced it from his back pocket, and Katrina removed the sleeve from the jewel case. She flipped through until she found the credits, and began scanning through.

Jason had personally thanked several people. The only names Katrina recognized were James Watson and Francis Crick. None of the people he acknowledged had Middle Eastern names.

She bypassed the acknowledgements from other band

members and found another section of the credits. And a line jumped out at her immediately. "Produced by Ziad Qattan at JDR studios, 4859 Prospect Ave., Santee, California." Katrina pointed to the name.

"Let's go," McMullan said.

"It's only two blocks away," Katrina said and engaged the gear shift of Josh's car.

Three minutes later, Katrina and McMullan knew they had found the right place. The crash of live heavy metal descended upon them even as they were still pulling into the parking lot. Katrina screeched into a parking space, and they jumped from the car. Following the sound, they climbed a staircase and opened a door.

The music they had heard was a full band, but only one young man was in the room. He was wearing headphones and playing a guitar. A microphone was inches from the speaker of his guitar cabinet. The guitarist stopped playing when Katrina and McMullan entered the room. The guitar dropped out of the mix, but the remaining music continued playing.

The guitarist shot Katrina and McMullan a look of rage. *"God damn it!"* he shouted. "You totally ruined a fucking awesome take on one of my solos!"

A moment later, the remaining music stopped as well, and a voice came over a loudspeaker. "What happened, Brian? I thought that was a good take."

"Some fuck-heads walked in," the guitarist shouted.

A door opened from within the studio, and a thin man entered the room. His tattooed skin was dark, but not black. He might have been Middle Eastern. "What's the problem?" he asked.

"Are you Ziad Qattan?" McMullan asked.

"Yeah, who wants to know?" There was no accent.

"Agent Sean McMullan, FBI," McMullan said and produced his badge. "And I have some questions for you." McMullan turned to the guitarist. "Sorry, but your recording session is over. Scram."

When the guitarist was gone, McMullan pointed to the CD sleeve. "Did you write these lyrics, the ones in Arabic?"

"Oh *shit*," Qattan said. "I *knew* something like this was going to happen. I *told* Jason it was a bad idea. At the time, we were both drunk, and he thought it would be hilarious. I went along with it."

Katrina looked wide-eyed at McMullan. Was this a confession?

"Something like what?" McMullan pried.

"You jackasses think I'm a terrorist because we wrote a song and I'm an Arab. Racial profiling at its finest. Freedom of speech at its lowest. God bless America."

"But you wrote these?" Katrina reiterated.

"Yeah, and I found out later that a bunch of the Arabic wasn't even right. Look, I barely even speak Arabic. My parents are Palestinian. But we're not terrorists. We're not even Muslim. We are Catholic—my parents come from Bethlehem—you know, the birthplace of Jesus Christ? I grew up here. I'm American. And I don't even pay attention to politics.

"Jason and his band wrote that song—in English. They thought it was a cool idea to write a song about terrorism from the point of view of the terrorist. In the metal world, that *is* cool. It's bad ass, actually.

"Then when we were recording it, Jason got the idea to put the lyrics in Arabic on the CD case. All I did was translate them—badly. That's it. You can confirm with Jason and his entire band that I had nothing to do with the writing of that song. And his whole band is American."

There would be no confirming of anything with Jason, but Katrina was inclined to believe Qattan. She and McMullan looked again at the CD case. Like Jason Fischer's, the names of the other band members were clearly of European descent. For a moment, McMullan looked toward her, as if asking her opinion on what to do next. Then he said to Qattan, "Don't leave town," and he turned and walked out of the studio.

Katrina followed McMullan as he walked briskly toward Josh Attle's car for the third time. To her surprise, McMullan approached the driver's seat. "Give me the keys," he said. "I'm driving."

Katrina raised one eyebrow in his direction.

"Look Katrina," McMullan said. "It's not a chauvinistic thing. We're in the middle of B.F.E. and I have training in high-speed driving. We're obviously going on some kind of wild goose chase today. So give me the keys."

Katrina handed them over and slid into the passenger seat of the car.

McMullan could barely fit behind the driver's seat, which Katrina had pulled all the way forward. He groped beneath the seat until he found the lever to adjust it. He pulled the lever. The seat inched backward, but only slightly. Something was blocking it.

McMullan leaned forward as far as his contorted position would allow and reached under the seat. He felt something beneath it. It was both soft and wiry. He groped around and yanked at the object from various angles. It did not budge. "Anyone who listened to the CD could have written the card and sent it to the White House," he said, "but they would also have to know about anthrax."

"I don't think Jason's band has that many fans," Katrina said, "but you're right. So I guess now we're looking for someone who has reason to frame Jason?"

"Yeah, that narrows it down. Sounds to me like half the world is pissed off at him."

"True," Katrina said. "But it has to be someone with connections to science, and it has to be someone who knows of *my* activators. Aside from that, remember: every indication suggests it was a *woman* who did all this. It's not me. So if we're still looking at members of my lab, then that leaves Li and Oxana. Maybe we should start with them."

With a final jerk on the seat, the obstruction beneath it pulled away. The seat slid rapidly backward, finally allowing space for McMullan's legs. He reached beneath one more time and pulled out the object that had been the source of his troubles. And in unison, McMullan and Katrina gasped. In McMullan's hand was a long, thick, black, tangled wig.

Outside the North Life Sciences Building at San Diego State University, Joshua Attle was pacing. The taxi was taking forever. *San Diego taxis suck*, Josh thought to himself. He should never have agreed to this. But what could he do? The FBI agent could have just taken his car anyway. And then he'd look suspicious.

Josh took a deep breath and forced himself to calm down. It would be OK. Katrina and the agent had found the CD. As long as they didn't find the wig in his car, everything would still be OK. They wouldn't find it. It was under the seat. They had no reason to look there.

And Jason would be mum on the subject. Josh had seen to that the previous day with a dash of scarcely visible powder sprinkled onto the glass of one of Jason's test tubes.

Can't you see what I go through for you? Josh thought. But he did not mind—it was a labor of love.

We have a whole new life in front of us now, both of us. A life that is full of promise. You have suffered enough.

You have struggled enough. You won't have to struggle anymore. I've taken care of it. I've taken care of you.

His graduation was eminent. After that, she would no longer be his advisor. He would no longer be her subordinate. There would be no reason for them not to be together.

You want it too, he thought. *I can feel it in the way you look at me. The way you smile at me. When he is not around, anyway. When he is around, you look at him instead. He might have more experience, but I have more passion. I am learning. And I know you better than he does, Katrina. He'll never understand you the way I do.*

Especially now. Josh smiled. Jason was finally out of the way.

The Doctor was terrifying, but he had been a blessing in disguise. It was fate that the Doctor had overheard Jason—that arrogant son-of-a-bitch—bragging about the activators to a table full of students at a meeting in Keystone all those months ago. It was fate that the Doctor had approached Josh. It was fate that Josh's youthful face had been so easy to disguise. And it was fate that Jason's CD had provided such an easy scapegoat. *That's karma, Jason.*

And the only people to die—except for Jason, of course—would be a handful of killers on death row. Men who deserved to die. Men who were going to die anyway. Men like the bastard who had murdered Katrina's son, and left the sadness in her eyes forever, along with the sparkling blue Josh loved so dearly.

But that was over now. It was time to move on. "*Fuck the taxi,*" Josh finally said under his breath and decided to take the Trolley instead.

As Josh gathered his belongings and began walking

toward the Trolley stop, an authoritative voice behind him shouted. *"Freeze!"*

A sudden panic consumed Josh as he turned toward the sound. And suddenly, he was staring down the barrel of a pistol. At the other end of it was Roger Gilman. Josh looked into Gilman's eye and turned to run.

12:20 P.M. PST

The engine of Josh Attle's faded red Honda Civic groaned as it climbed the steep hill leading to the North Life Sciences building at San Diego State University. When it reached the top, McMullan jerked the wheel to screech into one of the temporary parking spaces in front of the building. He quickly shut off the engine, and he and Katrina leaped from their seats.

They ran toward the entrance of the building. But then, just shy of the revolving glass door, Katrina quickly stopped.

There he was. A dozen or so yards away, Josh looked like he was running for his life. As McMullan ceased his dash toward the revolving door, a popping sound rang out and Josh fell to the pavement. Katrina and McMullan both changed direction and ran toward the spot where he had fallen.

Roger Gilman was there as well.

The bullet had strategically hit Josh in the lower leg. He writhed on the ground in pain, a maroon spot darkening his pant leg. Katrina knelt to tend to the leg, putting pressure over the wound. When she looked up, Roger Gilman's gun was aimed at her.

"He's the one!" Katrina shouted quickly. "He did it!"

"I know," Gilman said. "But what about you?"

"She had nothing to do with it," McMullan said rapidly. "We can prove it."

For a moment, Gilman glared intently at McMullan and remained still. Then, he took his aim off of Katrina and directed it at his partner. "Why isn't she in *jail*, McMullan?"

"Because I needed her help," McMullan said, instinctively raising his hands to cooperate with his crazed partner. "I needed her help to stop a biological terror attack at the biotechnology convention. And if you let us finish this, we *might* still be able to."

Slowly, Gilman lowered his gun and looked back toward Katrina.

She was still applying pressure to Josh's leg. "You killed Jason!" she accused. "And now hundreds, maybe thousands of innocent victims have been infected... including my daughter!"

Now, the pain on Josh's face was more than physical. "Katrina, I'm sorry!" he tried to explain. "I did it for you! *For us!* Jason had to die or he would have ruined it! And we needed to be free of him anyway! Can't you see that? *But I don't know anything about an attack at the convention!* There was never supposed to be a second attack at all!

"The prison was the perfect place, and it was enough! After that, the funding poured in, and we could focus on the *research*." He looked up at Gilman. "We still can, you know. If you guys can just see that and leave us to our work, we can find more antidotes for more diseases. More cures for more biological weapons. We can stay one step ahead of the terrorists. You know as well as I do that there will be more weapons. There will always be more weapons."

"Are you the one who broke into Jason's apartment as well?" Gilman asked.

"*I had to!*" Josh insisted. "The Doctor was demanding the activator data or he'd kill me. I looked everywhere. I never found it."

Katrina looked at McMullan, a look of dawning upon her face. "He didn't just want the Death Row anthrax strain," she said. "He wanted the activator data as well. He wanted to know how it was made. He wanted to know the science in detail. He wanted to be able to recapitulate it."

"Do you really think he had terrorist intentions?" McMullan asked.

"No," Katrina said. "That's not consistent with him. I think he had anti-terrorist intentions all along. He propelled my work forward to push the entire field of biological weapons defense to the forefront. To stop scientists like Johnson from blocking the funding.

"There was never going to be an attack on Christmas Day. He just made that threat so the funding would be granted and the work could go forward. He waited until the antidote was complete. Then he choreographed the attack at the convention to show the world that we could stop it. To show the value of the research. That was what he thought we had lost sight of.

"But he needed to know the science behind the weapons in order to continue propagating the antidotes after it was over. He needed that science to be out there. Not for the general public, but for collaboration among other infectious disease researchers. For future weapons. For future antidotes. In short, he needed the activator data for the same reasons that I did."

"Who?" Gilman was confused. "This kid?" He gave Josh a

half-hearted kick in his wounded leg, and Josh cried out in pain. "He couldn't do any of that if his life depended on it."

"Wong," McMullan said. "Wong is the Doctor. And if you don't believe us, ask the international press."

Katrina was grateful for Roger Gilman's sedan in lieu of Josh Attle's faded red Honda as she sat in the passenger seat. At the wheel, Gilman said nothing, his brow furrowed in concentration. Behind Katrina sat Josh, handcuffed with Gilman's cuffs and shackled with McMullan's. And next to him, McMullan was ready with his pistol in case there were any sudden moves.

"What exactly is your relationship with your students and postdocs, Stone?" Gilman finally asked. "I'm gathering that it's not all that proper."

Josh opened his mouth to protest and McMullan shoved his pistol into the boy's face. "We've heard enough out of you for now," he said. "You'll get your chance to speak in court."

"It's not like you think," Katrina said. "Josh has always had a crush on me. But there was never any inappropriate relationship between us."

"And what about Jason?" Gilman asked. "Why did Josh hate him so much?"

"Jason has been like a son to me," Katrina said. "I guess I've sort of emotionally replaced my son with my staff, and

Jason was the first one. He was also the highest up on the ladder within the lab, so he always had a lot of freedom and trust from me.

"Josh is *almost* as competent as Jason, but he was always in too much of a hurry. He was jealous of Jason scientifically as well as personally. It's like he wanted to 'pass' him but he never could. Jason was too smart. And Jason was more like a colleague than a subordinate with me, which Josh couldn't stand."

"So you're telling me that there was never anything inappropriate between you and Jason either?"

"Of course not," Katrina said. "Neither Josh nor Jason is my type at all. I tend to go after jarheads—God help me." She briefly glanced over at McMullan but then looked down.

By the time they arrived, the mayhem from the convention center had descended upon the emergency room of Scripps Hospital. Outside the sliding double doors, ambulances and police cars with lights and sirens roaring converged with medical staff, cameramen, and reporters with microphones.

An armored car, surrounded by police vehicles with lights still circling, stood just next to the entrance. In it was the bulk supply of the antidote, couriered over from Katrina's SDSU laboratory.

Gilman's car crept forward into the density of traffic until a uniformed police officer on foot blocked it from coming closer. Gilman rolled down his window and showed his badge to the officer.

"Oh, Mr. Gilman," the officer said. "I can take that one." He pointed to Attle in the back seat.

Sean McMullan stepped out of the car and signed the necessary paperwork, and the officer escorted Josh away for treatment of the wound on his leg. Gilman left his car parked where it was and showed his badge again, this time to a guard at the hospital's entrance. And he, McMullan, and Katrina stepped inside.

><

There were hundreds of them, thousands. Agonized, nameless faces and ransacked bodies writhing in desperation on white mattresses. An IV dripped into one arm of each.

The beds were clean, the facilities immaculate. The glaring white lights upon the brilliant white beds only accented the appalling conditions of the patients. They were crammed together, side by side and end to end. Thousands of adjacent hospital beds.

Nurses in white uniforms wheeled more patients in and aligned them tightly with those already present. "We're running out of space," one said quietly, removing an empty bag from the arm of a young man and then attaching a fresh bag of the antidote.

A phone was ringing. Katrina ignored it and walked like a zombie down the rows of beds; her eyes cast from one face to the next. Beside her, a feeble plea came forth from a teenaged voice.

"Please... "

Katrina stepped forward. She pulled a wheeled IV pole toward the bed and hung upon it a clear plastic bag, heavy with liquid. She tapped the child's vein and inserted a needle as gently as she could.

"I'm here, Lexi," she said. "And you will be OK now. All of you will." She gently squeezed the bag, and the solution inside it began to flow.

><

Four hours later, Alexis sat up in bed and smiled. Katrina was pleasantly surprised at the look of affection on her daughter's face, but even more pleasantly surprised at the look of health. Alexis was already recovering. The antidote was soaking up the poison as quickly as the bug, now dying from the antibiotics, could produce it.

As if reading her mother's thoughts, Lexi said, "I don't know what you gave me, but it *rocked!* I feel so much better already!"

From a chair next to the bed, Tom Stone rose and hugged his daughter. When he stepped away, Katrina took Alexis fiercely into her arms. Alexis, to Katrina's surprise, hugged back with as much intensity.

"You were going to take a bullet for me," Alexis whispered as she held her mother.

"In a heartbeat," Katrina whispered back. She lovingly brushed a stray hair from her daughter's forehead. Alexis pulled away from her mother's hand, but she was still smiling.

"There's something I should tell you," Lexi said then. "Some of my friends from the ALF went to your BSL-3 facility to break out some of the monkeys."

Katrina exchanged a look of shock with McMullan and Gilman. "Some of those monkeys were infected!" Katrina said.

"I know," said Lexi. "Anyway, it doesn't matter. I called them off. They never even went in. Considering that the entire San Diego chapter of the Animal Liberation Front is here right now for an antidote that came from your research on those monkeys, I think they might be a little nicer to you today than they otherwise would have been."

Katrina looked down for a moment. "Well that's good, I guess," she said. "But how are they going to reconcile this with their beliefs about that exact work? How are you?"

"I'm not going to lie to you," Alexis said. "I still hate what you do to animals. It's unfair and cruel. The animals don't know why they're being tortured and killed, and they didn't do anything to deserve it. They can't defend themselves. I still feel like someone needs to look out for them. And I'm serious about the fact that I would rather see your work done on criminals like the asshole who killed my little brother."

Katrina looked defeated. "But honey, you *know* that will never happen. In our society, there will *never* be legislation to do research on humans, no matter who they are. So what do you suggest as an alternative?"

"I don't know," Lexi said. "I hate the animal work. But, I think my friends will still be happy to get the shot in the arm, just like I was. So... I just don't know."

For a moment, nobody spoke, but Katrina was smiling as she looked at her daughter. It appeared that maybe, just maybe, Alexis had just opened some fraction of a door.

The silence was broken by Tom. "Nice shot back there." He was addressing Sean McMullan.

McMullan nodded softly.

"You were in the Corps?"

Another wordless nod.

"Let me guess—sniper?"

A final nod. McMullan's brow was furrowed. "It's amazing," he mused. "He guided us toward ISIL, which made sense at first, but then 'the Doctor' ended up being an extremist at the other end of the belief spectrum. ISIL fights to preserve what they believe to be the right traditions. Wong was fighting for advancement, for change. But in the end, Wong was no different than a suicide bomber. And just like them, he *believed* he was doing the right thing."

"So did Hitler," Gilman observed.

"And Einstein," Katrina said, and shrugged at the looks of shock on the others' faces.

"Einstein was a devout pacifist," Katrina continued. "He pleaded to Roosevelt, warning him about the threat of nuclear weapons. But those pleas led to the Manhattan project, which Einstein himself participated in only to spend the rest of his life trying to stamp out the very nuclear warfare he helped create. So was Einstein right? Wrong? Good? Evil? Who decides? I guess that's what conscience is for."

Conscience. Con science. With science.

Epilogue

·

The courtroom was silent when the verdict was read. Guilty on all counts. It had been no surprise. The formalities were tended to, and the crack of the judge's gavel declared the court in recess. Slowly, witnesses began standing from their pews and exiting the room, speaking to each other in hushed murmurs.

Katrina stood and turned sideways to hug Alexis. On her other side, McMullan wrapped a friendly arm around her. With his other hand, he reached forward and wiped the tear that had run down Katrina's cheek. Behind her, Gilman lightly tapped her and offered a sympathetic smile. It was over.

As they stepped out of the courtroom, the mid-September San Diego heat was stifling. Between the sun and the flashes of what seemed like a million cameras, Katrina felt dazed.

"Agent McMullan, how do you feel about the verdict?" a zealous reporter demanded.

"The incident was unfortunate, but I feel the verdict was just," McMullan offered, and began stepping down the courthouse steps.

The press turned on Katrina. "Dr. Stone! Were you truly uninvolved and unaware of your student's activities?" Katrina looked out at the sea of reporters. Surely, eventually, this would die down.

It was Gilman who came to her rescue, stepping forward and planting himself in the midst of the huddled microphones before her. "Dr. Katrina Stone has been neither charged with nor even accused of any crime," he asserted. "If you were paying attention to this trial, you saw that she had nothing to do with the generation of the Death Row strain of anthrax or its release at either San Quentin or the biotechnology convention.

"On the other hand, Dr. Stone had *everything* to do with the *containment* of the weapon, the production of the antidote, and the solving of these crimes. She performed these duties at her own risk and was almost killed in the process. The federal government is deeply indebted to Dr. Stone for her courage, her efforts, and her *ethics,* and we will happily fund her future research for as long as she needs it. Thank you very much. We have no further comments."

A grateful Katrina offered Gilman a sincere smile, but she herself did not comment. She leaned more closely toward McMullan, who wrapped one protective arm around her and the other around Alexis, guiding both toward his car. The press followed, yelling questions and comments.

When they were settled into McMullan's car, Katrina turned to McMullan. "Do you think they believe I didn't do it?"

McMullan smiled, but behind the smile there was

sadness. He shrugged. "You're exonerated, but I think you've just used your one get-out-of-jail-free card. I think you'd better stay out of trouble for the rest of your life. You can never, ever go to the authorities for help if you get yourself in a pickle. Not ever. Not for any reason. They won't believe you."

Six weeks later, the sentencing phase complete, Joshua Attle was escorted off a plane in San Francisco by an armed guard and then driven to the prison. It was a drive he had taken many times on his own. Today, there was no Muslim robe and hijab. There was no dark face makeup and gloves. There was no long skirt, chunky sweater, or black wig. Today, Josh was dressed in a blue prison uniform, and San Quentin looked much different.

Each step of the process felt like another bloody slice shaved neatly from his soul. The fingerprinting. The delousing. The new uniform. And finally, he was brought to his private cell in East Block.

Like so many before him, Josh had submitted his request for accommodations in North Seg, the very wing he had depopulated with a bioengineered strain of anthrax. Like so many before his, Josh's request was denied. North Seg was reserved for prisoners who had proven their model behavior. On the first day of his incarceration, he had a long way to go before he would be eligible for such a privilege. The cell door slammed behind him like the final closure of a metal coffin, and the guard who had led him to it disappeared.

In a cell across the hall, a man was leaning through the bars. The man caught Josh's eye and grinned, revealing a broken fence of rotting teeth. "Welcome to East Block, lover," the man said.

Josh turned away and surveyed the bleak cell that would be his home for the rest of his life. He sighed as he stepped forward and sat down on the bed, still avoiding the persistent gaze of the thick, heavily tattooed prisoner who had once been an identical twin.

Did you enjoy this novel?
A review on Amazon would be much appreciated.

For information about the next Katrina Stone novel, visit
www.kristenelisephd.com
and sign up for my monthly newsletter.

I hope you enjoyed the novel, and
thank you for your support!

—Kristen Elise, Ph.D.

Made in the USA
San Bernardino, CA
07 June 2015